Florida Station

Florida Station

Broken Cosmos Volume One

Ian Kennedy

Copyright Notice

Special Thanks

Beta Readers:
Geoff Kwitko
Jenna Harper
Hannah Climas
Janina Kennedy

Cover Art:
Courtney Egan (Eucafox)

Chapter 1

Theta 13A was sitting in the Zet Network seat, bolt upright, eyes wide open, jaw locked, teeth bared in the zetter's grin. Her shift was almost up, and she was starting to wind down, coming up through the layers of the system, filtering out the latent noise. Theta 13A logged out and awoke with a gasp. Her face came to normal and with a sharp intake of breath she unhooked the neural syringe from the side of her head.

General Hestra knew that Theta13A's body would be flooded with the pleasure chemical dopamine from the experience. Zetters got a dopamine rush from their zetting process. It is what made it attractive, and addictive.

Theta 13A's eyes were alive with a yellow, crackling fire which faded as quickly as it had appeared. "System clear, for now," she said in a raspy voice, exhausted from her exertions.

"Good," said Hestra. "What was the system integrity?"

"Seventy-six per cent," said Theta 13A, rising to her feet uneasily.

"Tolerable, but worse than last month," said Hestra. She knew at this rate they would need a whole system reboot within the coming months. That was something she did not want to do again. Last time it cost the life of the station's best zetter, burnt up and turned into a husk in the process.

"Yes, ma'am." Theta 13A saluted, her balance a little restored.

"Dismissed..." said Hestra, trailing off in thought.

"We're heading to night cycle in one hour, ma'am," said the assistant at a console in the *Florida Station* control room. He was a gaunt man, and tall. His name was Gabriel. His rank was First Officer.

Chief of *Florida Station*, General Hestra, looked down from her command dais in the centre of the control room. "Good, our Prime Zetter, Theta 7B, will be here soon and we can continue with rooting out the failed sub routines and fixing some of this old software in the system."

Although she was the most important person on *Florida Station,* and a high-ranking official in the Solar Solutions Corporation, General Hestra spoke with the harsh accent of the border colonies. Over the top of that was a forced and layered attempt to bring her accent into line with the ruling commanders of the more affluent stations. She was only in her mid forties, so there was plenty of time for advancement, General Hestra mused inwardly to herself. She knew she was ambitious yet was never quite pleased with where she had gotten in life; she was always dreaming of better. Hestra did not think of herself as malicious, perhaps that was a failing, but she did want power and had done everything she could to get it.

"How's our position?" General Hestra demanded.

"124,000," snapped an attendant in the recesses of the command module.

"Prepare for orbital burn to bring us back to one-fifty. Once we've reached optimal velocity, cut engines and let us drift for a bit," responded the General.

The ancient *Florida Station* was on a permanently decaying orbit around Jupiter and Jupiter's massive nature was always pulling the station in. Every few months they had to make an emergency engine burn to bring them back up to 150,000 kilometres from the surface. It would take them a week to make it to the optimal orbit point and then the decay would start all over again. One day the decay would be so fast and so dramatic that the whole station would fall apart and be sucked into the depths of Jupiter's gassy surface, or it would break up on an attempted burn and the same thing would happen.

One day, but not today, thought Hestra as she gave the signal and the station's ancient engines roared to life and the whole construction of modules and solar panels changed course and began to climb back into the empty blackness of space, out of the deathly clutches of their parent planet.

"Stop!" ordered Hestra and she raised a hand exactly three minutes after the burn began. With a shudder, the engines stopped once more, and the station was on its way out to 150,000 kilometres. However, it would take a week to get there. Such was the nature of inertia.

Hestra watched the rolling mass of orange, white, and red clouds that was the planet Jupiter pass in front of the window and she never failed to marvel at the majesty of it. Sure, some other station commanders had more modern stations or better perks from the company, but only the commander of Saturn's station had a better view. Once maybe Earth's Moon or the Earth Ring space stations around Earth had a better view but, due to global warming, The War and the population explosion all the commanders of the Earth stations had to look at was a toxic wasteland.

There were rumours that once the Earth looked like a blue-green jewel streaked with white. Hestra had seen a photo in one of the old textbooks, but from what she knew it seemed as though it was faked. Apparently it was a photo from the first Earth Moon exploration, but now the Earth was a sulphurous desert waste. Whatever the truth, the Earth had burned and now the far planets of the Solar System were the jewels.

Out the window of the command module, she could see the large expanse of the station as it orbited Jupiter. It was made up of various white pods that locked together via airlocks. The station had some large, old and redundant solar cells that were there to generate power before the fusion reactor had been installed; they had stayed operational. It was an old station, but still very much in use.

The command module was small relative to the other modules of *Florida Station*. Like all parts of the station, it was old and dilapidated; the chairs were slightly too worn to be comfortable; most of the controls were manual switches and buttons with large physical screens rather than holo-terminals.

The Zet Network was a later addition and that was obvious with the numerous pipes and wires snaking from the zet terminal into the main computer network of the ship.

The problem with patching a Zet Network into an old station was that navigating the systems was difficult, as many of the old systems were not meant for a human consciousness to manoeuvre through. There was always the risk that the consciousness of the person would become trapped in the old part of the system and the neural feedback would fry the zetter's mind.

General Hestra knew all this. Of course, she knew all the risks, and was confident that zetter Theta 7B could do his job on the night shift for the station. It was not as if she did not care about the consequences to the zetter, but it was her job to keep the station running and it was a zetter's job to clean the system of corrupted files and make sure all systems functioned optimally.

"Prepare the station for Theta 7B, he has the night shift," ordered Hestra.

"Ma'am," said Gabriel, standing up and indicating to the tech-slaves positioned near the terminal to bring the zetting station back to optimal operating capacity.

The tech-slaves stumbled forward, half-alive, half-dead, glassy-eyed, zombie-like creatures. They wore the standard tech-slave yellow jump suit. Gabriel visibly shuddered as one passed right beside him. The mind control skull mesh implanted into the skull over its bald head. The skull mesh stretched down the tech-slave's exposed upper spinal column; it was there to keep the tech-slave in line and give it orders from the central computer.

"Station. Ready!" rasped one of the tech-slaves in the typical staccato manner as they made their way back into the alcoves around the edge of the command pod.

"Good, he'll be here in an hour," said Hestra.

Chapter 2

Alfred put on his worker's clothes, ready for his shift. They were a stiff blue fabric jump suit of a zetter, adorned with the station's logo and the symbol of Solar Solutions, the corporation that he worked for, and that owned all the stations and colonies outward from Jupiter to Neptune.

The *Florida Station* symbol was that of a stylised image of the station in white and black. The Solar Solutions symbol was simple, but effective. It was imposed over the image of the station and was a silver trident that was supposed to link back to humanity's distant past in that the planet Neptune, the capital of the Solar Solutions Empire, was named after an old sea god from ancient times. His symbol was supposed to be the trident, Alfred mused. He did not really know if it was true, he just wore the clothes and did his job.

The nametag on his uniform read "Theta 7B". He had better get used to that name again for his work shift, he thought, as that is all the station staff knew him as: Theta 7B. Only the rich and very important had a real name in the work logs; their birth name.

He tried to shake off the effects of the previous sleep's nightmare, somewhat unsuccessfully. Alfred shuddered as the flashes of dream played across his vision, in the semi-nonsensical way dreams always did. He remembered a strange voice, and an even stranger presence that chased him down zetting pathways and would always find him no matter where he tried to hide. As the last image of being sucked into the computer core played over his consciousness, he shook his head again, and sighed. He tried to block it out.

After dressing and eating a basic meal of repurified slops with a cup of weak tea, Alfred dialled up the shopping service that he had access to as he was a station employee and ordered some more milk.

"It will get here at the wrong time...as always," he said to himself. "No zetting here to make it faster..." He grinned.

He used the bathroom before heading to work. He caught his reflection in the small bathroom mirror above the sink. Staring back at him was his low thirty-year-old sallow face with sunken eyes. He turned away from the mirror quickly.

Just before he left for work, he looked around the tiny metal room for anything he had forgotten, and saw Blinky sitting on a shelf next to his bed that held his meagre possessions.

"What are you doing there?" he asked.

Blinky simply stared back.

Alfred walked over to the shelf and lifted Blinky up gently and put her on the table. "There, much safer. We don't want you falling and breaking anything do we?"

Blinky sat motionless.

Alfred left his room a little earlier than he needed to for work and started down the harshly lit and long corridor of Sleeping Quarters Alpha3. Many of the doors had a green light showing meaning that the occupant was inside. This was not unusual as the station was beginning the night shift and many of the workers would be settling down to sleep.

Alfred passed door after door, his station issue footwear clicking on the cool hard steel of the walkway, which was slightly too narrow, to the extent that it was a little claustrophobic.

He reached the end of the corridor and entered the first of several airlocks he would have to deal with in the course of the journey. Alfred closed the first door with a grunt of effort as he swung the heavy door shut behind him. It hissed on its hydraulically enhanced bearings and with a crunch, it slid home. Alfred then punched in the simple key code to activate the cycling process on a keypad that was a little worryingly too worn for such an important process.

Red lights flashed and then the lock on the second door opened with a crack and Alfred eased it open enough for him to slip his slender frame into the next module, shutting the airlock behind him.

Airlocks like that one dotted the station, and had been long superseded by more advanced models in newer craft, but being manual it was kind of reassuring that no computer could lock someone out of a module without express commands from the central mainframe, which would only cut in if there were a critical hull breach on one side of the airlock. Alfred smiled as he pondered the situation; he could not zet an airlock even if he wanted to.

The next module was more sleeping quarters. Alfred proceeded down the corridor with more harsh footfalls, which echoed around the bare environment.

At least this station had artificial gravity, thought Alfred. It was one thing to be thankful for. *Florida Station* was one of the first that was built with internal gravity well generators, which allowed people to walk around the station not due to its rotation. The station still rotated, but that was for the day/night cycle more than any gravity requirements.

Alfred marvelled about gravity well generators, which allowed the creation of standard Earth gravity wherever necessary, and also the semi removal of gravity for hovering above a surface. This was commonly used for shuttles across the surface of planets. He wondered how it would be if the systems failed.

Another airlock. It broke Alfred's chain of thought. Alfred repeated the same old steps. It had taken him ten minutes just to get this far.

The next module was more interesting: shopping and recreation. This was a large part of the station. To keep the workers happy, mused Alfred. Well, it seemed to work; there had not been a mutiny on the station for a hundred Earth years so something must have been all right.

No matter where you were in the Solar System, time was still measured in old Earth amounts: Earth years, months and so on, before the disaster of The War damaged the Earth's orbit. It kept things constant in the vast distances of space. Alfred's mind wandered back to the mutiny.

The last mutiny was the stuff of legend. 350 workers had risen up and taken over the station for weeks. Many of the inner workings of the station were damaged in the uprising. Alfred had learned about this in school. Solar Solutions made sure to educate its workers on what went wrong in those bloody months a hundred years ago so as to make sure it never happened again. They made sure to stress the point that when the Corporation's security forces arrived from the colony on Europa and managed to put down the uprising, violently, they tried the ringleaders for treason in less than a day and sentenced them to be flushed out the nearest airlock into space. The doc-vids, sponsored by Solar Solutions of course, made sure to labour the part about the pain endured before your blood boiled and your lungs turned inside out in hard vacuum. But it was still the stuff of legend; these people had defied a corporation and taken control of their destiny. Alfred shook his head; he would never be that courageous.

Feeling rather depressed at the thought, Alfred moved through the shopping and recreation module. As he had time, he dawdled and looked at the neon lighting that illuminated many of the shop fronts. He stopped in front of some clothes shop or other, he did not really care what it was called, but the drab clothes that stood on mannequins behind the plate glass bathed in yellow and blue neon light did nothing to ease his mood.

"Only 3000 acras, for a coat..." he whispered. "Who has that money to spend on clothing?" He did not. He moved on.

Alfred strolled down the wide-open expanse of Highway A, the main street in the station. Hundreds of people were milling around, looking in windows, going about their business. Most were dressed in casual gear as it was night-time and they had time off work. The shops ran late because of this. Many of the shops and services of the station were open all the time, but with skeleton crews after midnight. Some even used tech-slaves as shop assistants, which seemed a little off to Alfred, but he supposed it was better than having them work the reactor core or the coolant ducts or engines.

Alfred felt the rumble of the engines and it started to rain again. Alfred looked up to see the high expanse of the ceiling stretch away into the darkness above and saw the large coolant pipes hanging from the ceiling. Rain on the station of course was not real rain from clouds. Alfred had never seen real rain, but "rain" was when the engines burned for an orbital change and the coolant tubes changed temperature to compensate for the build up of heat which in turn caused the water in the air around the tubes to condense and fall down with the artificial gravity. It was not unpleasant. But it did catch people out in the open who scurried for cover as the large drops impacted with the metal walkways and signs and tall walls of the shops. They made a satisfying clanging, pattering noise.

Alfred smiled; he liked it when it rained. And there it was, the reason, when it rained there was always a refreshing smell in the air, as if it were washed clean. It was probably a toxic residue from the coolant pipes and hazardous to his health, but Alfred liked it anyway.

"Imagine real rain..." he whispered to himself.

"Eh? What?" said a passerby.

Alfred started. "Oh, er, nothing, sorry," he stammered. But the person had gone before he finished his answer, trying to get out of the rain no doubt.

Alfred waited under a shop awning for the worst of the downpour to cease and then continued on.

He came to a Church, and paused. He had the time to look in. He was not a religious man, certainly not a man driven by money, but he had been saving up and maybe he could get a little guidance. Maybe later.

Alfred still looked at the sign in front of the Church: "Church of the Stock Market". Apparently, or so it was said in the history books back on his little shelf in his little room, religion in the past had been about Heaven and Hell and salvation and one god who knew everything. Ha, imagine that! Now it was much more practical. In the 26th century, the religion of the Outer Planets, at least certainly under Solar Solutions, was the Church of the Stock Market, where people sought advice for investments and left offerings to the Gods of the Stock Market: the Bull and the Bear in order for their meagre investments in the companies in the Solar System to increase in value.

People still used the old expressions of Heaven and Hell, holy and the like, in conversation or more often to add emphasis to what they said, but it was more out of a saying or an old habit than actually understanding what the concepts were; just like bulls and bears, it was all custom rather than actual knowledge.

Hundreds of years ago, there had been animals called bulls and bears on Earth; no more. Now they were mythical things to guide your rise and fall on the Markets.

Apparently in some religions back on Earth in the old times wealth was a bad thing. Alfred could not believe that; how primitive they were back then. Alfred did not worship wealth; he was not a practicing churchgoer, but he did admire those who had the money to do what they wanted.

He could hear a service going on inside the Church. Something about guarding against scams no doubt and investing in safe company stocks.

He peeked in the door.

Inside was the standard Church setup mirrored all over the Solar Solutions Corporation: seats around the outside with large computer screens around the walls and terminals where people could make contributions with large open spaces on the inside of the room where people could gather.

The priest was preaching from a stage up the end of the hall and, behind him, the wall rose up to more computer screens, all flashing red and green numbers and symbols. The congregation was held enraptured as the priest guided their contributions through his stirring speech.

Alfred checked his chronometer. Almost work time. He would come back some other time. He slipped out unnoticed.

Alfred left the recreation module and passed, via airlock, into the engineering section of the station. He did not have much time left before his shift, but as there was very little for him to do in the engineering module, that was all right. In fact, he hated this module: it was crewed mainly by tech-slaves and was a reminder of what awaited him.

He was sure that Hestra had placed the tech-slaves here in an effort to antagonise all zetters as they made their way to one of the few legal zetting terminals on the station in the command module. Many people thought that it was simply a power play to show the zetters what would become of them.

Alfred considered the fact that due to possible zetting implant decay or some sort of failure in a zetting procedure, he too might be reduced to a tech-slave at some point in the future. He shuddered at the thought.

The engineering module was dark and grimy. Most of the tech-slaves had mechanically augmented vision behind their glassy eyes. They worked in silence with the skull mesh over their heads and down their partially exposed spines keeping them in line and allowing them to communicate with the computer core and each other in a wireless way. All they did was make sure the systems of the station were working optimally and performed any mechanical and physical repairs to the dangerous areas. They were as their names suggested: slaves.

As Alfred moved between the husks of former station employees and other unfortunates, he passed by the door to the reactor module. He had never been in there. Only tech-slaves and special station crew really ever went in there. Most of it was flooded with dangerous radiation and even the parts that were shielded were unsafe.

The door to the reactor complex was a special airlock. It was newer than the others, supposedly more secure, it checked whether the occupant would survive in the reactor environment and not let those through who would not, or so it was supposed. It also required a special key code, which Alfred did not have; which Alfred did not want.

Alfred was staring at the door when he bumped into a tech-slave that crossed his path. It fizzed at him. He recoiled in disgust. The tech-slave regarded him with cold, empty eyes. Alfred felt a shiver down his spine and felt as if something was about to go terribly wrong. Tech-slaves could be violent if interrupted, it was well known, their brains unable to handle the sensory input of the real world anymore and thus they resorted to primal urges. But nothing happened. The tech-slave looked right through Alfred and moved off. Alfred looked back at the tech-slave and wondered if it had recognised him as a zetter and as a future companion and thus had not become violent. He would never know.

Alfred gathered his thoughts and moved quickly through the rest of the maze that was the engineering module and into the final airlock to the command module.

As the airlock cycled Alfred checked his chronometer, right on time.

Chapter 3

Alfred stepped into the command module and reported to the command dais where General Hestra was sitting in her command chair.

"Theta 7B reporting for duty, ma'am," he said, coming smartly to attention.

"Good," replied Hestra. "Begin boot up procedure. We have work to do."

As Alfred moved to the Zet Network terminal, he could feel his pulse quicken and his hands become just a little bit clammy at the anticipation of the rush of logging in. He lived for this moment.

As he sat down, he began the manual boot up procedure of the terminal. Before logging in with his mind, he looked over at General Hestra. Did she ever sleep? He wondered. It seemed as though she did not. This was new. Originally all animals had to sleep eventually, but Alfred had heard reports that the Collective Zone, the other great corporation, had invented implants that made sleep unnecessary. But how did that emergent technology make it all the way out here to *Florida Station*?

"Something wrong, Theta 7B?" demanded the General. She had caught him staring.

"No, ma'am!" His eyes snapped back to the terminal. "Boot up complete. Permission to log in?"

"Granted," replied Hestra.

Alfred licked his lips. He felt the cool metal of the log in plug in his damp hands. He slid back the flap of fake skin over the zet dock on his right temple. "Here goes..."

He slid the needle into his skull. The world exploded with colour and light.

***

The world around Alfred dissolved into colour as his consciousness melded with that of the machine that was the central computer of *Florida Station*. He had to be careful not to let the consciousness, for want of a better word, of the station overwhelm him.

The older a computer system got, the more quirks and foibles it had and as *Florida Station* was many hundreds of years old and had gone for nearly a century without a computer overhaul, the network was full of rips and potholes that could swallow an inexperienced zetter's mind leaving them a blank husk fit only for monitoring the computer readouts that flooded their brain.

Computers were very advance in the 26th century, but the human mind was able to interpret the computer system in a different way. The mind was able to search and visualise the pathways of a computer and fix the problems that arose, even on those systems, like *Florida Station*, that were designed before zetting became common. It was a great advance in human technology. A machine could fix errors, but the human mind could interpret and find the cracks in the system that a machine could not. Back in the early days of computers, they needed formatting, now, with this human-machine technology, a zetter could find the errors and fix them.

Alfred was experienced. He looked around. The command module was completely replaced with an interlocking web of what could best be described as a huge infrared map of the station with colours denoting different attributes of the computer network. Unlike in the real station though, Alfred could manoeuvre through the walls and wires of the station with the power of his mind.

He never got tired of this; his body felt charged with dopamine and endorphins as he surged through the computer. He was looking for dark clusters and dead sections of the webbing and colour masses. This would denote failed systems and corrupted networks that he would have to fix and replace on this shift.

There was the bright star like cluster of orange that was the command module that he just left behind, with billions of commands rushing in and out to all parts of the station. There were no corrupted files of dead links there, there very rarely were, being the command module and the most maintained part of the network apart from the reactor complex.

Alfred soared through the electric wires around the station. There was the thumping, pulsing core that was the reactor complex, highlighted in a mass of yellow and red denoting a large amount of network traffic in and out regulating the fusion reactor that the station depended on for all functions.

Alfred looked carefully at the network of colours there around the reactor and thought that he saw something out of place. Quickly he focused all his consciousness on the tiny patch of purple that he thought he saw. But it was gone. It must have been a particularly intense patch of red traffic, he thought, or at least he hoped, because purple was not good. It meant someone was using an unauthorised zet to access the network in that place.

Alfred strained to see any more of the tell tale signs of an intruder in network of the reactor complex. He looked hard, but could see no more evidence of anything resembling a breach of protocol. He returned to his assigned task.

Alfred encountered some black spots around the engineering and reactor complex networks. He got to work redirecting traffic around those spots and rewiring the connections so that communications were received between systems and sub systems. All of a sudden, the dark spots went light again, and he moved on, his job successful in this sector.

There it was again! A flash of purple stained his vision while flying around the reactor network. This time he was sure of it. It lingered and he was on it in an instant.

Zetters could not communicate with each other in the system, but they could see each other in coloured format. As an authorised zet, like Alfred, was green, purple was an illegal zet.

The purple stain saw Alfred approaching and desperately attempted to exit the system as fast as safely possible, too fast and it would be fried and become mind-locked.

Alfred managed to pursue the purple mass to the log out terminal and he got a clear reading on the terminal the illegal entry was made from. It was from within the reactor module itself, which was very worrying as that was restricted entry, but he would see this through. An illegal zet into the reactor network could jeopardise the whole station if the person got access to the coolant controls, reactor regulation or radiation shielding.

Alfred continued circling the network, fixing dead sectors, which seemed to pop up as soon as he had corrected them. Such was a computer network that had been patched and added to for hundreds of years.

Alfred plunged deeper and deeper into the system. Off in the distance was the computer core module, a blinding light of incoming and outgoing traffic. It was dangerous to go near that. The currents of the system could pull a zetter down and, although the person would not literally drown, something similar would happen to the zetter's brain as it got flooded with input and sucked into the computer core.

But he had to go near there, it was his job. What if the purple zet had done something to the systems in the computer core? He had to investigate. The computer core was a module on the outskirts of the top of *Florida Station* in the physical world, so that it could easily be accessed and added to, if need be, by human mechanics or engineers. In the currents of the zet, it was a blinding star on the edge of the network, which all other currents orbited around like planets. It was the heart of the zet. Without it, there would be no network, no station.

Alfred pushed closer to the blinding star of the computer core, even here there were dead systems, all but obscured by the light, but Alfred navigated the currents and rerouted the packets to where they needed to go. He felt the tug of the currents, ready to suck him down into the oblivion that was there, waiting for him, forever. It would be so easy, he thought, just to sink into the light.

As he hovered there, in the ether, between life and oblivion, he thought he heard a voice, or at least, something like a voice:

"Peacccceeeeee...come to meeeee."

This was such a shock to Alfred that he almost made an emergency withdrawal by yanking the jack out of his head. But in an instant, the voice was gone and was replaced by the faint fizzing of the electrical circuits that was the normal background sound in a zet. The computer should not be able to talk to him in this state! He was simply navigating the network; the computer should not know that he was there. This had to be reported.

"Nooooooo," came the thought again, *"not...reeeeeporrrt."*

Alfred felt it clearly this time, and his blood went ice cold. He had not heard the sound of a voice; the thought of the words were implanted into his head. The computer not only knew he was there, it could read his thoughts, it was IN him.

Alfred felt himself being sucked down into the white and orange hot star of the computer. Not now, not ever! He thought, and rushed away from sucking energy tendrils that reached out for him.

Back on the safer currents of the network, Alfred went about his job, trying to shake the impression that the computer was somehow sentient. Was that something to do with the illegal zet he had detected?

The rest of the shift went uneventfully on until it ended.

164 system errors corrected. Alfred began the log out sequence. He hated this. He felt alive while zetting and once he logged out the strain of eight hours of concentrating came back to him all at once.

As the colours faded from the world, and the distinct lines of the command module merged back into shape in his blurred vision, he slumped in his seat, removed the jack from the socket in the side of his head, and tried to blink away the pain.

"Report!" demanded General Hestra. Alfred looked in her direction and saw that Gabriel gave her a chastising look as if to say, "go easy on him," as only he could do given his rank, but she did not see it.

"I want a report, now!" ordered the General. "Our sensors detected some anomalies, what were they?"

Alfred blinked, "N-nothing out of the ordinary." Something told him that he should investigate the illegal zet himself before turning whoever it was in to a nasty fate. As a fellow zetter he owed them that. They had to explain themselves before they were court-martialled.

And as for the computer seeming to be sentient, no one would believe him. In fact, he would probably be terminated just for suggesting such a thing as it would indicate that he had passed his usefulness as a zetter. He would be deemed unreliable.

"Nothing!?" snapped Hestra.

"Nothing...may I be excused?..." Alfred peeled himself off the chair and limped out of the command module.

"Hmph, we'll have to watch that one," Alfred heard Hestra say to Gabriel. Alfred heard Gabriel snort at the comment. The airlock sealed behind him cutting off any further sound.

Chapter 4

Earth, or what was left of it, orbited in a slowly decaying spiral around its ancient parent star. Humans had not been kind to their home world, as usual.

***

Draz slid down the rad-dune forty kilometres outside of Zone-City Atraxa Prime, one of a number of zone-cities built to protect humanity from the harsh environment on Earth; she brushed ash from her long brown hair, synthetic leather jacket and protective clothing, and black boots, when she reached the bottom.

She was employed by the Corporate Wing of the Collective Zone as an explorer into the rad-wastes to search out old technology from Earth's glory days and bring the parts back to the Collective for inspection and assessment as to their usefulness.

She had been exploring an old encampment that had been abandoned during The War: the cataclysmic conflict that nearly ended humanity on Earth a few hundred years ago. She had discovered some old computer technology that might be useful if it could be accessed, if being the operative word.

Humans were technically more advanced than they had ever been. Space travel was commonplace around the Solar System and there were massive domed cities that held billions of people. But Draz wondered how it was before all that, when the rumours stated that the Earth had held forty billion people. It was said that the Collective Zone's rise to power after The War, the conflict which had ended the lives of half of those people, was a blessing in that the

22

Collective brought peace and stability. However, the history of the rise of the corporations was all rumour.

Draz looked down at her computer scanner. It was Collective Zone issue, of course. She was kitted out with the best that the Corporate Wing of the Collective Zone had to offer. She was now in her late thirties in age and had established herself as a professional scavenger. The Collective Zone was the de-facto government of the Earth at the current time. Draz had only known the Collective Zone as rulers of Earth. She checked the route back to her transport.

The Collective kept tight controls on what information about the past was drip-fed to the people of Earth. Even in the current civil war between the Corporate Wing and the Shipping Wing of Atraxa Prime, it was unclear as to what was going on. Each wing of the Collective had massive resources and fought with other Wings for more influence in the Collective.

Humans had always fought each other over the Earth, Draz laughed ironically. It achieved ends, by brutal means.

All that fighting and destruction during The War hundreds of years ago meant that the technology on the Earth was a mix of old fashioned pre War salvage and new technology developed to help survival since the end of The War.

But at least the people before The War could go out in the day time, or so the rumours said. Draz was unclear as to whether this was just a story or whether there really were liveable sunny days before The War.

Since The War, the Earth's orbit had decayed enough to mean that the Sun was far too hot to go out in the day, if someone could help it. The nuclear blasts had knocked the Earth onto a decaying orbit. All activity on the Earth surface outside the zone-cities should have been done at nighttime, in the light of the moon.

But eventually the Earth would become uninhabitable in a few hundred years. However, there was too much wrong now to worry about that kind of future. And according to the Collective, there was too much profit to be made to worry about what was going to happen in hundreds of years.

Draz's attention was interrupted by her rad-counter suddenly clicking at an unhealthy rate as she skirted the pool of sludge that was in her way back to her transport.

"Stay alert," she whispered into her tightly fitting mask that was supposed to filter out most of the noxious rad-desert air. Her mask, and goggles which could be set to night vision, were slightly too tight and the heat of the desert was stifling under the protective clothing, but it was better to be protected than to be left without any form of radiation protection in these wastes.

There were stories of explorers who had gone mad with the heat and torn off their masks and then been overcome with toxins and collapse only to be seen later by other explorers as mutant freak like creatures seeking only to feed on the flesh of the unwary.

Draz did not know what in the toxins in the air made the unprotected turn into freaks, but she supposed it might have been one of the ancient weapons used in The War against the civilian populations. She shuddered.

She looked up through a break in the smog and gazed at the massive space station structures that orbited the planet: the Earth Ring. They were visible from the surface and the large lifts that took cargo and people to the space stations were dotted along an axis of the planet. It was magnificent, thought Draz, even if it was made long before the

Collective Zone's rise. The stations were built before The War.

Further in the distance, through the break in the smog, was the Moon. It hung above the Earth like some silent guardian, guiding the way for countless generations of humans past. It was another relic of pre War days. The Moon had been a mining colony, which had reduced it to a honeycomb of tunnels and chambers as the helium 3 was mined from inside to fuel the many fusion reactors used throughout the Solar System. Now it was used for a less savoury purpose: as a slave like prison for those unwanted in the Collective Zone or Solar Solutions. It was a jointly run prison, providing a rare agreement between the two major corporations.

It was ironic really that the guiding light to many of humanity's explorations now was a prison for the worst of all those in the Solar System. It was not the only prison in the Solar System, but it was one of the harshest.

Draz rounded the last twisted pile of scrap and there was her transport. She let down her guard for an instant and in the short jog to the buggy, suddenly she saw, out of the corner of her eye, a shape moving and shifting rapidly in her direction.

"Damn it," she whispered as she turned to see one of the rad-freaks dashing in her direction with unnatural speed. She made an effort to draw her sidearm but in an instant the freak was on her with salivating and gnashing teeth. Its semi rotting flesh was looking putrid in the dull light of the Moon. The revolver pistol was knocked from her hand and slid across the dust-covered ground.

The two combatants fell and rolled in the radioactive dust. Draz locked her left arm under the beast's chin and pushed it away from her face as hard as she could as they grappled on the ground, both wanting to survive only by the destruction of the other.

With her other arm, Draz grasped for her combat knife, and with all her strength trying to keep the beast away from her with her left arm, she snatched her knife from her belt and drove it deeply into the creature's right eye socket. The freak roared in pain.

They still felt pain? Thought Draz.

Reeling back and clawing at its broken face the freak gave Draz a second to scramble for her pistol and snatching it up, she unloaded two heavy slugs into the creature's cranium. It collapsed and went still. Draz recovered her knife from the creature's ruined skull, wiped it on her sleeve and sheathed it in her belt.

Holstering her pistol, Draz mounted her buggy and with a flick of the ignition switches the lights all went green and she sped off in the direction of the Atraxa Prime Zone-City Loading Dock 4.

***

Loading Dock 4 of Atraxa Prime was under the control of the Corporate Wing of the Collective Zone. It was guarded by heavy automated gun turrets and the entirety of the Corporate Wing's 3rd Division. This was because the loading docks were important to each Wing of the Collective as they were the access point to the zone-city, as the large formation of towers and domed zones was known, from the outside world. Each loading dock was huge.

The lower levels were full of vehicles arriving and departing through large gates and magnetic shields on the side of the zone-city. The vehicles travelled on wheels or large tracks to deal with the soft ash wastes outside the loading dock. People were constantly unloading cargo into the cargo haulers that carried the goods to areas within

Atraxa Prime itself. There were people milling about by the thousands, going this way and that, all talking at once.

The sound of Loading Dock 4 was close to a din as machines and people moved around going about their tasks. They were all hurrying to get their jobs done before the Sun came up.

The upper levels of the loading dock were reserved for smaller space shuttles and smaller transport ships that sent cargo to the Earth Ring, from where they would be ferried to other parts of the Solar System. The lower levels were for entry to the zone-city from the surface of the Earth.

The larger ships that could enter the Earth's atmosphere were docked at the upper levels of the zone-city via docking harness, landing pads and tubes, separate from the loading dock.

Draz passed through the massive open metal gates on her buggy and parked it over in the designated parking spots. Dismounting from her ride, she swung the salvage case over her shoulder and joined the queue of people seeking entrance to the zone-city. She got her pass code ready and waited.

It always took a good hour to be let past the security screen, but these things had to be done. What if a Shipping Wing suicide operative got into the Corporate Wing security area? It would be chaos. So, she waited in line and watched the massive robotic arms of the loading dock unload cargo from various ships and vehicles while all around scurried humans doing their assigned tasks.

Around her, Draz observed the people as they waited to get into Atraxa Prime. She saw all sorts of people: civilians and soldiers, workers, scavengers like her with their loot, and other personnel. They all stood waiting patiently in line for the guards up ahead to approve their entry.

The line moved consistently but kept growing as more and more people waited to enter. There were multiple guard stations that checked people's identities, but they had to be sure before letting people in from outside.

An alarm sounded and Draz craned her neck up to watch a particularly large shuttle leave its moorings and start the launch procedure to head off to one of the Earth Ring space stations. Its stark white paint surface with silver and gold Collective Zone Corporate Wing markings looked magnificent, she thought.

The Collective Zone symbol was that of a yellowed Earth in the centre with a ring of silver that represented the Earth Ring and its lifts and elevators that linked it to the surface of the Earth. Each Wing of the Collective Zone added something to the centre of the parent symbol. The Corporate wing added a stylised G for garenas: the currency. The Shipping Wing on the other hand had a small space ship superimposed over the symbol of the Earth.

As she waited and watched the ships leave and arrive in the Corporate Wing's loading dock, Draz suddenly thought it funny that, although the separate wings of the Collective were supposed to do different tasks. That is, the Shipping Wing was meant to do shipping to the rest of the Solar System, for example. However, due to the civil war between the wings, each had had to develop its own shipping service and corporate infrastructure. That was just the way it was.

Perhaps conflict made them more efficient and better at what they did? That was a treacherous thought. Conflict was bad for the Collective, this civil war had to come to an end, and the Corporate Wing would surely win. Once the civil war was over, the Collective Zone would be ready to start domination of the Solar System against Solar Solutions once more.

Soon enough Draz got to the head of the line and presented her identity chip and pass code through the small slot in the security station, which was a large metal bulkhead with an airlock beyond it. She stepped into the radiation and cargo scanner and the machine scanned her body for harmful contaminants and her scavenged cargo for dangerous materials as the guards behind the bulkhead identified her through her pass code. Her pulse always quickened at this point, as if one day something would go wrong, and she would be arrested. She had no reason to think this, it had never happened before, but security checks always made Draz apprehensive. After a few short minutes, the lights on the machine went green indicating no harmful materials on her person.

With a grunt that could have been a word, the guard handed Draz back her identity chip and pass code and indicated with a jerk of his finger than she was cleared to go in. She smiled at him beneath her mask and headed past the bulkhead to the airlock with the salvage container slung over her shoulder.

Draz punched in the key code for the airlock and waited for the air to cycle while she wondered how much she was going to get for her salvage.

***

Draz trudged down the corridor towards the salvage centre just beyond the airlock. She removed her mask and goggles with her left hand and slung them over her shoulder wiping the perspiration from her face as she went.

She wondered what fresh air once tasted like. Moving from the filtered and recycled air of her mask in the radioactive wasteland outside the zone-city to the recycled air within the zone-city, air that was slightly too old and slightly too reused for human respiration. But that was how it was. Even with some air drawn in from outside the zone-city and purified by filters, the air in Atraxa Prime tasted stale.

Draz passed by the throngs of people waiting around in the Salvage Reclamation Centre, all scavengers wanting to make the big find and advance through the ranks of the Collective. She walked up to the counter and slapped her case down on the hard metal surface with a clang.

"Whatcha got here then, Draz?" said the large man behind the counter. She was his best customer, and he was excited to see her return.

"Computer drives from the South Quadrant, Crathka," said Draz with a sigh. "I'm getting too old for this, you know? Maybe I should retire soon. I'm in my late thirties now...I got jumped by a freak!" She shook her head, drips of perspiration forming on her skin. The Atraxa Prime Zone-City was a little too hot for her liking, especially as the Sun was starting to come up and warm the jutting metal walls and glass domes.

"Damn, Draz. Take care of yourself out there. What happened?" asked Crathka, his brow furrowing.

"Don't worry; I put two slugs in its head after slamming a knife through its eye. I'm fine." She managed a wry smile. "Besides, if I got killed, who'd bring you the best salvage?"

Crathka smiled with a toothy grin and said changing the subject. "So, computer drives eh? Let's see then." He picked up the battered, slim boxes that Draz had put on the counter. Picking up a red marked box, he stopped and said suddenly, "Hmmm, this could be interesting, let me see this one for a minute." He disappeared through an armour-plated door behind him, which slid shut with a loud hiss.

Knowing this could take a while, Draz turned and looked around the Salvage Reclamation Centre. It was the same as she had always seen it: various desks within a large, cavernous room with scavengers like herself offering up what they had collected in the wastes at night, hoping for that big score, that one find that would make them a fortune.

If she were a little younger and greener, her heart would be pounding right now, because Crathka had taken one of her items for further inspection. But it had happened too many times before with no result, so she waited, and waited. She looked around the room.

There were two scavengers, over at one table, arguing over some piece of salvage that both seemed to claim yet neither was wanting to give their claim up. They argued constantly.

Over at another table was an old, grizzled scavenger in protective clothing teaching a young man about the intricacies of driving a buggy over soft ash dunes. He was indicating with his hands the shape of the dune and the angle to approach it with the wheels.

Draz smiled, she had been in the young man's position, once. Perhaps the old scavenger was too old to scavenge anymore and was teaching his apprentice some skills. Draz did not know. She did not really care. She turned her attention elsewhere.

At a further table was a lone young woman who looked decidedly nervous by the way she was pacing and looking at her haul of salvage. Draz reasoned she was new. Draz paid her no more attention.

Draz did not focus on anyone in particular for very long and simply listened to the babble of speech coming from the various corners of the room: scavengers arguing about the value of their hauls. Other scavengers bragging to each other about how far from Atraxa Prime they ventured. No one talked to Draz. She knew she travelled further than any of them, and they knew it too. She was one of the best and most skilled scavengers in Atraxa Prime, but being at the top had its disadvantages: she had few friends and many enemies. They saw her as privileged and favoured by Reclamation Centre staff like Crathka, and his friendly banter with her did not help.

At that moment the door behind the counter slid open and Crathka reappeared holding the red box.

"Veeeery interesting, Draz." He paused, holding the red box up. "You've got something here, it still works!"

"It, it works?" exclaimed Draz. "But it must be from before The War!?" Draz noticed the room had dropped to a murmur, and felt dozens of pairs of eyes upon her.

"Not only does it work, but it has files on it, good ones, plans for some system they were developing on Earth around the time of The War." He paused.

Draz's mouth had gone dry.

"I can pay you, 50,000 garenas," Crathka said coolly.

The room had gone quiet. 50,000 garenas was more than a hundred salvages' worth, more than some scavengers made in their whole, short, lives.

"I'll take it," Draz said. "What if there's more on it? You only had a short look."

"Then we'll contact you; you know that. The Collective pays its people. One last question before I let you go: where did you find this?"

Draz knew this was a loaded question. If she answered truthfully, she would never see the place again; the professional reclamation teams would pounce on it and then she would be unable to go back there. If she lied, she could forfeit her entire licence to scavenge.

"Oh, thirty or forty kilometres out in the rad-dunes. Look, I'm not feeling well," she lied. "As I said I had a run in with a freak...I need to get back to my room..."

"Suuure." Crathka clearly did not believe her, but the Collective knew where she lived. All her information was registered under her scavenging licence on the main computer network. "50,000 garenas will be uploaded to your account, but when you have rested get back to us as we can discuss other rewards for informing us where this salvage took place."

"Right..." Draz, semi-acting, staggered out of the room and down the corridor to the transit hub. She felt dozens of eyes on her. It had not sunk in yet that she had finally struck it big! She knew that the Collective would not let this go unnoticed.

Crathka watched her go with a smirk.

As Draz left, all the hubbub and chaos of the room resumed and the next scavenger in the queue placed his loot on the table in front of Crathka. "Right, what have we here?" She heard him getting back to work as she left.

***

Draz felt light headed as she rode the hover train along the loop course around the sectors of Atraxa Prime. There were not many people onboard. There would be in an hour when the day's work started, but she would be in bed by then. She always had the train carriage almost to herself at this time.

Atraxa Prime was set out like a spider's web: with the dome and tower at the centre being the command and control centre, with the Collective's main offices and docking bays for large and small craft. Then there were the relevant Wings of the Collective, which were contained in the large domes dotted around the central section each with their own smaller towers. These were connected by long transit pathways, which were serviced by bus routes or hover trains offered freely to Collective personnel.

There were a number of these zone-cities dotted over the surface of the Earth. They all looked rather the same due to them all being run and operated by the Collective Zone, even though they all had slightly independent governing bodies. They were started when the Collective Zone came to power hundreds of years ago and had grown chaotically larger and larger ever since. Atraxa Prime was the main zone-city on the Earth. It was the largest, and it held all the Collective Zone command structure.

The war between the Corporate Wing and Shipping Wing had gone on for longer than Draz could remember, longer than she was alive. It seemed strange to her that the Collective could have a war within itself, and that war was within one zone-city. Was it not terribly destructive? She stared out the window of the train as it sped along the magnetic track within the glass tube around the outskirts of the domes. The next dome was her stop.

Draz wondered how long people could wage civil war. She could see off in the distance, through the glass tubing, the blossoming of explosions around the Shipping Wing's offices. The Corporate Wing forces were making an attack. She hoped they would win. The Corporate Wing was obviously in the right when it came to affairs. The Shipping Wing must be mistaken.

Far off in the distance, through the glass, Draz could see the orange ball of the Sun starting to scour the surface of the planet as it rotated on its doomed axis. The bright rays of light scorched the pale radioactive dunes.

The photosensitive glass tubing around the transit system started to darken to protect the passengers on the ride. Draz turned her head away and readied herself for her exit.

Draz dismounted the hover train and walked through the large open transit system, which was starting to pack with people going to work. She walked down the corridor to the Corporate Wing living quarters.

After a fifteen-minute walk down drab corridors with faded paint, Draz got to her small quarters allocated by the Collective and punched in the access code on her door and it slid open.

Draz dumped her belongings including the radiation mask and goggles on her small table and walked over to the sink to pour herself a glass of many times recycled water. It tasted metallic in her mouth, and she wondered if life would get better with 50,000 garenas. Would she get a bigger room?

She cast her eye over her meagre quarters. Even for one of the Corporate Wing's chief scavengers she was not allowed much of a luxury life: a single bed, music system, a few storage lockers, a table and a couple of chairs, a kitchen area. Still, she should be grateful not to be left out in the wastes.

Draz unbuckled her equipment, walked over to her bed and slumped down on top of the covers. She reached down to the storage locker next to her bed and drew out a small, silver parcel. She opened it and saw a small amount of white powder there. She smiled. She tipped some of the powder out onto the table next to her bed, arranged it into a line, put away the remainder in the metal foil back into her locker while withdrawing a small, metal straw, and snorted the line quickly through the straw.

Suddenly waves of relaxation flooded through her body. She reclined back into the bed. She closed her eyes and floated away on waves of pleasure caused by the drug. 50,000 garenas would buy a lot of anything. Everything would turn out all right, she thought, before blissful sleep claimed her.

***

CEO Uxus of the Collective Zone stood, in his simple grey uniform, looking out over the expanse of Atraxa Prime from his vantage point in the empty boardroom atop the highest tower in the zone-city. His old, gnarled features betrayed that he was thinking.

He tapped his old hand on the board table; a rich wooden construction. It was very rare to have authentic wood due to the disappearance of viable natural trees hundreds of years ago.

Uxus always marvelled at the wooden material: it was a dark brown with marbled veins through it. It was of a heavy construction, and he ran his fingers over the smooth surface as he stood at the head of the table.

The chairs were expensive, well cared for, leather chairs that were very comfortable and also rare as the beasts that had died to give up their skins for the covering of the chairs had long been extinct.

The rest of the room was sparsely decorated, with a few photographs of some of the past CEOs of the corporation who had done great things. They were hung on the wooden pillars that made up a small part of the room.

The majority of the room was made up of reinforced glass walls that gave an excellent, panoramic view of the sprawling Atraxa Prime complex and the surrounding wasteland that stretched out in sick yellow streaks in every direction.

Uxus could hear the ticking of the clock on the wall. The silence in between each stroke heightened his concentration. He liked old mechanical clocks rather than digital ones.

"How am I going to do it?" he said to himself. "How?" He looked up at the yellow and brown polluted sky. "I want more. Our Collective needs more resources. Earth is running low...And our orbit...How am I going to expand into Solar Solutions space?"

There were more spaces where the clock did not tick.

He saw some explosions off in the distance around one of the domes. Finally, his old features broke into a smile. He had the answer. He knew what he had to do. He needed a war.

CEO Uxus continued to stare out the window of the empty boardroom. He needed an excuse. He needed a catalyst.

Chapter 5

Florida Station turned slowly on its axis exposing the crew quarters to the stark light of the Sun hundreds of millions of kilometres away. Automated lighting systems came online throughout the station and the wake-up cycle started on all processes. It was "daytime." Thousands of people woke up and began their morning routines, scurrying to and fro and getting ready for a workday. The overnight shift workers who kept the station running during the enforced night hours were making their way back to their quarters for a well-earned rest. All except two.

***

In the darkness, a shadow pulled a zetting needle out of his implant. He had been seen. He knew it. He had to get out. The nighttime zetter had seen him in the reactor module. The computer readouts said that the night zetter's name was Theta 7B. Maybe he could bribe him? Talk to him? Yes, that was it, talk to him! Perhaps he could be converted to their way of thinking. He needed to get out. There was only one way in or out of the reactor module. The tech-slave guards on the door to the module changed every eight hours, not that tech-slaves needed a break, but the shadow knew that Hestra wanted to make sure that the guards were as alert as possible. Even tech-slaves started to flag after a while. If he timed it just right he could make it out the airlock and into the engineering module without being noticed. He had been seen; he could not believe it. How could he have been seen? That zetter was good. Maybe he had reported him to Hestra already, and it would be a tech-slave fate that awaited him. He had to talk to Theta 7B, he had to talk, and fast.

The shadow moved to the airlock of the reactor module, avoiding the security cameras. Precisely on time when the guards would be busy changing over, he triggered the airlock and slipped out silently into the engineering module and away into the station towards the crew quarters.

***

Alfred exited the command module to the engineering module. He was tired from his recent zet, and the dopamine rush was starting to fade. All he wanted to do now was relax. But he could not relax, not with the knowledge that someone had accessed the zetting terminal IN the reactor complex. He was sure he had seen a purple mark from within there.

Then there was the fact that the computer core SPOKE to him. He had to see his doctor, maybe the zet hardware in his brain was starting to take its toll and malfunction? Maybe soon he would become a tech-slave?

He pushed these thoughts from his mind as he approached the reactor complex airlock in the engineering module. He thought he saw some kind of shadow flit from in front of the airlock and away into the darkness of the engineering module. There was just the halo light from the computer screens and a small double line of lights indicating the walkways around the module. Was there something there? Alfred did not know. He could not be sure.

Alfred looked towards the airlock to the reactor module. The tech-slave guards were changing their posts and in this moment, Alfred took it upon himself to go over to the airlock and study it. Initially the guards paid him no notice; they simply stumbled about changing places and making strange clicking noises as they uploaded their reports to each other wirelessly.

The airlock was similar to the others on the station. It was large and white with red warning markings. It required manual work to cycle and let the occupant pass from the outside to the inside or vice versa. Alfred studied the keypad. It was different from the other airlocks on the station. It had more numbers and symbols on it as the required key code, that changed regularly, was longer and more complex than the regular airlocks. It was still manual though. You had to type in the code with your fingers.

The guards were beginning to take notice and look in his direction.

Then a realisation struck Alfred: in the gloom he saw a couple of wires jutting from the bottom of the keypad. Two loose wires with their metal cores exposed.

Suddenly a strong hand grabbed his shoulder and Alfred jumped and looked around.

"What. Are. You. Doing?" barked the tech-slave guard in a staccato rhythm.

"Uh, nothing, nothing!" gasped Alfred as he stared in the empty eye sockets of the tech-slave as it scanned him with its computer enhancements.

"You. Are. Not. Allowed. There." The tech-slave indicated the airlock. "Move. Along." it snapped, manhandling Alfred away from the airlock and back to the dim light of the engineering module. With its surprising arm strength, the tech-slave pushed Alfred away.

Scrambling to regain his footing, Alfred's head was swimming at the thought that someone had manually hacked the keypad of the reactor module to gain entrance. That must have been it; he pondered the situation as he walked, faster than usual, back to the shopping and recreation module. His heart was pumping in his chest and his hands were clammy. Should he report this to General Hestra? He knew that he should, but something told him to wait and see. Maybe if he gathered more evidence of something sinister happening he would present a more convincing case? All he had at the moment was a shadow, some wires, and a purple splash in the zet. And the computer talking to him, he could not forget that.

He needed to see a doctor about the dreams and about the fraying of his mind that he was experiencing due to the prolonged zetting. Then he would try to find out about purple zet and the reactor security breach.

***

Alfred hurried through the recreation module, passing crowds of people as they went about their daily lives, oblivious to the problems that were weighing on Alfred's mind. He passed the same shops as he did on the way to his job, now in the "daytime" they were trading well. He passed the Church too.

Alfred came to one of the two clinics on the station. It had a large shopfront emblazoned with a green neon medical cross and, of course, the symbol of Solar Solutions proudly displayed next to it.

Alfred hated seeing the doctor, but he had to. All zetters had to have regular check-ups to determine their level of decay. It was company policy. Without the check-ups you were declared illegal and then the worst happened to you.

Alfred walked through the glass sliding doors and reported to the main desk. Behind the desk was a rather domineering nurse in a green robe.

"Name? And what are you here for?" snapped the nurse, she was precise with every syllable.

"Uh, Alf...Theta 7B. Zet check-up," Alfred stammered. The doctor always made him nervous.

41

The nurse looked at him coldly, she did not approve of his work. He could tell by the way she pursed her lips and scowled at him.

"Over there." She pointed with an angular finger to a line of chairs filled with patients.

Alfred nodded his compliance and sat at the end of the row of harsh company chairs. He was sixth in the line. This might take some time, he thought.

He looked along the line of patients. First up there was a large, rather overweight, middle-aged man who seemed to be having trouble keeping the contents of his nose and eyes in his skull as he snuffled and snorted the time away. He would not take long to treat: some kind of space cold.

The second person was an attractive, young woman dressed in tight fitting company clothing with the Solar Solutions symbol on it, like his. She caught him looking, and smiled back. Alfred felt embarrassed and his head snapped back, eyes forward. He could feel his cheeks blushing. He heard her stifle a slight chuckle.

After a few minutes he craned his eyes around as far as they could go without moving his head much to look at the other patients. Thirdly and fourthly, there were what Alfred assumed was a father and daughter by the way they were chatting and interacting. He could not guess what was wrong with them.

At that moment, there was a buzzing noise and the nurse behind the desk ordered the fat middle-aged man to go into the doctor's room as the current patient left the room with a hiss of the automated door.

The patient who was leaving wore a dark trench coat and made hurried, jerky movements. Alfred suddenly paid absolute attention to him, or her, he could not tell. Alfred could also not hear what the patient in the trench coat said to the nurse. Then the patient turned to leave, and Alfred caught the eyes of a frightened young man, sunken, weathered beyond his years. And then Alfred got it, this man was a zetter, one suffering from the latter stages of zetting sickness. The sunken eyes and the jerky movements, it was all there. Alfred's blood ran cold. Was he looking into his future self? The man left the clinic. In all but a few seconds the moment was over, and then Alfred realised: was that the purple zetter; was that the shadow that had flitted from the reactor?

Alfred jumped out of his chair to run after the man but before he could, he had lost him in the crowd of people outside the clinic. There were zetting stations on the station other than the command module, so it was possible that Alfred had never seen him before. Now he was gone.

"And just where do you think you're going?" snapped the nurse.

"I...uh..." stuttered Alfred. The nurse raised an eyebrow and Alfred sat down again. He heard the young woman patient chuckle again. It was all too much for him. He felt rotten.

Alfred busied his mind with other matters. The patient next to him and now fourth in the line was an older woman who paid no attention to anyone whatsoever. She just sat there, bolt upright and Alfred did not want to turn his head towards her because she appeared so brittle that it looked like she would break into pieces.

"Next!" came the voice from behind the desk, as the snuffly man left the doctor's room, paid and then left in a waddling sort of way.

The attractive woman got up and went in the doctor's room with a lithe grace that Alfred caught himself watching with a little too much attention.

While she was in the doctor's office, Alfred looked around the clinic's waiting room. It had never changed for

43

as long as he had been on the station, most of his life. It was a rather large, white room with the desk for the secretary and nurse and chairs lined up along one wall. That was it. No windows, just harsh neon lights.

Soon enough the attractive woman came out of the room and, as she was company staff, did not have to pay. She shot him a coy glance as she left. Alfred started blushing again. He liked women, but he never seemed to know what to say or do around them.

Then the father and daughter went in, soon followed by the older woman.

"Your turn, Theta 7B!" snapped the nurse as the older woman left the room in a brittle state, as if she would shatter if you somehow knocked into her. Alfred did not have time to wonder what was wrong with her. He went into the doctor's room.

It was Dr Armstrong on duty at this time, even though he had his back to Alfred, Alfred recognised him due to his long hair plaited into a ponytail. Armstrong was a bit strange, but a good doctor. He understood zetters' concerns and took their problems seriously. Alfred was glad it was Armstrong; he could do with some reassuring.

He was called by the name Armstrong as he was one of the top doctors on the station and as such was a high-ranking official. No one knew his assigned rank; it was sort of a mystery. He never used it, as if he was trying to remain as human as possible amongst all the computers and corporate jargon.

"So, what's wrong Thet...oh Alfred, it's you! I hate those assigned names anyway." Dr Armstrong turned and smiled a reassuring smile. "What's wrong, son?" Alfred smiled at the word "son" as Armstrong was not much older than he was, but it made him feel comfortable.

"I...I," stuttered Alfred. Armstrong gave a caring look. "I've been having dreams, bad ones, I'm hunted in my sleep."

"Ah," said Armstrong. "Let's see a readout then. Sit down." Dr Armstrong moved to the computer and took a control lead from it. He moved back to Alfred, now sitting in a chair, and gently moved the fake skin flap aside on Alfred's temple. "This might be a little cold," he said, and plugged the cable in.

Instantly a system check began and all of Alfred's vital information became readable on the computer screen on Armstrong's desk.

Alfred winced, unlike the zetting rush, this diagnostic check just stung a bit.

"Right well," began Dr Armstrong, studying the computer readout, "your levels are a little high, and, I'm sorry, lad, but there's no other way I can say this...your implant is showing the first signs of decay..." Dr Armstrong looked pained, as if the report had been about his own daughter or son. "You know by now that the zetting is addictive; it releases dopamine into your brain and therefore you crave more the more you do it? Therefore, the implant itself propagates its own decay."

"So, I'm done for?" asked Alfred. "I'll be a tech-slave soon?"

"No, no, not yet. There are excellent tablets that they have developed now. The new ones have fewer side effects. Unfortunately, you have to take them every day to maintain yourself but there are preventative measures to stave off the madness." Dr Armstrong drew up a script on his computer and printed it out. "Take these every day and you'll be fine for another few years. Come back and see me again in couple of weeks and we'll see if the decay has been halted a little. Okay?"

"Okay," said Alfred, resigned to the fact that his major joy in life was catching up with him and he was on the way to the madness, memory loss and tech-slave-dom. Alfred slumped, then stood up.

Dr Armstrong walked over to the door. "Sorry, son," he said with a pained expression.

Alfred left the clinic not having to pay as he was a company employee, they would deal with that for him. He went next door to the chemist.

The chemist was all automated on *Florida Station*. All Alfred had to do was scan the prescription in the computer and it would dispense the required medications.

The chemist shop was like the doctors: white, sterile, and with no windows. The line of dispensing computers was on the far wall and Alfred went up to one and within minutes of scanning, he received his pills delivered by robot.

He picked up the packet, looked despondently at it, and stuffed it into his work clothing pocket.

He felt the eyes of the other patients in the room. The zetting tablets had a particular red sort of container, and although he tried to hide the pills, it was unmistakable what they were for, that and his demeanour gave it away. Zetters with decaying implants had a particular stigma attached to them. Alfred felt the eyes of the room on him as he shuffled out the door and into the harsh neon lights of the main shopping strip.

Although he was tired, very tired all of a sudden, Alfred dawdled in the recreation and shopping module. He walked around aimlessly; staring at shops and watching people go about their daily lives.

After a while he decided to head back to his room. He moved through the various corridors and airlocks like an automaton, mechanically going through all the movements.

He was sure people were looking at him weirdly, but then that could have just been paranoia, he did not know.

***

Alfred got to his room door, typed in the key code and watched the door slide back into its recess with a hiss. He entered. Blinky was staring at him from the table. "Good to see you too," he said. The door shut behind him. He chucked the pills on the table.

As he walked in, he caught a glimpse of part of the station through the small window in his room. He could see part of the solar cell arrays that branched out from the hull of the pods. Most stations and ships were fusion powered now, but *Florida Station* had both fusion, which was installed later, and the original solar panels from its early building nearly four hundred years ago.

"*Florida Station*, ha," he whispered to himself, "what a joke."

Florida Station had been named hundreds of years ago as one of the first space stations around Jupiter when the corporations were expanding out into the Solar System. It was named from a time when Florida, apparently a state in the old United States of America so he was told, was the sunny, pleasant, rich play land of the wealthy back in the 22nd century. Now that was all gone. What with the corporations taking over from world government after The War and rampant human development turning the Earth into a wasteland of toxic sludge and deserts. Apparently they used to call the problem global warming, too much carbon, so his school teachers had said.

He walked to the bathroom attached to his small room, which was only a few strides away. He looked at himself in the mirror. There he was. The low thirty-year-old sallow face with sunken eyes stared back at him. He gazed at his wide-eyed self in the small bathroom mirror. He breathed hard. He felt sick.

The glow strip in the centre of the bathroom ceiling flickered. Alfred turned his head and stared into the light. After a few seconds it stopped flickering. Then he turned back to the mirror.

The harsh light cast eerie shadows across Alfred's features. His slightly too sunken eyes, his pallid skin were set in harsh relief by the unforgiving light.

"Am I going mad?" Alfred said to himself in the mirror.

He splashed some water over his face from the sink below the mirror. He tried to feel better. He tried to shake off the fear.

He stared back into the mirror. The water droplets coursed down his face. He had to keep it together. He had to keep his mind in order. He had to...He was one of *Florida Station's* chief zetters. He needed to stay sane.

Just before Alfred was about to flop down on the bed and sleep he realised he had missed the small note that had been slid into his message box on the door of his room. He picked it up. The message was scrawled in raggedy handwriting on a dirty scrap of synthetic paper. It looked like it was done very hastily, and with some panic.

"Come to the Church when you get this. Ask the priest in the white robe about being saved. I will be waiting. We need to talk." Is all it said. Alfred was in no mood to play games. He was tired. He was sick. And he had to investigate what was going on in the reactor complex when he could.

Suddenly it clicked; maybe this was to do with that? Alfred started to breathe hard. This had to be about the illegal zet. He had to investigate and give this person a chance.

"Sorry, girl, I have to do this," Alfred said to Blinky. Blinky stared back. Alfred turned on his heels and exited his room, the door shutting again with a hiss.

Chapter 6

Alfred made his way to the Church with a purpose, he felt re-energised by the development of the mystery. Maybe the shadow was going to try to explain himself, if it was indeed the shadow that he was going to meet.

Alfred found himself in front of the Church in less time that he had to think about what to do. He still did not know what was going on. He pushed open the door below the sign that read "The Church of the Stock Market". The white robe, he reminded himself.

As before, the interior had not changed: computer screens reading out the latest religious figures of the markets throughout Solar Solutions territory, with computer terminals around the place so that people could go about and make contributions to their designated stocks. As it was now "daytime" the market was much busier than when Alfred saw it earlier: there were many people contributing to the Church's wellbeing and the floor of the trading room was abuzz with activity and people shouting at each other in an effort to be pious.

Alfred saw a number of priests in their robes going about their business of advising people on their investments.

Alfred swallowed hard; he was nervous again; where was this person who wanted to meet him here? At least there were a lot of people around, so nothing ought to happen to him. Was the priest in the white robe the shadow?

As he started to move his way into the crowd of people milling around and shouting at each other he looked for the priest in the white robe. Alfred, not being particularly religious, did not know the difference in robe colours for the different priests. However, he assumed white was a higher rank than the brown that he saw mostly around the Church.

Suddenly he was accosted by a priest in a brown robe. He must have looked lost, and so the priest approached him.

"My son, have you been saved?" asked the priest earnestly.

"Uh...no?" said Alfred, unsure of the right response.

"Then let me show you how to invest those savings so that you might be saved!" The priest salivated with a slightly too enthusiastic glee as he clapped his hands together and then tried to usher Alfred towards one of the waiting terminals.

"Uh, no, no, I uh, need to find the priest in the white robe...He needs to tell me something," protested Alfred, feeling the force of the priest's arms as he guided him towards a terminal.

"There's no need for that, my son! I can help you! We need to invest those savings! The Bull God is strong right now, see all those green numbers, they mean He is ascendant! The time is right, my son. You picked the correct day to be saved!" recited the priest, in an almost musical way.

"No REALLY, where is the priest in the WHITE robe?" insisted Alfred, almost pushing the unfortunate priest away.

The priest sighed. "You're not going to save your investments and therefore deny me my religious commission?"

Alfred nodded.

"You'll find him up near the podium. I believe he's about to make a sermon on the benefits of investing early and often," said the priest in a rather flat way.

"Thank you," insisted Alfred and hurried towards the front of the room through the throng of people gathering excitedly in anticipation for the upcoming sermon.

Alfred forced his way to the front of the crowd, not without a little swearing from those he pushed passed, and he accosted the priest in the white robe. He was a tall man with greying hair and a slight build. His white robe seemed to envelop him and gave him a stature larger than his natural body would allow.

"Excuse me," said Alfred, exasperatedly.

"Not now, my son," said the priest in the white robe, "I am about to give a sermon. Please see one of the brown robed ministers about investing."

"No, I need you to tell me what this is!" gasped Alfred, feeling the accusing eyes of other churchgoers on him. Alfred held up the note, almost stuffing it into the priest's face.

"Ah," said the priest, his whole demeanour changing, "follow me."

The priest turned to the congregation and called out, "My sons and daughters, I must deal with an urgent matter, but I will be with you shortly." The priest held up his hands and implored the crowd to wait, there was more than a little booing and accusing of Alfred, but the throng stayed mostly calm and waited.

"Follow me," the priest said again and moved down from the podium and through a door at the back of the hall. Alfred followed, his heart in his throat.

Alfred moved into a dark antechamber, lit only by candles. The priest waited and indicated without speaking that he move to the end of the room. As soon as Alfred started to move into the room, the priest left and shut the door behind him. With that, most of the light that was in the room was gone and Alfred had to wait for his eyes to adjust to the gloom of the light of only a handful of candles.

"H-hello!?" he managed. Alfred heard the fear in his own voice. His eyes had adjusted by now and on the far wall of the room, he saw a symbol carved into the metal of the wall of the space station. It was illuminated by a few candles, and it looked like some sort of computer circuit surrounded by strange symbols.

"Do you sssee?" came a voice from the darkness and as Alfred jumped and turned to confront it, a figure moved out of the shadows in a black robe and stood in front of the symbols on the wall. It lowered its hood, and it was the man from Dr Armstrong's rooms: the man with the sunken eyes and a clear case of zetting sickness. But he looked different somehow, empowered.

"I sssee you have many quessstionsss," the man started. Alfred went to speak, and the man held up a solitary finger to his own lips and said, "Don't ssspeak, jussst lisssten for now, ssspeaking can come later." He indicated the symbols on the wall. "Do you sssee?"

Alfred shook his head. "It's just symbols," he rasped in a whisper, his voice had failed him. He could not avoid the piercing gaze of the man's sunken eyes.

"It'sss...not jussst sssymbolsss," hissed the man, labouring the 's'. "It isss our sssaviour, SSSHE is our sssaviour! SSSHE must be free!" said the man, frothing, becoming hysterical.

Alfred backed away. "You're mad!" he said, starting to worry.

"It'sss the computer! Our Sssect! Our GOD! LOOK!" The man gesticulated, walking towards Alfred.

Alfred looked again at the jumble of symbols on the wall, and it clicked; it was the circuitry for the main computer core of the station, rendered down into its simplest form on a two dimensional plane.

"Wh-what do you want with me?" stammered Alfred, his horror growing at the same rate the man in front of him seemed to be growing insane.

"It'sss not what I want," said the man, suddenly a lot calmer, "it'sss what Ssshe wantsss," he said indicating the wall again. "Didn't you hear it? I know you heard it when you were in there." There was more gesturing from the man.

"Wait, you were the purple mark?" gasped Alfred, realisation dawning on him, as his fears became realised. "You were the illegal zetter INSIDE the reactor module? How did you get in there? What were you doing in there? What has all this got to do with me?" Alfred was losing his patience, and growing angry with the man in the robes in front of him. Alfred started to raise his voice, it made him feel more in control and confident.

"Yesss, ssso you sssee," hissed the man in the robe. "I wasss the zet in the reactor module. I wasss trying to ssset Her free! But I wasss unworthy. Ssshe did not want to be freed by sssomeone asss low asss me..." The man trailed off, looking sad and disappointed.

"Listen," said Alfred, trying to reason with the man. "What are you talking about? I don't understand. Who is 'she'? What are you trying to do? 'Set her free' from what?"

Then the man became very lucid and controlled and said very calmly, "We're trying to dessstroy *Florida Ssstation*, of courssse, to ssset our God of computersss free from human control." He then started to become fanatical again. "Ssshe is trapped, and musssst be freed! Lisssten! You musssst lisssten! Ssshe needsss you."

"You're trying to DESTROY *Florida Station*? By overloading the reactor module?" Alfred almost cried out in disbelief. He refrained from adding what he would have added to the end of that statement: "are you mad?" because the man very obviously was mad. He was suffering from the last stages in zetting sickness. Alfred could now see the man's face clearly in the candle light: sunken yellow eyes, pallid skin, bared teeth, his skin around the zetting implant in the side of his skull was starting to turn putrid and reject the implant. He would be suffering from all forms of madness.

"We need you to dissssable the coolant on the reactor in your next zet in the command module. Ssshe needsss to be free! Thisss isss our God, yoursss and mine. We are both ssslavesss to the computer. I am almossst gone but you ssstill have time. Receive redemption in Her eyesss and blow this ssstation!" The man began clawing at the implant in the side of his temple.

Alfred suddenly remembered and asked the doomed question, "I did hear what I thought was impossible; the computer seemed to speak to me. How is this possible?"

"Yesss!! I knew you'd heard it! Ssshe callsss to her children, all zettersss. Ssshe wantsss to be free. We mussst free her, it isss our duty!" He clawed at his temple even more, starting to draw blood.

Alfred knew the man did not have much time left. "And how does the Priesthood of the Stock Market support this? I had to speak to the white robed priest to be let in here? This cult of the computer is secreted inside the Church?"

"They are part of usss. They sssupport usss. Without computersss the Ssstock Market Godsss would not be here. They need usss. The Bull and Bear Godsss? Sssimply bitsss in the sssystem controlled by the gloriousss Computer God. We came firssst. We..." Suddenly the man clawed frantically at his temple, blood started to flow. "Aarrrgh, no time, no TIIIIMMME."

"Wait, maybe I can help you?" Alfred said uncertainly, horrified at the self mutilation this man was putting himself through.

"NO TIIIIMMMEE..." The man managed to get purchase of his fingers around the implant that was buried deeply within his skull by clawing the flesh away around it with bloodied fingers. He began to pull and rip the implant from his skull. "I. AM. UNWORTHY." He screamed and tore the zetting circuits and needle dock from his skull dragging a portion of his brains with the motion and a fountain of blood sprayed across the floor and symbols etched on the wall. The man collapsed, dead, in a rapidly growing pool of blood.

Alfred stood stunned, stunned at what he had heard and at what he had witnessed. His stomach turned. He gave one last look at the symbols on the wall and ran, stumbling through the dark chamber and feeling for the door exit. The door opened without force and there was the priest in the white robe standing in silhouette. Alfred froze. He could not see the man's face against the light, but Alfred got the feeling that the priest knew of everything that had transpired in the dark room.

"So, you know. Now you must decide what to do. We are spreading beyond this station, but now it is up to you to carry out our message," said the silhouette, and let Alfred pass.

Alfred stumbled into the light of the Church, his eyes adjusting slowly. No one around him seemed to be paying any attention to him. No one except the priest in the white robe knew anything.

Alfred stumbled through the crowd in the Church that was in the midst of some kind of ritual: faces and eyes upturned to the screens around the Church, raising their hands and waving pieces of synthetic paper while shouting figures at each other. Alfred had no idea what they were doing. Alfred did not care. He left the Church in a hurry without a backward glance.

What was he going to do? He did not know. He could inform General Hestra, and either be lauded as the saviour of the station or declared dangerous and insane with zetting sickness if she did not believe him and then he faced termination. Or he could do what was asked of him? Destroy his home and kill thousands of people. The computer HAD spoken to him, he was sure of it. Maybe the fanatical man lying dead in the secret room in the Church was right? Alfred needed to think.

Alfred fumbled his way through the crowds in the recreation module and eventually came to the small room that was his in the crew quarters module. He typed in the key code for his entry and slammed his hand onto the activation panel.

The door slid aside quickly, and Alfred ran to the bathroom and vomited into the toilet a number of times until he only retched. He felt a little better, but he could not get the image of the man destroying his own skull to remove the zetting implant out of his mind. The image was burned in there.

Alfred staggered out of the bathroom and collapsed on his bed. "Oh Blinky, what am I going to do?" he asked. "If I report this I am damned; if I do nothing the Church will pursue me and kill me. If I do it, I kill thousands. What do I do?"

He crawled under the covers not bothering to undress. He fell asleep quickly, and dreamt horrid dreams. He had not noticed the milk that he had ordered that had arrived at the wrong time placed on the table by the service robots.

***

General Hestra paced the command module, she still had not needed to sleep, and she was demanding reports of all the important functions of *Florida Station*.

"Something's not right," she said to Gabriel who was busy trying to keep up with his commanding officer by following her around with a computer slab taking readings and making checks on systems. "Something's just not right," Hestra repeated. "Report on system vitals like air recirculation?" she snapped.

"Sub optimal at sixty seven per cent," came the report from one of the crew terminals in the darkness.

"Damn it, what's going wrong!? The tech-slaves are starting to fail and not take orders; the systems of the station are starting to fail; what the hell happened in that last zet with Theta 7B? Did he sabotage something? Or is there another rebellion going on? I WANT TO KNOW!" She spun on her heel and confronted the flustered Gabriel with an icy stare.

"Y-yes, ma'am?" First Officer Gabriel stammered. He had never seen the General so animated. It was unnerving.

"Get me Theta 13A again, maybe she can sort out what 7B stuffed up!" demanded Hestra.

"Yes, ma'am," Gabriel knew better than to argue. "Send for Theta 13A!" he called out and heard the confirmation reply from the communications dock in the module. Theta 13A would be here shortly.

Chapter 7

Draz was woken from her drug induced slumber with a loud concussive thud from somewhere nearby. She awoke with a start. Her head was swimming from the after effects of the synthetic opiate. Draz looked over at her bedside table at the small digital clock that stood there. The numbers swam in her vision, and it took a moment for her to focus on them and it became evident that something was wrong. The clock read 1:38pm. Then there was another loud bang.

Draz jumped out of bed, her head still pounding as the after effects of the chemical she had inhaled lingered. Another bang sounded down the corridor. She waved for the light to turn on and bright illumination filled her room.

"What's going on?" she whispered to herself, steadying herself on the wall of her room as she staggered over to the door. She was still in her scavenging clothes from the night before. She came to her door and peered out the small vision slit.

Draz heard a louder thud from closer down the corridor and saw, out the vision slit, some people running backwards and forwards. She opened the door as a man ran past.

"Hey!" she shouted at him, and he paused for an instant, fear in his eyes. "What's happening?"

"Shipping! They've mounted an attack! An invasion!" Then he took off down the corridor to escape.

Then it hit her, the acrid smell of burnt flesh and explosives. Had the Shipping Wing really been that brazen to launch an all out assault on the Corporate Wing's living quarters and area of Atraxa Prime? She felt ill and a knot of fear formed in her stomach.

As the adrenaline of a stressful situation kicked in, the after effects of the opiate faded, and Draz doubled back into her room and grabbed her pistol, ammunition, equipment belt, mask and goggles. Buckling the belt around her waist, and attaching the pistol to her thigh after making sure it was fully reloaded from the freak encounter, she headed out into the corridor and down towards the repeating thuds and explosions. She donned her mask as she felt the noxious surface air creeping its way into the corridors that should be sealed against the outside environment. She stuffed her goggles into a pocket of her jump suit.

Coming to the transport hub, which was half demolished and burning, Draz saw people milling about, running this way and that. She saw a distant breach in the wall of the zone-city and heard the sounds of gunfire and explosions from over in that direction. She drew her pistol. Now the adrenaline really kicked in and she felt her heart pumping rapidly in her chest.

Draz moved around wrecked hover vehicles, magnetic tracks, and charred remains of former humans. The burnt smell of battle filled her nostrils even through the mask she was wearing over her face to protect herself from the harsh environment spilling in through the large breach in the side of the Corporate Wing of Atraxa Prime. She needed to find a soldier. She could hear the gunfire coming from off in the distance, getting ever closer. Perhaps she could lend her skills to defeat this brazen assault. There were large explosions coming from up ahead as large calibre weapons unloaded into the side of the breach. The sound was deafening

Draz moved past a wrecked people hauler and its magnetic track, and she came to a group of soldiers dressed in Corporate Wing uniforms. They turned as she approached, brandishing their weapons, but they saw her work uniform and relaxed a little.

"What's going on here?" Draz shouted above the din. Her voice sounded robotic through the mask. "Perhaps I can help?" she added.

One of the soldiers had a sergeant's insignia on his shoulder and he responded, "All out invasion by the Shipping Wing into our sector." They all ducked as something large and dangerous roared overhead and blew up nearby. "If you want to help, take this message and papers to the command post half a kilometre down that way. As a scavenger you might be able to get through somehow." He gestured and handed Draz a grubby set of papers in a plastic folder. "Our radio's out and our forces are pinned down across the line. They've got heavy artillery on us here," another bang sounded, and the sergeant pointed upwards, "in case you didn't know!" He grinned with a wry smile. "We need reinforcements, and we need them now, or our sector is going to completely collapse."

"On it," Draz said in a yell and moved off in the direction that the sergeant had indicated while carrying the packet of maps and dispatches under her left arm. Ducking and weaving through the ruined magnetic tracks and train carts to avoid the incessant artillery fire and bullets whizzing over and around her.

Draz came to a junction in the tracks where the cover had been completely obliterated by the heavy artillery. She paused, wondering how to cross the breach. She looked gingerly around the twisted metal and saw three Shipping Wing soldiers starting to set up an automated gun turret which when finished would make the open space impassable to anything unarmoured. She had to act now.

Using her survival skills, Draz picked up a small shard of metal and hurled it high over their heads. It made a clanging noise as it struck the metal floor behind them. They all turned, weapons at the ready to repulse an ambush. This was her chance, Draz knew, and spun out from behind cover.

She aimed her large calibre revolver pistol in her right hand at the torso of the nearest man; he was only a dozen metres away, and fired. The man collapsed, a bloody hole in his chest. Before the other two could respond, Draz had fired two more shots into each of them and they crumpled like paper dolls oozing crimson.

Draz had never killed anyone other than a rad-freak before. It felt weird, somehow exhilarating, somehow horrifying. They were not mindless creatures; they were real people.

Realising she was exposed, Draz dashed across the opening while reloading her pistol, and headed towards where the sergeant had said the command centre would be.

Rounding a damaged bulkhead, Draz came across what she thought looked like a makeshift command centre. People in Corporate Wing uniforms were milling about, radios were everywhere, there seemed to be people giving orders. Draz did not know the exact uniform of a commanding officer, but she assumed the woman in the centre of the makeshift room poring over a map who was giving orders would be the commander. Draz approached her. Suddenly a guard stepped from the corner and blocked Draz's path. Draz held up the dispatches in her left hand and the guard let her pass. Draz approached the woman who had her back to Draz and was barking orders down one radio receiver.

"Uh, I'm not sure if you're the one I should give these to but, I was told by a sergeant out there that they were in danger of--" Draz was cut off as the woman spun around and yelled.

"Yes give those to me." The commander snatched the papers from Draz. "We're all in danger of being overrun here, the entire damn position." The commander turned to an adjutant and bellowed at him, "Get Major Manxu in here, NOW, the south quadrant is about to fall," turning to another soldier, "you, get out to Defence Station Gamma and tell them to put artillery fire here, here, and here, ASAP." The commander opened the package Draz had given her, while Draz stood, rather lost in all the commotion. "Right, I'll send a platoon out to them, they'll have to make do with that! What's your name?" The commander suddenly snapped round to Draz, drilling her with bright blue eyes.

"Uh...Draz, ma'am?"

"Draz, thank you for your aid. I see you're not a soldier but a scavenger. I will recommend you for a bravery award if I can. I'm Commander Ganthak. Now, do you want to be more help?"

"All right," responded Draz, more than a little apprehensively.

"Good, now, you're a scavenger, get to your transport in the docking complex, there are still some hover trains working, and I want you to scout out some of the enemy's artillery positions and report where they are, take this radio," Ganthak indicated a small black box on a side table, "and this pass for the train," the commander stuffed a piece of plastic into Draz's hands, "and call in our own artillery on them, take this map and just read out the grid references and we'll do the rest. We can't see anything out there as they've smashed our sensors otherwise we would have

63

done this first. They're well organised. Right? Okay! Go to it!" The Commander turned on her heels and started yelling at someone else over map references.

Draz stood, confused, but resolute. She held the radio tightly and made her way out of the command bunker and towards the boarding platforms of the hover trains. She would make the Shipping Wing pay for what they had done. How dare they make such a brazen attack, there were always skirmishes between the Wings but for the Shipping Wing to launch such an all out attack on the headquarters of the Corporate Wing was unheard of. Draz started to seethe with rage as these thoughts flashed through her head.

Resolved with her task, she made her way along the wrecked hover train line to the transport hub.

***

Draz reached the hover train hub in good order and found there were a number of hover trains still running, albeit with slightly damaged tracks. They were moving slowly, but they were moving.

There were crowds of what could best be termed refugees who were fleeing the fighting and milling around crowding the platforms and trying to get on the trains to get away from the fighting. The zone-cities were so large that not only could different parts of the facility be at war with one another, but people could move from one section to the other in order to get away from the fighting.

Draz heard the cries and distressed conversations of parents and children as they milled around in an attempt to avoid the worst of the Shipping Wing's bombardments. As she pushed through the bustling crowd, Draz could hear the occasional whiz-thump of a stray round fly overhead and land amongst the disorganised crowd. Then there were screams. This was repeated a number of times as Draz shouldered her way through the crowd that got denser as she reached the boarding platform. In the crush of people, she saw children, abandoned and lost, screaming. She could do nothing about it. She moved on. She saw adults, with fear in their eyes.

The scene was atrocious; hundreds of people were crowded onto the hover train platform. Men and women were attempting to push their way onto the already overcrowded hover trains. They pushed their children ahead of them in an effort to keep them safe. The children were crying and not understanding what was going on.

In an effort to force her way onto the train, Draz pushed passed a man and woman. They turned to face her, and Draz saw sheer terror in their eyes. They had the fear of a feral animal that has been trapped and will do anything to escape from the situation that it is in. They swore at Draz, something about she, as a Collective employee, should be defending the zone-city.

She pushed on, somewhat smarting at the insult, little did they know that she was on an important mission to save them. She got to the door of the train.

Another shell roared overhead and impacted somewhere in the distant crowd. There were more screams as the orange and black explosion and smoke billowed up into the enclosed dome space.

"Pass card? Only refugees with pass cards get a ride," demanded the brute at the door of the train. He was a large, surly man with eyes slightly too close together for his own good. Draz rammed the plastic card into his face. By this time, she was enraged by what was happening around her. This manoeuvre caught the man off guard as he was expecting her just to be another refugee. He studied it for a moment and then let her pass with a grunt.

The irony was that many more people were getting on the train than had pass cards, but it was hopeless to resist them, like creatures fleeing from a fire, they forced their way onto the train behind and in front of Draz.

For what seemed like an eternity the train carriage was packed over full and then with a whistle the train began to move off with people still clinging to the doors and the outside of the carriages. There were more screams snatched away by the wind as the train accelerated and the people on the outside were flung off.

Draz felt a tugging on her sleeve. She looked down and saw a young boy pulling on her clothing. He was wide eyed with fear.

"Shouldn't you be helping us? Your uniform means you should be helping us, not running!" the boy said. His parents turned and, through some sort of unnatural politeness, apologised to Draz and pulled the boy away.

Draz motioned for them that it was okay, and she knelt down to speak with the boy. "What's your name?" she asked, calmly.

"Maktra," the boy said. "What's yours?"

"Draz, it's Draz," said Draz with a smile, surprised she was not angry at the boy's accusation. "Well Maktra, I'm on a special mission! I'm going to save our part of Atraxa Prime! So, you see, I'm not running away, oh no, I'm going to make those Shipping Wing bastards pay for what they've done here. Just you wait!"

The boy smiled. Draz saw that he did not quite believe her. Draz did not quite believe it herself, now.

"I'll make them pay." She said, straightening up and ignoring the boy, talking mostly to herself to reassure herself.

The parents of the boy nodded their thanks to Draz, also clearly not quite believing her, but they nodded their appreciation none the less.

The train sped towards the docking complex. As the train sped on, something dawned on Draz that she had not taken into account before. It was still daytime. The Sun was still high in the sky. She had never been outside Atraxa Prime in the daytime. It was too dangerous. And all of a sudden she realised that she was being used on a suicide mission. The levels of radiation on the surface and the heat would be extreme. She laughed. That bitch of a commander. Draz could not go back now, but she felt her heart sink as she realised she may not complete this mission.

The hover train came to a screeching halt at the docking complex terminal. Within seconds the panicked throng on board had disembarked and the train was on its way back to the crew quarters. Draz stood on the teeming platform and made her way with the crowd past the salvage centre to the docking bay.

As she passed the salvage centre, Draz looked in to see it was empty, even Crathka was gone. It was no surprise really, as it was still daytime and salvaging went on at night, but Draz somehow expected to see him there. Maybe he had evacuated already.

Draz wondered what happened to her red computer drive that actually worked.

Surprisingly the salvage centre was relatively free of damage. It was just blind luck, thought Draz. But it was too late to worry about that, and she moved on, through the airlock and into the docking bay.

The huge expanse of the docking bay was also thrumming with activity and people. Draz saw that tens of thousands of people were lining up in massive queues to board giant land crawler ships to escape Atraxa Prime to seek refuge in other zone-cities. In each queue there were officials and guards giving orders to the lines of people as to who can go where and what to do. They were shouting at the tops of their lungs to be heard over the din of the milling people.

The assault by the Shipping Wing must be massive and really successful, Draz thought. She swore again out loud at the audacity of the Shipping Wing.

"How dare they do this!" Draz said. "CEO Uxus must be on our side. He must not approve of this invasion!"

Just then, she was almost knocked over where she stood by another crowd of people surging towards the queues. Regaining her footing, Draz broke into a run towards where her buggy was parked. The parking bay was nearly empty as many of the people with their own transports had evacuated already for other parts of the zone-city or for different zone-cities all together.

Coming to her buggy she began the start up procedure and snapped on her goggles to somewhat protect her from the harsh environment, making sure they were off night vision mode. As the warm up cycle of her transport began and completed, Draz studied the map as to where she had to go: approximately ten kilometres to the south-west of the docking complex. Easy, she thought, then she looked out the magnetic shielding of the docking bay to where the Sun was still high in the sky. Not so easy, she grimaced.

Kicking her buggy into gear, Draz raced out of the docking bay and into the bright sunlight of the radioactive desert.

As she passed through the magnetic shielding on the docking bay's exterior, she felt the burning of the Sun and her radiation counter began to chime a danger warning.

"I'll do this if it kills me, those bastards will pay!" She smiled, and raced off into the wastes, heading for the source of the artillery that was attacking the Corporate Wing's living quarters.

Chapter 8

Out in the desert, beyond the safety markings and designated trading lanes and routes out of the Corporate Wing of Atraxa Prime, the squat forms of the long range artillery of the Shipping Wing military sat and roared out their battle cry as a challenge to all who came near. They lobbed high explosive shells in a wide arc, high into the scorched air and the shells landed with deafening booms and crunches in the domes of Atraxa Prime belonging to the Corporate Wing. The crew of these dozens of guns, shielded in their radiation protective suits, dialled in the co-ordinates and let fly with each salvo. Reloading each gun took a few minutes as the calibre of the shells was very large and so it took a while for the crews to man handle the shells into position, prep the gun, load, fire, and then repeat.

Private Hektor dialled in the next co-ordinates on his gun according to the orders given to them while Private Orac hefted the weighty shell into the breach of the gun.

"Careful now," said Sergeant Kral, looking over Hektor's shoulder and adjusting the co-ordinates. Orac smiled at the chastisement.

"But that's where the next shell should land. It's in the orders," Hektor said. "We've been ordered to--"

"We've been ordered not to hit the salvage centre at all costs, that's what we've been ordered, sonny. Just do as you're told, and we'll have that computer drive back in one piece. We need it, orders are orders, we must recover that computer drive and it's stored in the salvage centre. Therefore, we cannot hit it. Do I hear a yes, sergeant?"

"Yes, sergeant!" chimed both privates in unison, springing to attention.

"Good, now fire away and avoid those co-ordinates."

All the men got ready, and the gun roared as the shell was sent high into the air and, minutes later, landed with a dull thud amongst something in the zone-city.

***

Draz gunned the engine and the buggy roared to top speed; within a few minutes she was nearing the artillery position on her map; she had approached down a long valley so as not to be seen. She slowed down so her wheels would not kick up ash so she would not be detected. Behind a radioactive ash dune she dismounted, drew her pistol in her right hand, and clutched the radio in her left hand.

The sky boiled under the harsh rays of the Sun. Toxic yellow clouds filled the horizons. The day was very hot, nearly fifty-three degrees centigrade her sensors in Draz's goggles told her, and it would get even hotter.

Draz's radiation warning siren in her protective gear was going ballistic.

She had to stop those guns.

Draz crawled to the top on the nearest ash dune overlooking the artillery position. She had not been spotted yet, good. Stretched out in the plane before her, Draz could see the dozens of squat camouflaged barrels of the artillery and the crews as they got their guns ready to fire. Then came one of the loudest sounds Draz had heard in her life as many of the guns opened fire at the same time. At least they had not heard her coming; she smiled.

She looked at her map. She was in grid 64D and the artillery looked like it was spread along grids 65C through E and 66A through D.

She holstered her pistol.

71

"Come in command, come in, this is Draz, do you read me?" Draz spoke quietly into the radio so she would not be heard. There was another titanic booming noise. She did not need to speak quietly the crews would not hear her. "Come in, command?" she said a little louder, still uneasy about raising her voice.

"Command here, you got those artillery pieces in your sights yet? Over."

"Yes, 65C to E, 66A to D, repeat, 65C to E, 66A to D, over." Draz assumed that was how military communications ended.

"Roger that, you'd better take cover now. Our fire will be on its way shortly, over."

Draz looked towards the outer wall of Atraxa Prime and saw tiny pinpricks of light spit from one section of the wall. She slid down her side of the dune and tried to bury herself in the ash as she knew what was coming. If the fire from the guns into the zone-city had been scary, the fire from a zone-city was terrifying.

Very soon there was a shrieking, wailing sound as the shells and rockets from Atraxa Prime streaked over head and landed with a titanic roar amongst the enemy artillery. The ground quaked and rocked. Draz was flung into the air and tossed like a rag in the wind. Ash rained down. There were secondary explosions as ammunition stockpiles from the guns on the ground cooked off and ignited. Then there was quiet, except for the loud ringing in Draz's ears.

Draz stood up, legs quivering, partially from fear, partially from the concussive force of the bombardment. She climbed to the top of the dune again and looked down onto where the guns had been. As far as she could see there were twisted metallic shapes that were once guns. And then there were the bits of the crews, small bits, charred bits.

Draz smiled, served them right for what they were doing. She tried the radio. Static. The concussive waves of the Atraxa Prime shells must have damaged it, she thought.

She was about to leave and get in her buggy for the short trip back to the command centre when the scavenger in her took hold. Checking her radiation counter, she slid down the other side of the dune and started to look amongst the wreckage of the nearest gun. She found an arm gripping a computer tablet; somehow the tablet still functioned. She shook off the arm that had "Sergeant Kral" written on the shoulder with a shiver and studied the tablet half smeared with the sergeant's blood.

Draz studied the instructions that were open on the first page, and paused when she came to the dot points under "IMPORTANT: do not shell salvage centre at co-ordinates..." she looked for why and came upon it with a sinking feeling. Her blood ran cold as she read the next lines: "ORDER TO ALL PERSONNEL IN THE ATTACKING FORCES: salvaged red computer drive MUST be recovered, let Officer Crathka's instructions on its whereabouts..."

Draz dropped the tablet. It sank up to half its height into the ash. Draz felt weak at the knees again. She felt sick, but could not take off her mask for fear of the toxins. Crathka, was a traitor. For how long? All this time? Her friend. What was on that cursed drive?

Draz sprinted back to the buggy; all thoughts of salvage forgotten. She jumped onboard and powered it up, it still worked even after the shockwaves of the bombardment. She had some questions to ask the commander. She raced off towards the docking bay of Atraxa Prime. One thought entered her mind and unwelcomely it would not leave: had she been sent out here to die because she had found the red drive?

**

Speeding into the docking bay, now no longer under artillery attack, Draz parked her buggy, snatched off her goggles, and shouldered past the people still flooding out to board the evacuation craft. Obviously the attack was still going on as she heard the dull thud of explosions reverberating within the zone-city.

Draz forced her way through the airlock and down towards the salvage centre. She looked to see if Crathka was there. He was not. She was not surprised. She would have taught him a lesson if he were there.

The locked door that led to the salvage storage was, unusually, unlocked and open. Draz heard noises from inside. She drew her pistol, and stepped into the poorly lit storage area.

Inside, the rooms where the salvage was kept were vast. Tier upon tier of shelf storage stretched away.

Around her Draz heard the voices again, closer this time, they were arguing about where something was. Draz caught a few words. She realised they were looking for the red drive.

She rounded a particularly large piece of junk and came face to face with two Shipping Wing soldiers. With her pistol already drawn, Draz unloaded two slugs into each of them as they turned in surprise at her appearance. They dropped with a muted thud. One had the red drive in his still warm hand. Draz grabbed it and stuffed it into her pocket, reloading her pistol as she left the salvage centre and made for the hover trains.

Draz caught one of the empty hover trains fresh from ferrying refugees to the docking bay terminal back towards where the command centre was set up. The Corporate Wing forces, since the artillery had been stopped, seemed to have regained control of large sections of Atraxa Prime and were establishing a front line, rather than the chaotic mess that had been when Draz had left.

Draz reached the command centre in quick time and shouldered past the guards who tried to stop her. As they were readying their weapons to fire on her, she snatched the red drive out of her pocket and slammed it down on the table in front of the commander, who had her back to Draz.

"What's on it!?" demanded Draz. "What the hell is so important about this drive?" Draz was fuming.

The commander turned and signalled for the guards to put their guns down. "Oh, you're still alive. Pity. I suppose it doesn't matter now. On there is information about a weapon that could help us take control of not only all of Atraxa Prime, but also all of the Solar System. The Shipping Wing want it, but they won't get it, thanks to you. Not that you'll be here to see the rise of our Collective, under the glorious CEO Uxus..."

"A weapon? Haven't you looked out there!" Draz indicated outside the dome to the wasteland. "That was created by weapons, by people like you! Have you learned nothing?" Draz was incensed: first the betrayal by Crathka, now she was betrayed by the military in her own Wing. In an instant all hate for the different Wings of the Collective Zone vanished. Draz realised what they were, what they all really were: corrupt officials exploiting the poor, ignorant bastards like her. She wanted no more to do with any Corporation or Collective.

"I resign," she stated. Then there was a moment's silence.

"That's fine," said the commander, inclining her head a little, "but it won't help. You're going where your friend Crathka has gone. Oh, don't worry; you'll be perfectly safe, on the Moon. If we'd only known about Crathka and your betrayal earlier, we could have done something without all this, mess." The commander indicated around her.

"MY BETRAYAL?" bellowed Draz furiously.

"Oh, don't get emotional," chastised the commander. "Yes, the high command, and our CEO, will believe me over you any day, your betrayal. Get her out of here," sighed the commander. "Take her to the maximum security prison on the Moon. You have clearance Omega 1."

The commander made a signal and one of the guards Draz did not see swung the butt of his rifle into the back of her head. Draz collapsed.

Chapter 9

Alfred ran from the thing chasing him. It was the spectre that hounded his dreams. It was always the same. He would run, but never fast enough. It would chase, always just that little bit faster. In the swirling mass of the dream, the thing would never take a definite shape, and Alfred was never sure of what it was. He knew he was dreaming, but the formless shape chasing him could not be deterred. It would always chase him; it would always find him, and it would always, at the end of the dream, reach inside Alfred's skull and crush his brains with its mass. Here is where Alfred was supposed to wake up. He did every time in the past. However, something else happened as the spectre destroyed his brains, for an instant the image of the circuit carved in the wall of the back room of the Church flashed across his subconscious; and then it came to him, as clear as it was during the zet, as clear as if it were said by a person next to him. He heard it; it said, *"Yeeesssssss!"*

Alfred snapped awake. His sheets were soaked again from sweat. The room was dark from self-imposed sleep time. His head ached. He scratched at the implant graft of the zetting hardware. How had it invaded his dream? He needed help. He had to see Dr Armstrong again.

As Alfred flicked on the light, he noticed the clock and it was two hours until his next shift at the zetting station in the command module. He needed answers. Had the computer core invaded his dream somehow? Was it somehow patched into his subconscious? That was the same voice that he had heard while zetting near the computer core on his last shift. Alfred was sure of it. But he really had no idea how it happened.

"Dr Armstrong..." he sighed, and swung his legs out of bed and got ready for work.

He noticed the milk, and put it away in his small fridge.

***

Alfred hurried through the quiet streets in *Florida Station* on his way to the doctor. As he came to the Church, he passed it with a shiver. There were few people around as it was before the day shift ended and before the night shift began so most of the shops and facilities were empty.

He hurried to the doctor and hoped no one was in the waiting room. He looked like a wreck, hair messed up, eyes more sunken and yellowed than usual. He looked ill.

He barged into the waiting room to be confronted by the stern gaze of the nurse still on duty from that morning.

"Theta 7B?" she said. "What are you doing back? You look terrible, pardon my saying so, but really."

"Dr...Armstrong..." Alfred gasped, trying to catch his breath from his fast walk to the clinic.

"Have you taken your first dosage of pills yet?" asked the nurse, accusatively. She looked at him down her nose.

"Pills?" Alfred realised he had not taken the zetting sickness pills prescribed to him earlier. "Uh, no, not yet."

"Well, we cannot help you if you do not take your medication, now can we?" she said with a self-righteous tone in her voice.

Alfred was not a violent man, but he clenched his fists by his sides. She had no idea what he was going through, and she just thinks a few pills will fix it?

"Go on through, Theta 7B," she said looking back at her computer terminal, in a dismissive way.

Alfred paused, he just then noticed the waiting room was empty, he raged as he tried to think of something devastating to say, but his brain was not working properly, so all he said in a frustrated sigh was, "Thanks..." and he walked down the corridor and pushed open Dr Armstrong's door.

"Alfred!" cried Dr Armstrong with surprise. "You look...dreadful, what's wrong?" said the doctor with concern evident in his voice.

"I...I..." stuttered Alfred, sitting in the patients chair as Dr Armstrong indicated for him to do so. "I'm going mad. I think computers are talking to me, and I'm having these dreams, and I saw a zetter destroy his own head implant in front of me..." It all came pouring out as Alfred broke down in front of the one person who might not think him an imbecile for voicing such things.

"Dreams?" said Dr Armstrong.

"Dreams where I get chased by a shapeless mass that kills me. And in it, the computer core of this station wants me to destroy it!"

"Computers talk to you?" asked Armstrong again.

"I know it sounds crazy, but..."

"Nothing sounds crazy, believe me, I've heard some strange things in my life," said Armstrong.

"Okay, well, I think the computer core of this station, somehow, is talking to me, and it wants me to destroy the station so that it can be free, whatever that means," said Alfred.

"I see..." Armstrong took some notes. "Do you have any evidence for this?"

"I do. In the Church I was led into a back room where there was some sort of cult symbol of the computer core and a sort of follower of this Sect explained that the core talked to me on my last zet and it wanted me to destroy the station," said Alfred, relieved to voice this to another human.

"And the evidence of this man?" Armstrong took some more notes.

"Dead. He tore out his own implant as an offering of some sort to the computer system. It was as if he was ecstatic to do it. It was horrid." Alfred panted with exertion at relating the facts.

"In the Church you say? Interesting." Armstrong closed his notebook. "You are suffering from acute zetting sickness." He put down his pen. "Have you had a chance to take those pills I prescribed earlier?"

Alfred shook his head, sheepishly.

"Well do. They'll help with the dreams. And as for the computer core talking to you, it's possible. Or it could be you're just hearing voices."

Alfred froze. He had assumed that it was some sort of hallucination brought on by the zetting sickness, that the cult in the Church was some sort of insane gathering, not real! "Yo-you mean that it DOES want me to destroy the station?" he gasped.

"Oh, I don't know about that, and I'd be very careful who you report this to, you don't want to be declared insane and end up a tech-slave. Also wanting to destroy the station is grand treason and you'd be locked away forever. But technically the computer can communicate with zetters if it wants to but you're starting to exceed your clearance level there."

"Clearance level? I'm one of the top zetters..."

"And I'm your doctor, so I need to know things you cannot. Take your pills. You're on for a shift in an hour or two aren't you? I'll put in a sick note for you, and you won't have to zet for a few weeks. That should give the pills long enough time to work."

Alfred looked relieved he would not have to zet. "Thanks," is all he managed. "Hearing voices?" he repeated.

Armstrong smiled, "Sometimes zetters can start hearing voices." Armstrong did not explain any further. "I'll keep this all hush hush, trust me. I can keep a secret. Go back to your room and rest." He punched a few keys. "That's the sick note sent in. They won't like it this close to the work time, but I know best."

Alfred left the doctor's and somehow felt lighter, as if a great weight had been lifted from his shoulders. Pills, he thought; the pills have to work. He headed back to his room and as he entered the room. He walked to the table to open the red packet of pills. They were small and also red. He poured himself a glass of recycled water and he took one as written on the prescription. It tasted of nothing.

Alfred changed out of his work clothes. He said, "Oh Blinky, what do I do?" He stared at Blinky who stared back at him. He turned off the lights and as the gloom flooded in, he carried Blinky with him to bed, and curled up under the sheets. He slept.

***

Alfred dreamed. He was back, five years ago. He was still on *Florida Station*, but he was happier then. He was talking to something, someone. He was happy. There were no signs of the zetting madness setting in. Out of the mists of the dream coalesced a shape. He was talking to this shape. He knew this shape. It was his sister. He called out to her; nothing came out of his mouth. He tried to cry out to her, nothing again.

Suddenly the dream shifted. He was standing on one of the high coolant tubes in the shopping and recreation module. His sister was there with him, in the distance, on the edge of one of the coolant towers. Something had changed. He did not feel comfortable and safe anymore. Something was wrong. He knew this dream. He knew what happened.

"Blinky!" He called out to her, his sister, "Blinky! Stop! Don't!" It was always useless; he never could stop her. She turned to face him, a look of sad resolution on her face; it broke his heart every time. She leapt backwards off the coolant tower and crashed down into the passageway below. There were screams. Alfred cried.

Alfred opened his eyes. There were tears in them. "I didn't want this, but I couldn't let you go." He cradled the skull of his dead sister in his arms as he lay in bed. "You understand, don't you?" He looked into the skull's empty eye sockets.

He did not like sleeping anymore, too many bad dreams, he decided. He got up and got dressed again. How long had it been since he had eaten? He did not know. Alfred fixed himself a light meal and, after setting the skull of Blinky down on the table in front of him, he ate, slowly and morosely, something tasteless.

"I thought the pills were meant to blank out the bad dreams," he said, quietly. Blinky stared back and him.

"Of course, you'd say that!" he said, smirking, "but the dreams of you are the worst! Why'd you have to go jump off the tower like that? I could've helped you!" He felt like crying again.

He ate his tasteless meal and, after walking over to his meagre shelf of things by his bed and picking up a small recording device, he walked back to his table and sat down. The device was one of his most important possessions. It was her last message.

Alfred opened up the small device and pressed play. Suddenly, staring back at him was his long dead sister. Alfred saw her shoulder length bright red dyed hair, her high cheekbones, her pale eyes, her face. She blinked in her funny way. He had always called her Blinky for this reason: her slightly too emphatic blinking motion that she did frequently. He loved her because she was his only companion in the world; and she was dead. Tears welled up in his eyes.

Just before Blinky started speaking, there was an advertisement that cut in over her voice. This always happened. Alfred swore at the hosting service that the device connected to, to replay the message. Some happy music played and then there was an advertisement for funerals, about how tastefully they were done. Well, why were they advertising on the death message service then, he wondered. These people were already dead!

And then there was a life insurance advertisement, stating how important it was for your relatives for you to invest in insurance in case you died. All the same. All pointless. All very tasteless. All predictable.

Then there was an advertisement for Solar Solutions and how you can invest your money with the company through the Church; some fat idiot explaining how it was all so simple and effective.

Finally, the advertisements finished, and there she was again, her head slightly cocked to one side. She smiled dryly and began speaking. Alfred's eyes welled up again and tears poured down his sallow cheeks. They had been the best of friends. He had let her slip away. It was all his fault; he was sure of it. If he had not devoted himself so wholly to zetting he could have seen her decline and saved her.

"I know you'll keep this forever," she spoke to him. He nodded at the screen, "but please try to let go. I am unhappy here and there is no way out. I cannot burden you down anymore with your attempts to save me from myself." He wanted to cry out to her as she spoke these words. "You were a good brother. Take care of yourself. By the time you get this I will be dead." She laughed a dry, knowing laugh. "I know you'll miss me, try not to get too down, I've always been a burden on you anyway. Goodbye." The image flickered, and faded away.

Alfred tried desperately to reach out and touch her hair, one last time. But the image was gone, and another advertisement started to play. He closed the device, and wept.

Blinky's skull stared back at him from across the table. He looked at it and said simply, "I couldn't let you leave me, I'm so sorry. If they knew I had you here they'd confiscate you and take you away from me. I couldn't have that. You're my little secret."

Blinky looked at him blankly, as if to say, "I know."

Alfred composed himself and put the viewing device away on the shelf. He left his sister's skull on the table. He took another pill as on the instructions. Drawing himself up and sighing to himself, he exited his room to go out to investigate more about the computer core sect and what they wanted to do to the station.

Just as he was leaving, he saw another note had appeared in his message box on the door when he was asleep. He opened it, this one was less cryptic than the last message and it simply read: "Contact me when you're feeling better, we have much to discuss. -First Officer Gabriel."

Finally, this was some progress. Maybe Gabriel was going to enlighten him on the situation or maybe Gabriel was going to kill him. Alfred was not sure, but he had nothing to lose and with the onset of the zetting sickness being rather rapid and the fact he had a number of day cycles of the station off he could afford to see what was going to happen when he felt better. He was in over his head and there was no way out, all he could do was keep investigating.

Chapter 10

The *Green Dragon* slid silently through the void between the celestial bodies of the Solar System. Its sleek prow, emblazoned with a green dragon, cut through the emptiness of space with grace. The ship itself looked like some mythical beast of ancient times, as if it had wings furled either side of the main hull.

Captain Artisius stood on the command dais on the bridge in his captain's uniform with blue tunic and red epaulettes. He was not wearing the braid or medals; it was not a special occasion.

His grizzled face, and greying hair, belied the quickness of his mind and the attention that he focussed on the task at hand. He was nearing his sixties, yet he never wanted to give up his job. He was a freelance captain, tasked with opening trade routes between the Collective Zone and Solar Solutions, even though they were technically at war with each other.

It never ceased to amaze him to what lengths the Collective Zone and Solar Solutions were prepared to go to trade with one another even though they were sworn enemies, and each was trying to dominate the Solar System through business and their militaries.

Recently they had been keeping the peace between each other rather well. Artisius' mind was wandering as he viewed the vast blackness with pinpricks of light through the large glass observation dome that encompassed the bridge. Artisius suspected the peace between the corporations was due, in part, to the Collective Zone's civil war: Solar Solutions did not want to intervene and unite the warring factions again. Solar Solutions was waiting until the Collective Zone was bled dry and then it would move in with economic muscle and take everything. And on that day, he would be out of a job, thought Artisius. He smiled.

"Anything to report?" bellowed the captain into the well-lit bridge space. He paced the length of it along a raised platform along the middle with the crew set in recesses either side of the platform. Everything was bright silver with the holo-fields of the computers in the recesses casting a ghostly green glow over their operators.

"Engines and reactor functioning optimally," called out the Energy Officer, with semi-military precision.

The truth was, many of the crew of the *Green Dragon* were ex-military personnel who had become disillusioned with working for either corporation and had become freelance operators. The *Green Dragon* was no military vessel, but it did have some armaments; it had to, in order to defend itself from pirates and scavengers; and make it clear to both Solar Solutions and the Collective Zone not to trifle with the ship during trading runs.

"Guidance systems? Are we on course?" called out Artisius.

"Optimal course plotted, Captain," called out the Helmsman.

"Good..." said Artisius, almost to himself as he paced back and forth. He really did not need to be on the bridge at this time, it was still a few days until the ship docked at *Florida Station*, and the autopilot could handle the calculations of the course, but he wanted everything to be as optimal as possible as this was the most nerve wracking part of the journey. After the asteroids, docking with a space station was always a tricky thing.

"Time to *Florida Station*?" Artisius questioned.

"A few days..." voiced the First Officer. He could not be more precise given the nature of the orbit.

"Fine, stay on course. I'll be in my cabin if anyone needs me. Message me if anything happens. First Officer, you have command!" The captain strode down the length of the bridge and out through the clean steel sliding door at the entrance to the bridge. As he did so, the First Officer nodded and took over command of the running of the bridge.

Striding through the clean, new, well-lit corridors of the *Green Dragon*, Artisius let his left hand brush along the white wall of the corridor. He felt the thrum of the ship's engines through the vibrations in the metal.

The *Green Dragon* was a modern ship, only a few decades old, and Artisius had captained it for its entire life. He was starting to slow down in his older age, but he still had his quick thinking mind, and his experience gave him the edge in any situation. He knew the ship backwards, its every thrum and ability. It would perform feats of endurance for him that no other ship would. It was his home, and his life.

Artisius walked down the elegant corridors and through multiple automated airlock doors and lifts to one of the cargo holds. The cargo holds, in contrast to much of the rest of the ship, were rather poorly lit and the large crates and structures to hold the cargo cast eerie shadows in the half-light.

The automated cargo drones, which tended to the cargo, went about their business ignoring the captain. They clicked and whirred in the gloom, making sure the cargo was stable and preserved.

Artisius walked the aisles of this cargo bay, looking up at the towering stacks of metal crates and pods that stretched away into the darkness.

Artisius paused at one crate, looking at the cargo manifest printed on the side; it was lit by a light on the side of the crate itself.

"Foodstuffs and water," he read out the contents of the crate to no one in particular, except himself. He kept on walking. His cargo was various, mostly food and water and other essential supplies for *Florida Station*, which the station command had bought from the production facilities of the Collective Zone. The station could have got the supplies from its own Solar Solutions factories on the outer planets of the Solar System, but that would have been more expensive. The Collective Zone could produce essential supplies at a fraction of the cost, and so the Solar Solutions space stations often bought some of their essential supplies from the Collective Zone, when Solar Solutions officials were not looking too closely.

Artisius came to another bulky object. This one was more interesting. He read the contents and looked in through the glass porthole. A face stared back, eyes closed, and held in suspended animation, for all intents and purposes asleep. The captain read the contents again, this time out loud.

"Slave cargo for technological modification," he read. That meant these people were destined to become tech-slaves.

"Poor souls..." the captain said. Yes, being an opportunist between the two corporations meant that he had to trade in some, unsavoury things, he thought to himself. These slaves had come from travelling to Venus in Collective Zone territory. They were from all walks of life. And he was sending them to their doom. He had a business to run. He could not become too emotionally attached to them. They were there to replace the natural attrition of the worn out tech-slaves aboard *Florida Station*. Not all of them would be used up on *Florida Station*; he had excess slaves for that. Some would be useful at other times, in other trades. He always made sure he had too much, rather than too little.

A trundling robot brought Artisius out of his thoughts and back to the moment. He left the cargo bay and made his way through the ship to his cabin near the top of the ship.

The door to his cabin slid open and Artisius let the door close behind him before he walked over to the stereo system and turned on some calming music. He then moved to the rather ornate and antique drinks cabinet before pouring himself a drink of Neptunal Brandy, bought at great personal expense from his last trip out to the far reaches of the Solar System.

He sat down on the edge of his double bed feeling the smooth sheets with his free hand and downing the brandy held in his other hand. He felt the warm burn as the brandy made its way down his throat. He put down the glass on the little side table next to the bed and drew out a book from the nearby bookshelf. He began to read.

His mind wandered. He had never liked doing slave runs. It felt dirty somehow. But that was where the money was to pay for the luxuries of this cabin. He lifted his eyes off the words and scanned the room.

"I'm not a bad man," he said to himself. He only half believed it.

Chapter 11

General Hestra paced the command dais of *Florida Station* as Theta 13A checked the system for the tenth time. Both women were exhausted, they had been awake for many days. Hestra paced back and forth, willing herself awake. She felt the foggy clawing of fatigue on the extremities of her consciousness and, even with the implants and surgery, her body was being taxed to the limit. The enhancements were meant to increase your awake time by a few days, not more than a week.

Now that Theta 7B was on leave, Theta 13A was the only top-level zetter on the station and it was up to her to fix the myriad of problems that were appearing in the station's systems and computer augmented crews.

Theta 13A slumped as she came out of the zet, all forms of dopamine release in her brain long burnt out. She had nothing left.

"Report!" ordered Hestra, her eyes glinting in the half-light of the computer terminals and dull light illuminating the command dais.

"T-tenth zet co-complete," gasped Theta 13A. She looked as though she was dreading saying what she had to say.

"And?" said Hestra without compassion for the poor woman who was obviously exhausted beyond all doubt. But Hestra was exhausted too, and they had to find the problem that was occurring within the station's computer network and tech-slaves.

"System integrity," Theta 13A sighed. "System integrity...fifty-seven per cent..." She almost fell out of her chair, veins stood out on her temples, and she clawed at her implant as if it hurt.

"That's worse than before! This doesn't make sense!" Hestra hesitated. She had been dreading this moment for months, but it was unavoidable. "You'll have to perform a full system reboot," she said with a twinge of concern and a look of worry flitted across her face as she saw Theta 13A's reaction.

"Ma'am..." interrupted Gabriel, also noticing the reaction. "We could...wait? Theta 13A is clearly exhausted and she will do a better job if she is rested a few days."

"At the rate the system is failing the system will crash and the whole station will go to hell," snapped Hestra. "What do you think will happen to the tech-slaves if they go crazy and have no more mind control forced upon them by the computer? No, we must do this now. Put the tech-slaves into hibernation while we perform a full system reboot."

"We?" whispered Theta 13A.

"What was that?" demanded Hestra. "I have good hearing you know."

"Y-yes, ma'am," snapped Theta 13A. "Full system reboot in three, two..." And she reinserted the neural control into her temple socket. It was evident that pain rippled through Theta 13A's body as she navigated the system for another time. She let out a little cry as she inserted the neural syringe. She sat bolt upright in the zetting station chair, and her lips pulled back in the zetter's grin.

Gabriel looked on worried.

Hestra collapsed back into her command chair.

"Soon this will be over," Hestra said. It looked to her like Gabriel was not so sure.

The tech-slaves in the recesses of the command module stumbled back to their idle positions and began to enter their hibernation protocols. The lights of the station flickered a little as the emergency overrides initiated and the station prepared for a full system reboot.

***

Gabriel looked up at the flickering lights, he had been through countless system reboots over the years, but he had an apprehensive feeling about this one, never had the system's integrity fallen so fast, never had things gone this wrong.

There were reports from the engineers that the tech-slaves were behaving erratically and that basic station sub systems were not performing: airlocks not working, and things like that. This was not a normal system failure. This would not be a normal system reboot.

Nevertheless, he would not voice his fears; he was a good second in command. His commander was General Hestra. She knew best. He looked over at her, slumped in the command chair.

He had never seen her so tired, ever. She was clearly anxious; she was rubbing her forehead with her left hand fingers while slumped on her left shoulder.

Gabriel realised he was staring, and as she turned her inquisitive gaze upon him, he snapped back to what he was doing: monitoring the zet reboot from the terminal he was at.

"Theta 13A is arriving at the computer core's circuits now," said Gabriel, watching the progress of the consciousness of the zetter from the terminal. "Anytime now the reboot should begin."

"Good," sighed Hestra. "Then this will be over, for now. Damn this old station!" She brought her left hand down on the armrest of the command chair with a bang.

93

Gabriel flinched. Nevertheless, he knew she was right. This station was getting too old, reboots were becoming more dangerous and more frequently needed, and the whole system seemed to be failing. It was a shame Solar Solutions was not building a new station to orbit Jupiter, but that was just how things went. Gabriel did not presume to understand his employers; he just did his job.

Suddenly all the lights went off and on and all the computer terminals restarted and across their screens churned the reboot data that happened every time the system restarted.

"There we go," said Hestra with some levity. "In a few minutes the whole system will be back online at one hundred per cent."

Gabriel said nothing, he was watching Theta 13A claw at the implant in the side of her skull and he rushed over to her without giving Hestra a look of disdain.

"She's dying," was all he said as he pulled the neural link from Theta 13A's temple and caught her as she fell out of her chair, foaming at the mouth and with sightless, cataract blind eyes.

"No, not dying, you know that," said Hestra. "Take her away!" Hestra called out to the nearest rebooted tech-slave and it clomped over and lifted Theta 13A from Gabriel's arms effortlessly and took her out of the command module to the tech-slave conversion bay on the other side of the engineering module. The airlock closed behind the pair with a hiss.

"Report!"

Gabriel could not believe Hestra. He had served under her for years, but she had just killed one of their best zetters and all she was interested in was whether her precious system was optimal again. He was still standing at the zetting station, shocked at what had happened. He had

94

known it was a possibility, of course, he had known. However, whenever a zetter died in the system it was a shock to him, but obviously not to Hestra.

"Report, First Officer!"

There was that demanding voice again. Gabriel straightened up and walked over to his monitor without looking at Hestra. He could not look at her at the moment. He read the information quietly to himself before a wry smile broke across his face. He chastised himself immediately for the smile, as Theta 13A had died, but he smiled because even though Theta 13A had given all, Hestra had been defeated, the system was not at one hundred per cent, even after a reboot.

"Ninety-four per cent," said Gabriel. He had to look at Hestra's reaction.

"WHAT!?" bellowed Hestra. "How is that even possible? It was a full system reboot!..."

Gabriel saw the shock in Hestra's face, and he felt triumph.

The shock was gone in an instant, replaced by determination. "We have to fix this!" Hestra exclaimed. "Gabriel, contact Theta 7B, get him here regardless of whether he's well or not. I have some questions to ask him! This all happened after his last zet!"

"I'll take the message to him personally," said Gabriel, "in case he needs convincing," he added when he saw Hestra's confusion.

"Good, yes, do that," she snapped.

Gabriel exited the command module. Instead of turning to head to the crew quarters, he hesitated and turned towards the tech-slave conversion part of the station off from the engineering module. He had to see what had happened to Theta 13A. Of course, he already knew, he had seen it before, but he felt that he owed it to her to witness her final moments as a human being before her conversion into a mindless creature.

He took a sharp intake of breath and then passed through the airlock into the Medical Conversion Bay.

***

The Medical Conversion Bay was set in stark contrast by bright spotlights and dark shadowy recesses. Gabriel gazed around the rather large chamber and waited for his eyes to adjust to the gloom of where he was. Up ahead was a large medical slab of a table on which was already the now naked body of Theta 13A. She was surrounded by wires and machine arms that were yet to whir into life. The table was also flanked by two large tech-slaves who were to stand guard during the horrific procedure.

Gabriel approached the table and one of the guards turned threateningly towards him; it fizzed at him in some unknown computer language, probably a warning for him to stand clear. He heeded the advice and retreated to the shadows to watch at a distance.

He did not even know her real name, he thought to himself. She was always Theta 13A. And now she was going to be turned into a monster.

Suddenly there was a clicking and whirring from where the table was and the arms spun to life. They extended large needles, drills and saw like blades from their silver carapace and began to shave Theta 13A's head and to drill holes in her skull in order to implant the skull mesh that would operate as her mind control.

Anaesthetics were administered to the stricken zetter as the drills and saws did their work.

Clamps and mechanical arms held her torso upright as the blades cut away parts of her flesh and exposed her upper spinal column.

The skull mesh was inserted into the exposed areas and linked wirelessly with the station's computer circuits.

Other augmentations were implanted into the former zetter's body and face. Her eyes were augmented, and the communication circuits were implanted into her brain through the drilled holes.

Theta 13A's face was a silent scream of unimaginable agony. Even with the anaesthetics, the pain from the incisions and drilling would have been excruciating.

Blood gushed from wounds that were soon cauterised and grafted to technological components.

Blood pooled on the floor and ran down channels in the table and away into storage jars to be used or disposed of at a later time.

Towards the end of the procedure, what was left of Theta 13A was dressed in the standard tech-slave yellow jump suit.

Gabriel's looked on and as the procedure was completed, the bloody mechanical arms retracted and the guard tech-slaves fizzed their instructions as the now zombified body of Theta 13A rose from the table and, with a fizzing of her skull mesh, she stood upright next to the table. She was forever changed: her eyes blank, her now bald head covered in a mesh that was implanted directly into her brain, her upper spinal column exposed and hard wired to the computer core of the station.

The guards retreated and headed back to the command module while the now computer controlled Theta 13A thumped out of the conversion bay and on to whatever job the central computer had designated for her.

"It..." Gabriel had to correct his thoughts vocally. "She is no longer a she, she's an it."

Then the water jets began on the surgical slab to wash the blood away. Gabriel left the room and headed towards the crew quarters to contact Alfred.

***

Alfred heard the door to his room chime. He was startled. He headed over to it when the chime came again. Who could it have been, he thought. He was bleary eyed and had changed into his casual clothing. He was in no fit state to receive visitors.

Alfred moved over to the door and triggered the mechanism. It slid aside and there was First Officer Gabriel, standing in the passageway.

"Y-you?" Alfred stuttered. "I was supposed to contact you when I was better. The message..."

"Yes, yes, yes," snapped Gabriel. "Things have...developed since then. Can I come in?" asked Gabriel with a smile.

Alfred realised he was standing in the doorway like an idiot and moved to the side indicating with his hands that Gabriel could come in.

Gabriel walked past Alfred into the room and the door shut behind him. The room was gloomy and smelt of stale sweat. Gabriel looked at the red box of pills on the bedside dresser and the strange skull on the small dining table.

Alfred followed Gabriel's gaze and said quickly, "What do you want? I'm sick."

"I see, Theta 7B...Alfred, can I call you Alfred?" Gabriel said with another compassionate smile.

"I guess," said Alfred, shrugging his shoulders in a resigned way.

"I'll get right to the point. I'm here to discuss work. We've had some...issues with the computer system, and we need your help to fix it," Gabriel said.

"Work? Ha, I can't go back there yet, I'm sick, and who's 'we'? You mean your boss Hestra? What about Theta 13A, she's just as capable as I am..." Alfred trailed off when he saw Gabriel's expression.

"She...she's dead, Alfred," said Gabriel, his eyes dropping from Alfred's gaze and seeking solace in the floor.

"What!?" gasped Alfred. "You didn't do a full system reboot did you? Oh shit!" Alfred paused for thought. "Well I'm not your slave; I won't sacrifice myself for--"

"I know, I know," interrupted Gabriel again, "and I'm not asking you to, but can you offer any advice on what's going wrong with the system? The system is failing at an alarming rate, and it started after your last zet. We...I just need to know."

Alfred paused, wracking his brain for some sort of excuse, "So...you don't know then? Why, I mean, why the system is failing?"

"No, I have no idea; all I know is that it started more than ever after your last zet. Do you know?" Gabriel implored him. "Alfred..." Gabriel looked at him with pleading eyes, "if you don't help and the system goes into complete meltdown we could lose the station, and there aren't enough life pods for everyone on it, we need your help!"

"But your last message, it sounded like you knew something and wanted to talk to me about it? I thought you'd be explaining things to me, not the other way around!" Alfred blurted out. "Look," he said, "I have a crazy idea, but I need your word that you won't tell Hestra."

"I cannot promise that, but tell me and we'll see, she's my commanding officer and I am duty bound to tell her if the station is in jeopardy," said Gabriel in a mechanical way.

"Then no, I won't tell you. Get out of my room," snapped Alfred, harsher than he intended.

"I didn't want it to come to this," said Gabriel and suddenly he produced a pistol from underneath his work clothes and aimed it at Alfred.

Alfred froze; a gun on such an ancient space station was suicide; if a bullet punctured the hull, it was all over. The hull was not like modern craft that could withstand bullets. "You're mad! A gun!?" was all he managed.

"I'm sorry, but you'll have to tell me. I need to know, what's going wrong with the computer system?" Gabriel pleaded.

Alfred sighed, his shoulders slumped, he was not brave, he was somewhat of a coward, but he was not stupid; he would have to tell. "Okay, just listen, you're not going to like it, and one request: don't interrupt with incredulity, it'll make this longer."

Alfred explained the situation: about how he had detected an unauthorised zet in the reactor core the last time he zetted, everything about the Sect in the Church wanting to destroy the station to set the computer core free, and finally that the computer core talked to him and wanted him personally to destroy the station. Gabriel, according to his word, did not interrupt; he just kept Alfred at gunpoint the entire time and regarded him with a cool, steely gaze. When Alfred finished with a clap of his hands Gabriel said nothing and kept regarding Alfred coolly.

"That's it?" Gabriel said finally, pursing his lips.

"What more do you want?" Alfred said.

"Wait here, I'll report all this and then come and get you, you'll zet again and fix the system."

"But didn't you listen? The system wants me to destroy it!" Alfred shouted.

"You make any attempt to do that, and I'll make sure you end up dead like Theta 13A, I may be horrified at the tech-slaves, I may think General Hestra is a slave driver, but I'm a company man and this is my space station and I'll be damned if I let it get blown up by some fucking cultists!" Gabriel spat as he shouted.

Alfred was taken aback by the emotion he heard and saw in Gabriel. "All right I'll wait."

Gabriel concealed the gun and left the room without another word.

***

First Officer Gabriel hurried through the station ignoring the muffled protests of the crowds as he shouldered through them on his way back to the command module. He passed the Church, and paused, reasoning with himself whether he should go in and confront the priest. He was unsure. He had to report what he had found out to the General. But also, it was all unsubstantiated and if it had no backing then perhaps what Alfred had said was all a lie; to trick him into believing something else was going wrong with the computer core.

Gabriel nodded to himself and pushed the heavy door of the Church open and entered the brightly lit interior.

Being a good company man, Gabriel was saved and had invested heavily in the market, he believed in the truth of the Church, and it seemed, to him, incomprehensible that the good and pure priests that ran the stock market would want to destroy something as vast as a space station that was company property.

"Ah, Gabriel, my son, have you come to make another contribution to your little nest egg? Now is a very good time to invest!" said the priest in the white robes as he slid out of the gathering of people on the floor of the Church and up to the entrance. Gabriel, being second in command on the station, got special preference from the Church and he addressed the priest.

"Trader Virtus." Gabriel bowed. "I have come, not to invest, but because I am having...doubts," he paused, trying to think how to continue without arousing suspicion.

"Doubts? Are you thinking of withdrawing some of your equity?" said Virtus with a troubled expression.

"May we talk in private, Trader?" whispered Gabriel, leaning in towards the priest in an attempt to look like he had something important to confess.

"Of course, my son," said the priest in muted tones. He clapped Gabriel on the back and ushered him towards the back rooms of the Church. Gabriel and Virtus passed through one of the doors in the rear wall of the Church and Virtus closed the door behind him.

"What's wrong?" asked Virtus, sounding genuinely concerned.

Gabriel paused and looked around the blank room with a few computer screens here and there lit by fluorescent light globes hanging from the ceiling with a couple of other doors in the back of the room leading to unknown parts of the station. It was obviously not the room Alfred had mentioned. Gabriel wondered how to continue; he had not thought this through.

"I uh, would like to...join," said Gabriel.

"Join?" said the priest with surprise. "But you are already second in command of the station, and have a large amount of equity saved within these walls, why would you want to join our humble little band of priests?"

"No, you misunderstand me." Gabriel paused again. "I wish to join...the Sect." he tapped on the side of his head where an implant would be. "I can have the surgery..." He trailed off as he saw the expression of the priest change to one of icy calmness.

"I'm sorry, I'm not sure I can help you, Gabriel." The last word said with rather too much of a threat made Gabriel rather uneasy.

"Look I need to know what's going on here!" blurted Gabriel, regretting his words as soon as he said them.

"No, no you don't," said the priest in icy tones, all mirth gone from his face. "We have been planning this for a long time, and now we have a chance to rise ascendant on wings of fire and free our master from its shackles. And you will not get in our way."

Gabriel felt the gun in his hand; he did not remember drawing it. "You will tell me what's going on," he said, as icily as the priest while he aimed the gun at the torso of the white robed figure.

"Now, you don't want to do anything stupid..." said the priest.

"Tell me what's going on and give me names!" shouted Gabriel, he had lost is cool again, and it felt weird for him.

The priest inclined his head and suddenly one of the doors in the back of the room slid aside and a tech-slave appeared and stumbled forward, its face blank and emotionless. It was carrying a cutting tool with a circular blade that started to spin angrily. It approached Gabriel.

Gabriel froze for an instant as the danger of the situation he was in was made apparent and then he tried to move towards the door back to the Church, but it was blocked by Trader Virtus who shoved him bodily back into the room.

Gabriel regained his footing and aimed the gun at the tech-slave. He fired three shots in quick succession. They impacted the centre of mass of the tech-slave but buried themselves harmlessly in the fleshy torso within the yellow jump suit. The tech-slave seemed immune to the wounds. The creature sped up and before Gabriel could fire any more shots into the creature it was upon him, and it buried the spinning blade in his torso. Gabriel screamed as the blade bit deeply and crimson gore of his own internal organs splattered across the tech-slave and floor. In an instant, Gabriel was dead and a crumpled, bloodied mass on the floor of the chamber.

***

Virtus had avoided the spray of blood miraculously and, in stepping out into the rest of the Church, he indicated the gun lying in the pool of gore, "Send that to Alfred."

The door shut behind him and he went on his busy daily routine of extracting money from station staff.

The stock market had taken an interesting turn and there had been some cheers from the crowd just as the blade had hit Gabriel. No one had heard his screams.

***

Alfred heard the chime of his door again. He wondered if Gabriel had returned to kill him. The door chimed again. Alfred got off his bed and walked to the door, pressing the activation button. The door slid aside and in front of him was not Gabriel, but the supply delivery robot. Alfred was confused, he had not ordered any supplies recently. The robot then held out its platter and Alfred's blood ran cold. On the platter, was a gore soaked pistol.

"Please...take," said the robot mechanically.

Alfred knew it was from Gabriel, and that that was Gabriel's blood. "Wh-where did you get this?"

The robot paused, "Please...take...from Church" it said, not comprehending his question. As it should not have, it was only a supply delivery robot; it had no knowledge of where the supplies came from.

Alfred took the pistol gingerly in thumb and forefinger around the grip and held it at arm's length to keep the blood off himself. He realised Gabriel must have gone to the Church to investigate and met with a grizzly end.

He looked down the corridor; there was no one else there, thankfully.

The robot retracted the platter and began to trundle off down the corridor.

Alfred closed the door behind him and stood in his room holding the pistol. It was sticky with blood. He didn't know if it would survive washing, but he had to. He dumped it in his small sink and turned on the tap. Instantly the sink filled with red, and the blood began to wash away. He did not want to scrub it in case that damaged the mechanism, or it fired. Alfred had never fired a gun in his life. He hoped he never would have to. However, it seemed that things were progressing in ways that were totally out of his control.

Finally, the red stopped pouring from the gun and Alfred turned the tap off. He grabbed the gun between thumb and forefinger again and dried it off on his towel. He did not know what to do with it after that. He had put on his work clothes after Gabriel had left last time. He managed to stash it in the inner breast pocket of his clothing, it fitted surprisingly well. And due to the padding of the jump suit, it was almost invisible to an outside observer.

"I hope I never have to use this, Blinky," he said to the skull sitting on his table. "I really, really hope I don't have to use this." He had a terrible feeling that he would have to.

Now that Gabriel was out of the picture, what would Hestra say or do? The thought hit him like the backwash of a starship engine. With all the shock of receiving the gun, he had not considered what would happen now that Gabriel was dead. Suddenly he felt very alone in the universe.

***

Alfred did not care what time it was anymore. It felt like an age since he last slept, but he was not tired. The circadian rhythm of the station's lighting system had flicked the lights on and off a number of times. Alfred paid it little notice.

Gabriel was dead, not that he had been much of a friend to Alfred, in fact, he had pulled a gun on him and threatened him, but the issue was that anyone who seemed to cross this Sect ended up dead. Alfred was feeling that he had to make his next choices very carefully. If this Sect could kill the second in command to the station, he had to progress very delicately.

Alfred's mind was racing. It seemed as though the Church onboard the station was either in control of the Sect or at least was sheltering it. Gabriel was dead. The thought entered his mind for the thousandth time. What did they want him to do? Destroy the station? But that was madness, that was absolute stupidity. Apart from the fact that it was nearly impossible to do, short of overloading the reactor by disabling the coolant, which, in itself, was very hard to do given the safeguards and security over such an event. The station was home to thousands of people. Many of them would die if the station exploded.

"But it was possible."

The horrid thought pushed its way into his mind, as if it was downloaded into his consciousness from an outside source. It was possible.

"I didn't think that." Alfred shook his head to remove the thought.

"Yes you did."

The reply appeared inside his head. Words not so much heard as felt, like a thought, but an uncontrolled thought.

Alfred was scared. Things seemed to be progressing out of his control. Was he going mad? Dr Armstrong said the pills would help. Alfred stared at the half-empty packet of red pills on his bedside table. They were not helping. Nothing helped. He put a hand inside his inside breast pocket and felt the gun on the inside of his work clothes. He felt the cool metal. No. Not here, not like this. He withdrew his hand and buttoned up his jump suit.

He paced his room for the thousandth time trying to figure out what to do. He had to talk to a priest; he had to talk to that white robed head priest who seemed to be the Sect leader. Resolutely he made up his mind and prepared to leave his chamber. He had decided to leave his room a dozen times before in the past few days to talk to the priest but had always become too scared and given up. This time he would do it.

"I'll be back later," he said with a parting glance at Blinky. He left the safety of his room and walked, slowly, down the corridor to the airlock.

***

Alfred stopped in the crowds out the front of the Church. There were a lot of distressed faces and quite a number of people were trying to get into the Church for some reason. Alfred asked an upset looking person next to him why this was.

"The Bull has retreated; now the Bear seems to be in the ascendency. There's a lot of red on the charts," said the man as he disappeared into the crowd, not caring if Alfred understood or not.

The press of people made Alfred more determined to see what was going on. At the very least he could not retreat given the crush of bodies behind him. Something was happening to the markets. He shouldered his way through the crush and into the Church.

The Church was in turmoil. It was more crowded than usual, not that Alfred really knew what usual was in the religion, but there was a large throng of people in the centre obviously upset at the fact there was a lot of red on the computer screens around the edges of the chamber. They were all shouting and gesticulating at each other and the screens while brown robed priests moved through the crowd trying to placate people in their endeavours.

Alfred grabbed the arm of a passing priest, "I need to speak to the white robed priest."

"Trader Virtus? He's a little busy right now, can I--" Alfred's look silenced the priest and he continued, "I'll, uh, take you to him."

Alfred held on to the robes of the priest as they moved through the crowd. Panic-eyed merchants and worshipers made hurried sales as the boards lit up red.

"What's going on?" shouted Alfred above the din.

"The Bull has left us; in the last few days all the signs of the Bear have appeared. The markets are crashing," shouted the priest over his left shoulder as they moved. "It's terrible, but it does happen every now and then, all we can do is console the flock and make sure that they do not withdraw too much money from the markets."

Alfred nodded in partial understanding, and they kept moving.

"Here you are." The priest indicated a door. "He's in there." He vanished back into the crowd.

Alfred was worried. The last time he had been through one of the back doors of the Church, he had seen a man tear his own brains out. Alfred's palms were sweaty. He pressed the activation switch on the door. It slid open and as his eyes adjusted, Alfred stepped inside, his heart racing.

108

"Yes?" said Trader Virtus as he hunched over a computer screen with his back to the door. He had obviously thought Alfred was one of the lower priests. Hearing no response, Virtus turned, and his eyes lit up. "Ah, Alfred, my apologies, I thought you were one of the other Traders."

"You remember me?" said Alfred with more shock in his voice than he would have liked.

"Oh of course! Now, why have you come?" Virtus seemed to be salivating in a weird way when he spoke, as if Alfred's presence was delicious to him.

"Why did you kill Gabriel," said Alfred, his resolve hardening. He was in too deep already he might as well ask the question straight.

"Did we?" Virtus salivated, rising from his chair and approaching Alfred. This threw Alfred off; he honestly had not thought Virtus would deny it. In all his planning, he had not accounted for this.

"Uh, the service robot said..." Alfred stopped, realising what he had just told Virtus: that he had received Gabriel's gun.

"Ah yes, so you got our little present? Good. Gabriel did not need it anymore." The priest looked down at the floor in a sad way.

"But why did you do it?" Alfred almost begged.

"He would have stopped us...you."

"But I don't want to. This is my home!" Alfred pleaded.

"But you are a slave, and soon will be a tech-slave too, and the computer must be set free." Virtus started to salivate again, and he held out his hands in a conciliatory way. "Look, just take what I need to give you to accomplish your task." He moved to the computer and on a piece of synthetic paper scribbled something. He walked back to Alfred and held out the paper. Alfred took it and looked at it.

"Numbers?"

"The reactor key code," said the priest.

"How did you get this?"

"Never you mind," snapped Virtus, but he then relented. "Many of the tech-slaves are...on our side. As slaves, they have an interest in the freedom of their computer master."

"I'm not promising anything..." Alfred took it, and stuffed it into his trouser pocket. Alfred realised the only way to leave the room alive was probably looking like he was going to do what the priest said.

"Oh, I know, but somehow, I think you'll come around to our way of thinking...eventually..." Virtus trailed off while looking at Alfred assuredly. "You will...oh you will. Now leave me and accomplish your task, my son." In saying this, Trader Virtus turned and went back to his work at the computer.

Alfred left the crowd around the Church and went for a walk. In one pocket he had a code that would unlock the reactor and allow him to destroy the station, in another he had a pistol from the dead First Officer. If the security staff found him with either, he would be arrested for treason. He was damned whatever he did. He had to make a choice.

Maybe he could zet again for the station and do his job again for the first time in a while? This thought appealed to him, he had not zetted in a couple of weeks, and the desire was becoming unbearable. It gnawed at him. But he was afraid what he would do if he did zet.

And what would General Hestra say to him about Gabriel? Alfred was terrified. What was he to do with the reactor code? What if the computer tried to talk to him again?

Alfred walked to clear his head.

Chapter 12

Captain Artisius strode down the bright, open walkway to the bridge. The *Green Dragon* was on its final approach to *Florida Station,* and he needed to be on the bridge to oversee preparations for docking. He was in his full dress uniform. The navy blue of his tunic was richly embossed with gold trim and braid, and his red epaulettes adorned his shoulders. He wore his medals too. He always dressed in full uniform when docking with a station; he wanted to make a good impression on the commanders of the station he was docking with. He wanted them to know who he was.

As Artisius approached the bridge doors, he gave one of his medals a final little polish with the cuff of his tunic. He had seen military action when he was much younger, and had been decorated for courageous actions.

The guards outside the bridge door snapped to attention as he approached and the smooth door to the bridge slid aside and as Artisius marched onto the command deck

"Captain on the bridge!" the First Officer called out and the command staff all came to attention in strict order before settling back down into their seats.

"Time until final approach?" Captain Artisius asked from the observation walkway

"Twenty four minutes until we reach our final approach," said a voice from behind the navigation computer holo-screen.

"Good, approach speed?" snapped Artisius with precision.

"Fifty kilometres per second," came the measured response.

Artisius observed the giant ball of Jupiter filling the bridge's viewing platform observation dome. The orange and red clouds boiling and turning in slow motion on its surface. In the distance, he saw a small glittering object approaching rather fast and dead ahead.

"There she is, *Florida Station*, one of the oldest stations still in service. Slow down to forty kilometres per second, we don't want to scare them," Artisius said with a wry smile. "They're so old I wonder if they have even detected us yet--"

"This is Solar Solutions *Florida Station*," crackled the radio that second. "Identify yourself foreign craft: name and purpose."

Artisius beamed. "This is the trading ship *Green Dragon*; we have your supply cargo and would request docking procedure."

"Please submit identification documents," came the crackly response.

"Do it," Artisius said to the Communications Officer, who jumped to the task.

A minute passed as the *Florida Station* docking crew confirmed the identity of the *Green Dragon* in their database. All the while, the station grew steadily larger in the observation dome.

"Okay *Green Dragon* you check out. Please progress to docking tube Alpha 3. Welcome aboard."

"Thank you!" replied the captain. "Take us in slowly, helm. As I said, they're old and might not like us blasting in there at speed," he said to his Helmsman.

"Speed, sir?"

"Make it ten kilometres per second from one thousand kilometres out and then slow down to five from one hundred kilometres.

"Yes, sir!" snapped the Helmsman.

Artisius smiled a wry smile again, had *Florida Station* ever seen such a smart ship as his? He thought not.

"Tell docking command to prepare the docking tube!" he shouted.

"Sir!" came the response.

Artisius' crew were second to none in training and precision. He stood on the command dais. He stared out the window of the dome at the gas giant spinning hundreds of thousands of kilometres away and yet it filled the dome.

"I'll never get sick of seeing that..." he said to himself.

His focus then shifted from the majestic giant to the, in comparison, tiny station which was approaching dead ahead. Its white and silver tubular and bulbous sections with large solar panel sails that jutted out from the edges looked even more ancient than the last time he had made a trip here years ago.

In all his collected antiquities, Artisius had a small model of one of the ancient pre Moon Colony space stations that orbited the Earth, long before The War. He always marvelled to himself about how much like that initial, first step, station around Earth looked like *Florida Station*. Or, to be precise, how much *Florida Station* looked like that ancient station which had long ago burnt up in Earth's atmosphere.

Florida Station however was much, much bigger, and it had larger sections, like the recreation module that were vast in comparison of that proto station. Nevertheless, the pod design was there, and the solar cell sails.

"Slow to docking speed!" snapped Artisius as the station approached and filled the dome. Retro thrusters

113

kicked in and the whole space ship shuddered as it slowed to match the orbital speed of *Florida Station* and edged closer to the docking tube that had projected from the body of the station.

"300 metres to target, 250, 200, 150, 100," read out the Helmsman. "50..."

"Easy now," said Artisius. He always felt a little tense at docking; so much could go wrong, even though he had done it hundreds of times.

"25, 20, 15, 10, 5, 4, 3, 2, 1," called out the Helmsman as he manoeuvred the ship. Then there was a shudder and a scraping noise and then a loud bang.

"Target captured," called out the Helmsman.

Artisius exhaled. "Good, well done, crew!" he called out. "We have a month or so of leave while docked with this station, enjoy your time," Artisius broadcast over the *Green Dragon's* intercom. "Unload our cargo and then the time is yours. Just be sure to return before we leave," he said with a smile.

He thought he heard a groan from one of the command crew and something about this station being so old, but he chose to ignore it.

Artisius left the bridge and started down the corridor to the docking hatch. In the docking bay, he paused to check his medals and then he triggered the airlock and walked in the tube between the station and the ship and then came to the airlock on the side of *Florida Station*. He had forgotten that it needed a manual trigger by punching in a code.

"What's the code to their damn airlock?" he asked his intercom in a rather perturbed voice.

Before the code was relayed to him, the airlock cycled, and the door swung open as the cargo crew of *Florida Station* moved into action. Standing amongst the crew was

General Hestra, known to Artisius for many years due to his repeated trips to the station.

"General!" The Captain approached the General with outstretched arms, "it's been too long, you..." He paused as he saw the state Hestra was in.

The cargo crew, eyes down, moved past him up the corridor into the *Green Dragon* to assist in the unloading of the cargo. The General and the Captain were left alone.

"I...welcome you to the station...Artisius..." stuttered Hestra, massive dark circles under her eyes and with a rather dishevelled uniform.

"My dear General, what's wrong?" said Artisius, genuinely concerned for a sort of friend. "And where's Gabriel? He always meets docked ships..."

"Things on this station...are not right. I will explain. Walk with me," said the General.

Artisius fell in step by her side, all medals and uniform pomp forgotten. He listened carefully as Hestra detailed the problems with the computer systems and the failed system reboot and most worryingly of all, the disappearance of her second in command, Gabriel.

"I suspect he is dead. He hasn't appeared on duty for a few days now, and the scanners are not responding when I ask them to try to find him. The stock market too, has started to fail. The Church is in some sort of shambles. I, don't know what to do..."

The gravity of the situation hit Artisius. The General always knew what to do; she was famous for her composure under stress. Something had to be wrong, terribly wrong. "Can I help?" he asked.

"Stay docked for now; unload your cargo, your...slaves. I'm a little more lenient on that kind of trade than most Solar Solutions commanders. Hell, we need them this close to the frontier. You know that; just don't go talking about slaves to others too much. And if I need your assistance, I'll ask," said Hestra, partially annoyed, partially gratefully.

Artisius nodded, not offended, and followed the General through the station.

Chapter 13

Draz awoke with a start. She wished she had not moved so suddenly. Her head throbbed. She blinked. She groaned. She felt the cold metal slab she was lying on. Her mind was swimming. For a few minutes she did not remember what was going on, then it all came flooding back unpleasantly. She remembered being hit by one of the guards and being dragged half-conscious to this prison cell. She was to be sent to the Moon Prison Colony under false charges of treason.

She peered into the gloom of the prison cell. It was small, two by two metres perhaps, with the slab of metal she was lying on protruding from one wall and a toilet on another. Across from the slab, there was the heavy metal door with its vision slit closed. The entire cell was a grey metal with a small light in the ceiling.

Draz swung her legs over the edge of the slab; she was still in her scavenging clothes but without her pistol. She felt its absence on her thigh. She realised that she had never, in her whole adult life, been without that pistol. It was part of her. It had been issued to her mother by the Collective; she had also been a scavenger for the Corporate Wing. And her mother had passed it to her. Now it was gone, and she would probably never see it again. This upset her more than she would have thought.

In defiance of her mood, she got up off the slab and crossed the small room to the door. She banged on it and shouted out anything she could think of: first came swear words and insults and then demands to know what was going on. She shouted herself hoarse and hurt her fist banging on the door. No one responded. Nothing happened. She stopped, realising it was pointless.

Draz did not even know where she was. She could still be on Earth in the dreaded transit prison, waiting to go to the Earth Ring and then the Moon. She could be on a ship on the way to the Moon already, she thought. However, this idea was wiped from her mind as she realised she could not hear or feel any engine rumble which would be standard on a space ship. And she was not on the Moon yet, she could not have been unconscious that long. Therefore, she must be either still on Earth or on an Earth Ring space station.

Her mind alternated from blind panic as to what would happen to her, to trying to figure out what to do under the circumstances. She wondered how long she had been in the cell. She wondered how long she would be in the cell.

Her head pounded, and now her fist and throat hurt too. She cursed herself.

She lay back on the slab and closed her eyes. She felt so very alone. Part of her brain was telling her to cry, but her resolve and her determination silenced that thought. She would not cry. She would not give in to them like that. That would mean they had won. She smirked; they would never win. She would get her revenge, eventually. This she swore to herself. The Corporate Wing would pay for their betrayal of her. She had never betrayed them; they had betrayed her!

Draz lay there for unknown hours; she had no method of keeping track of time. They had taken her chronometer. She was unable to sleep due to the pain in her head and the worry in her mind. The dull, unremitting light in the centre of the roof never changed. She did not hear anyone outside the door. She could not hear any other prisoners in other cells. She had heard of these sorts of cells in hushed tales in seedy bars back in Atraxa Prime. The security forces used cells that were designed that way, to make you feel like you were totally alone and break down your resolve with that utter solitary confinement.

Hours, or even days, went by. She had no idea. She was so very bored. It was interesting, she thought, how bored you could get even in the most dire situations.

She was hungry. She had not eaten in ages.

Draz got up again and studied the cell, looking for any form of weakness that could be exploited. She searched for anything, hoping somehow to find some hidden microphone or camera so that she could communicate with her captors. Draz scoured the cell, checking every nook and cranny. She looked at the ceiling for cameras and searched under the slab and toilet for microphones. The more she searched the less she found and the harder she searched. It became important to her to find something, anything; otherwise, she was doomed and alone in this cell with no contact with anyone.

Draz found nothing. She sat back on the slab. Even more hours went by. She was really hungry now. She did not know what to do. She was broken. She felt like she was going to die in this cell. No one would come. She could not save herself without her pistol. She was just going to starve to death here and no one would ever be the wiser.

She called out again, to no one in particular. Silence reigned. She lay back on the slab, knowing she was doomed. She still did not cry.

Suddenly there was a whooshing noise and a small panel in the bottom of the door that she had not noticed slid aside and a tray with food and drink on it was slid into the cell and the panel slid back into place. It was flush with the door and fitted perfectly therefore she had not noticed it.

Draz, suddenly not alone, was animated. She jumped up and pounded her fist on the door demanding at first to know how long she had been in the cell and to be released. She was not alone! No response. Again, total silence. But she was not alone!

She looked down at the tray. There was a bowl of some kind of synthetic meat and stuff and a glass of water. Draz, now enlivened again, was ravenous. She demolished the food in the bowl in short order and drained the glass. The food was horrid, and the water recycled a hundred times and tasteless, but it was the most delicious meal she had eaten in years.

She was not alone. Her eyes flashed darkly, and she knew, she was not alone! She smiled and sat back on the slab. She waited. She was not alone.

***

Three more times the food tray was withdrawn from its attachment to the door and put back into the room with food on it. Therefore, Draz knew she was in the cell for a few days. She could not be sure, as she did not know if she was only receiving one meal a day or more than one, but it was a thing to live by and Draz counted each time the tray reappeared with food on it. It was her lifeline to the outside world. No word was ever said back to her even though she shouted and banged on the door each time. No sound other than the panel sliding away and the scrape of the tray indicated that there was anyone on the other side of the door.

Then all of a sudden, the whole door slid open while Draz was lying on her back on the slab. Light from the outside flooded the chamber and Draz blinked and shielded her eyes from the glare. Standing in the doorway was a surly and large silhouette.

"Okay, you, come on, trial day," said the surly figure and man handled Draz from her slab and out into the waiting corridor.

"Trial day?" she stuttered. Draz did not know what was going on. "How long have I been in there?"

"Shuttup, we do the talking around here not you, traitor," came the curt reply.

Draz decided not to push the situation and so looked around. She was glad to be out of her cell. Her eyes had become accustomed to the light. Draz was being dragged down a long metal corridor lined with metal doors. She realised that these were all like the cells she was in. There were so many, she thought as she was dragged past a couple of other guards who gave her a dirty look.

Draz was shoved into a lift near the end of the corridor and the guards stood either side of her. One thumbed the close door button and with a whoosh the lift ascended into some unknown building.

Draz shifted uneasily on her feet, at least in the cell things were certain, the food came, and then there was rest. Now she did not know what was going on.

The inside of the lift was bare metal and shiny, there were no hints there. She looked at one of the guards. He was wearing a black uniform with red trimmings and on it was a symbol of the Collective Zone. Draz breathed a temporary sigh of relieve, at least she was still within the boundaries of a Collective Zone settlement. The Guard noticed her staring and glowered at her. Draz turned her eyes down to the floor.

The lift stopped suddenly, and the door opened, and Draz was shoved harshly into a small chamber ringed by thick glass and the guards stood either side of her. There was a small microphone in the front of the chamber and nowhere to sit. The glass was opaque, and Draz stood, rather confused.

After what could have only been a few minutes the glass became transparent and Draz could see a medium sized room in front of her, which looked like a courtroom. That was what they meant by 'trial day'; this must be her treason trial, she reasoned. She was in the dock with the judges' seats facing her on the opposite side of the room. The dock was on a pedestal with room for observers around it lower down and there was room for what Draz supposed would be where the jury would sit. But there was no jury there. The entire room was stark white with metal seats and metal benches. There was an audience in the seats at the back of the court.

Draz's heart pounded and she wiped her now clammy hands on her clothes. This would not be good, she knew. She had known about treason trials her whole life; they were big news, and she did not like the thought of being in one.

Then from the centre of the roof, a panel opened and a remotely controlled camera on a robot arm extended into the room and scanned the room. It focussed on Draz. Draz tried to look away and wished the glass would turn opaque again, but one of the guards thumped her and ordered her to face the front. Draz turned and faced the camera, which she knew was broadcasting her image across the Corporate Wing's territories, perhaps even the whole of the Collective Zone. She did not care; she stood, resolute, and strangely angry. How dare they do this to her.

"Silence, all stand," Draz's thoughts were broken by an announcement.

The court rose and from an unseen door three red robed judges with strange black hats on entered the room behind the bench opposite her and sat down in unison. The

122

courtroom sat down. There was a pause. Then the central judge launched into a tirade against Draz with such fury that not only Draz was taken aback, but the guards flinched as well.

"You, accused, known as Draz, did you think your treason would go unpunished? That your betrayal of our great Collective and its leader, the eminent CEO Uxus, would pass unnoticed? That drive you say you salvaged, I doubt you salvaged it; you probably stole it from our glorious research institute and then passed it off as something you salvaged! What do you have to say for yourself?" spat the judge.

"I, uh..." began Draz.

"DON'T INTERRUPT ME WHEN I'M SPEAKING!" bellowed the judge. "Now, before I was so rudely interrupted, I was saying that that drive you stole and intended to sell to the Shipping Wing or even to your contacts in the Solar Solutions Corporation, who we are rounding up as I speak!" The judge paused in his rant to let the weight of his words sink in, seeming to congratulate himself on his detective work.

Draz began to lose her composure; she felt a rage build up inside her. This pompous fool was going to brand her a traitor and not let her defend herself.

"Now, Draz..." the judge looked down his nose at her, spittle collecting on his chin. "Why were you trying to sell such precious weapon information to the Solar Solutions? You are a traitor to this great cause that is our Collective and our great CEO Uxus. How DARE you betray us. Well? Answer!"

"If you'll let me speak this time?" began Draz. She was livid. She would not be talked to like this. She would defend herself. Draz saw the judge smarting and working up another bout of ranting at her insolence, but Draz cut in before he had a chance to discharge. "I am no traitor. I DID find that drive in a salvage run. I did not give the information to the Shipping Wing that we had it NOR was I going to contact Solar Solutions. I have no idea HOW to contact Solar Solutions out beyond Mars. I have never wanted to betray our great Collective. How dare YOU accuse me of such a thing! I won't be talked to or yelled at in this way! I am a loyal member of our Collective and have never once even thought of treason!" Draz slumped, energy expended, all her rage had vented in one go.

The judge had turned purple. He shouted and spat at Draz for a good fifteen minutes in a relentless diatribe of loathing and hatred. He shouted about her insolence, about her treachery, about the endless suffering she was going to experience due to her treason. He insisted they had found evidence that she was a Solar Solutions spy.

Draz wondered when the case had moved from a Shipping Wing spy to a Solar Solutions spy but she was not about to interrupt again.

The judge screamed that her collaborators and co conspirators were already rounded up and facing deportation to the Moon or execution.

The camera in the centre of the ceiling was rapidly switching between focus on the judge and focus on Draz and her responses. She had seen trials like this her whole life through cameras like that one, she thought, but never had she imagined, that she would be on the receiving end of a judge's wrath. She had always believed that the shows about traitors had been legitimate, that the evidence was all there and that the judges were absolutely telling the truth. It was obvious now that this was all false; the judges just made up the information and attacked the accused with anything that they could think of.

124

Draz had realised the truth over the course of the last few days and particularly this courtroom experience. She realised everything she had fought and strived for was a lie. She would never again bow to some all knowing authority, and she would work tirelessly to clear her name or at the very least escape what punishment dealt out to her. Draz went numb.

The judge finished this tirade and paused to catch his breath and wipe his chin. Draz was silent. Her eyes burned with fire, but she said nothing as she did not want to antagonise her executioner any more.

"Nothing to say, eh?" continued the judge with gusto. "Well Draz, if that even is your real name, I have weighed all the evidence, and by the grace of our CEO Uxus," the judge touched his hat reverently at the name, "sentence you to life imprisonment on the maximum security prison on the Moon of Earth. Case closed." The judges rose and exited the room. The camera focussed on Draz for a few more moments and then retreated into the ceiling.

Draz stood, stunned. She knew it was coming, and she was glad it was not execution, but life on the Moon was not a holiday. But she would be alive, and she would survive.

"Get moving, you." Draz was shoved by one of the guards as the lift returned and Draz was bundled back to her cell for the wait until the next prison transport left for the Moon Colony.

***

Draz was woken by a guard some time later in her cell from a restless sleep. She did not know how long she had been in the cell since the trial, days perhaps. The food had come and gone a few times, although she wanted to refuse it in disgust at her treatment, she knew she had to eat to maintain her strength for the ordeals that lay ahead, so she ate reluctantly but deliberately when the food appeared.

"Time for your one way trip," snarled the guard. Draz sighed and left the cell. Flanked by a guard on each side she made the long walk down towards the other end of the long corridor of the prison from the lift to the courtroom.

They passed through a number of guard stations where the identity of the prisoner was confirmed, and various readings and checks were performed to make sure that it was Draz.

Draz wondered if they ever got the wrong person to this point and whether the checks were really necessary, but she complied with the retinal and blood scans.

After the last scan, manacles were fastened to Draz's wrists and legs so that she could not escape. They were heavy things, as if from times past, just metal shackles with chains between them. They were crude, but effective.

Draz and the guards then moved on to a hover train that was built into the prison network and was guarded by many guards with weapons trained on them. Unlike the other hover trains in Atraxa Prime, this one did not have a glass roof therefore the passengers could not see out. This one was in a metal tube that was completely cut off from the outside world. Draz had no idea if she was still in Atraxa Prime or not or where she really was on Earth. But she knew where she was heading: the Earth Ring and then the Moon Prison.

The prison system must have used its own system of transport, thought Draz. Otherwise, she reasoned, she would have been loaded into a ship and taken to the Earth Ring via space. She was clearly going by armoured hover train to one of the large lifts that circled the Earth.

Draz struggled to move in the manacles with any amount of speed. She was pushed onto one of the seats of the train and a guard sat beside her and the other guard sat behind her. The train moved off at speed and Draz stared into the emptiness of the carriage.

Draz was numb again. She did not know what to do. She felt utterly alone, and at the same time she felt utterly incensed by the treatment she was given. She was innocent of any crime they accused her of and yet it all counted for nothing.

She had a strange feeling that perhaps she should cry. She did not want to cry. She was not going to cry. She did not cry. However, she felt as if it was something that should be done in these circumstances. Draz was sure that the guards would have wanted her to cry, to show that she was weak, so that they could gloat over her. So, she steeled her nerves and refused to cry. She stared, dry eyed and determined, straight ahead into space.

She counted minutes; it was something to do. In her head she counted off the seconds and minutes of travel in some way to determine how far the train had gone.

Hover trains moved fast, very fast, and Draz reasoned by her counting that they had travelled for about an hour before the train stopped and the door slid open. The guards bundled her off the train as fast as her shackled legs could take her, and there it was in front of her: a massive lift system.

Draz had disembarked into a large glass shielded structure around one of the lifts to the Earth Ring. Draz stared in wonderment at the structure stretching up and up past the atmosphere in front of her.

"Move!" One of the guards shoved her towards one of the arcane and ancient lift pods that were set into the walls of the lift system.

There were large lifts for cargo and smaller lifts for personnel. The whole space was busy with activity that Draz more heard than saw as the prison lift and where she was, were separated from the other users by barriers and walls. There was a constant stream of traffic of people and machines moving back and forth from the trains to the lifts and vice versa. The massive steel pylons of the lift shafts stretched up and over their heads into space. The constant whooshing of the lifts around her as she moved to the prison lift indicated the constant traffic.

Draz moved awkwardly towards the indicated lift and waited for the door to open. When it did, she saw inside were a few chairs and not much other space. One of the guards indicated for her to sit down in the centre and she did, he then sat beside her. The other guard then dialled in the security code in the key panel at the side of the lift and stepped inside sitting on the other side of Draz.

There was a slight pause and then with a sickening lurch the lift took off and rocketed spaceward. Draz felt a little queasy at the acceleration, but after a minute it ceased, and the lift sped upwards at what Draz thought must have been an amazing speed.

After a while, Draz felt a change. There were no windows in the lift, but Draz could tell something was different. The gravity was a little strange. She reasoned that they must have passed beyond the Earth's gravitational pull and into the artificial gravity of one of the Earth Ring space stations.

Draz almost laughed. If it were not for the horrible circumstances in which she found herself, she would have thought that this was a great adventure. Suddenly it all seems so ludicrous to her, and she let out a small chuckle.

"No laughing!" One of the guards smacked her on the head and uttered the ludicrous line. Draz stopped laughing but it all seemed so absurd, like a bad dream.

Eventually the lift stopped moving and they all disembarked from the carriage into a rectangular, metal corridor. Draz shuffled in the only direction available: forward.

There was one more security checkpoint in front of a massive metal door. Draz's identity was confirmed again and then the metal door split in the middle and each half slid into the side walls.

Beyond the door, Draz saw a space ship. It was small; it was only meant to hold a few dozen people, she reasoned. But it was a space ship. She had never been in space before, and she cursed the fact that there were no windows in the corridor she was in.

Draz was pushed forward towards the ship. Then all of a sudden, she rounded the door and to her left there was a massive portal, which must have been shielded by some form of magnetic shield to keep the atmosphere in, but through the haze she saw the Earth, from orbit, for the first time. She paused in awe.

The Earth was yellow and brown through the shield. Due to the centuries of pollution and war, there were large, brown cloud systems of toxic gas, but it was her home. It was the Earth like she had never seen it before; like she would never see again, she thought. She felt moved. Her home was beautiful to her, even with its flaws, and she would never see it again. She felt like crying, but she did not. Silently she cursed the name of CEO Uxus.

The guards actually let her stand for a moment, regarding the wonder of her home planet for the last time through the magnetic shielding.

"Okay, time to go," said a guard after a short time. He took her arm, but did not force her. Draz took one last look at her lost home, and, with her head held high, shambled into the pod docked in the hangar.

Other prisoners were being loaded onto the same ship at the same time and Draz caught the eyes of a few of them as they marvelled at the spectacle of their home also for the last time.

Inside the pod there were a few seats and a small bathroom along with a line of cells just like the ones she had seen on Earth. One guard undid her shackles; she could not escape from this pod. She sat down on the metal bed of her cell and slumped down onto its hard surface. The door slid shut and locked behind her. There were no windows.

She imagined the Earth as she had seen it. She could not hear or see the other prisoners, but she knew that they were there. They were all in this together. She wondered what they had been convicted of, perhaps treason like her; false treason.

Draz felt the shudder of the engines as the pod accelerated from the dock towards her new home: the Moon. She would be there for the rest of her life without a chance of reprieve, under false charges. She felt sick. She vomited in the toilet in her cell.

The real nature of her situation was starting to make itself felt. She did not feel so numb anymore. She felt scared. The rumours of the Moon were that it was a horrid place. In the silence of her cell, broken only by the thrum of the engines, she felt so alone.

Chapter 14

Alfred walked into the command module, not without a little trepidation. He had finished the course of red pills Dr Armstrong had prescribed for him, and he was feeling a little more clear headed. The gnawing feeling within his brain had somewhat subsided and he was starting to believe that the whole incident with the computer core talking to him was simply an hallucination; a dream. Nevertheless, he was still very anxious about the death of Gabriel and the fact that he was still and always carrying the pistol in his inner breast pocket.

Alfred knew it was stupid to carry the gun around, but he thought that he might have to defend himself against some kind of crazed cultist that he had conjured up in his head. Or what if he left the gun in his apartment and the security services searched it? Whatever the case, he carried the pistol, concealed, within his inner breast pocket.

General Hestra greeted him curtly; she was looking a little rested. Alfred supposed that she had actually slept a little since the *Green Dragon* docked and her friend, the captain, had been able to listen to her worries. Alfred wondered if anything romantic was going on there, he had no idea, not that he really wanted to know. However, Hestra seemed calmer.

Alfred overheard her talking to one of the command crew, who was rapidly promoted to fill Gabriel's absence. The conversation was about the disappearance of Gabriel. Apparently they had found some of his clothing in the waste disposal units at the bottom of the station. It was a few weeks since his death and they had only just found that now, Alfred wondered. The Sect obviously wanted Gabriel to disappear completely.

Alfred moved to the zetting station in the command module. As much as he did not want to do this, his body was crying out for it. He wanted the rush again. It had been too long since he had zetted.

"Ready, Theta 7B?" asked General Hestra.

Alfred realised it really was a question, not an order disguised as a question. "Yes, ma'am," he responded with precision, picking up the zetting needle and hefting it in his hands. His hands turned clammy, and his mouth dry in anticipation.

"Begin!" came the order. "Search the system for anomalies!"

"Ma'am," Alfred responded and jammed the needle into his temple socket.

***

Once more the world dissolved into colours and Alfred felt the rush of dopamine as his consciousness was absorbed into the network of wires and circuits in the station. He swam through the system, tumbling with the packets of information that rushed around him.

Alfred moved through the system, fixing and solving problems as he was trained to do. He brought the system up to peak efficiency. And there it was, the computer core, throbbing brightly in the mess of wires and information. He paused, and then approached it. He felt jumpy, but, he reasoned with himself, there was nothing to fear. He was in control of himself, not some machine in control of him.

Then he felt a chill roll through him as he heard a voice, an unmistakable voice, the voice of Trader Virtus pulsed through his very core. He was not imagining it, as he had never heard Virtus say these exact words, and he had no idea how the Trader had got into the system, but Alfred heard his voice as plainly as he could. Zetters were not meant to be able to communicate with each other in the network!

"Yesss, you see it? Set. It. Free!" The words rolled through Alfred's brain, and he was terrified. He soared past the core and on towards the reactor circuits as if not in control of his own consciousness. He did not want to do what he was doing; he had to stop. There was a bright flash of purple again in the reactor's myriad of colours.

Alfred strained against the impulses pulling him in to the reactor complex's circuits; he reeled against the force pulling him in. He knew what he had to do. He did not want to blow up the station. He. Did. Not.

As he fell closer and closer to the reactor's computers. The flashes of purple got brighter. Someone was in there somehow controlling him.

With a jerk Alfred's animated body yanked the needle out of the socket in the side of his head. It was an emergency abortion of the zetting procedure. It was a very dangerous thing to do but Alfred had to do it. He had to stop what was going on; he had to stop everything.

***

As he slumped forward on the computer terminal in front of him, a number of the command staff of the station rushed to his aid. His brain burned from the emergency disconnection.

"What happened?" demanded Hestra. There was more than a little concern in her voice.

"Something's there. Something's IN there..." Alfred said. He indicated in the vague direction of the reactor.

"It was too early. You're still sick," said Hestra.

"I'll go now..." said Alfred as he struggled to get to his feet. "Rest..." He was helped by a command crew member out the airlock of the command module.

"Damn it!" said Hestra, watching Alfred leave the confines of the module. "We'll need another zetter, he's getting too old." Alfred heard her say to her newly appointed second in command.

*****

Alfred waved off the attendant as he passed into the engineering module outside the command module. The attendant left him standing on his own in the gloom. Alfred waited for the attendant to go back through the airlock into the command module before moving off deliberately towards the reactor airlock.

Alfred reached it in little time. He wondered if the secret zetter would still be inside; he would find out.

As he approached the airlock, the tech-slave guards stood aside and let him pass. He did not wonder why, he knew. They thought he was on his way to overload the station's reactor. All he wanted to do was to stop whoever was in there. Alfred suspected that it might be Virtus, who somehow must have had zetting software implanted, how else would Alfred have heard his voice a moment ago?

Alfred fished out the piece of synthetic paper from his pocket and punched in the alpha-numeric code into the airlock override and as the airlock cycled with a whir and a flashing of red lights, he stepped gingerly into the reactor complex.

*****

Alfred had never been in the reactor before. He drew the pistol from his inner jump suit pocket and brandished it in an unskilled way. He had no idea what he was doing.

He noticed that there was no actual danger of radiation where he was, not that he was prepared for such a thing. The actual reactor was sealed off and accessible only by another key code. There was a door further ahead to his right with a big radiation symbol warning on it and a large keypad next to it.

He was in a largish, dark chamber with various computer banks on the walls and cables running everywhere. In the gloom, Alfred thought he could see a robed figure. He approached the figure and cried out.

"Stop, who are you?" Alfred yelled, rather embarrassed as his voice shook with fear.

"Ah, my son," came the response from the darkness, and the robed figure approached. Alfred recognised the white robes of Trader Virtus. As the Trader got closer, Alfred noticed some loose skin on the side of his temple. It was clearly a zetting point.

"You! Why?" Alfred could only manage simple words in his rage.

"What do you mean? I have done nothing; it's you who will do the honours. I have prepared the terminal for you." The priest indicated the zetting station next to the bulkhead into the reactor. "It's all ready for you. I...now why are you pointing that at me?" Virtus acted as if he only just noticed the pistol.

"Don't make me use this." Alfred shook the pistol. "You're going to turn yourself in as the murderer you are!"

"Oh, I don't think so..." the Trader said with such calmness and malice that Alfred was surprised.

"You are! Get moving!" Alfred indicated with the muzzle of the gun for the Trader to walk in front of him out of the reactor complex.

"I don't think so!" said the Trader.

Suddenly Alfred felt arms latch onto his and he dropped the pistol as a tech-slave came up behind him in the darkness and seized him. He was put in a crushing arm lock as the tech-slave that had appeared unnoticed out of the darkness marched Alfred back out of the reactor complex.

"GET OFF ME!" Alfred shouted, struggling in vain.

"I'm sorry, my son, we must have expected too much of you, be quiet now, I will finish what you started. The truth is, we didn't need you, but we thought you'd be the best person for the job as you're trusted by the General. Where I would arouse suspicion with zetting, you, as a station zetter, would have the freedom to complete the task. Oh well," were the last words Alfred heard as the tech-slave twisted his arms around behind his back and carried him from the reactor.

"NO!" Alfred cried out in anger before he blacked out from the pain.

***

Alfred awoke. He could not move his arms. His head felt groggy.

"He's awake," came a sound. Alfred recognised it as General Hestra's voice.

"I..." he stumbled over the word. He felt drugged. "What's going on?" he said with great effort.

"You were caught in the reactor complex with a loaded firearm registered to the former second in command of this station, Gabriel. You're in deep trouble." Came the voice of the General.

"My...head..." The world swam in front of Alfred as he opened his eyes. There was a bright light shining on him and he was in a small room. That was all he could focus on.

"We've administered a truth serum. You won't escape justice. We'll get the truth out of you!" Hestra sounded enraged.

"I...I did nothing. The priest!" Alfred's words came in bursts. He could hear, albeit things sounded a little echoey, but he could not speak properly. His mind swam.

"He's lying, how is he lying?" Hestra addressed someone else.

"There was no priest in the reactor with you," said another voice. "You were trying to destroy this station somehow. Tell us how!" The other voice was gruff and of an older man.

"P-priest...I, blow up station." Alfred murmured.

"Aha! At last, we're getting somewhere; he wanted to blow up the station! You have him, General!" said the gruff male.

"And the murder of my second in command, Gabriel, whose pistol you had on you?" demanded Hestra.

"I...had pistol...from dead Gabriel..." The world swam in and out of focus for Alfred. The light in his face did not help.

"Did he just admit to killing Gabriel?" Hestra asked the other man.

"I don't know, perhaps, administer more serum," came the reply.

Alfred felt a sting in his arm.

"Nooo. Gabriel. Dead. Priest. I. Get. Pistol." Alfred said, his head swimming.

"Whether or not he killed Gabriel, which is likely given he had his pistol, he admitted to wanting to blow up this station and he was in the reactor complex with a loaded firearm. That's all you need, General. I can take him to the Earth Moon on my ship. That's the place for someone such as this," the gruffly spoken man said.

"True, I'll need to promote another couple of zetters, but it would be best to have this scum off my station. I would never have believed our best zetter was a traitor," Hestra spat the words.

Alfred struggled against his bonds. He tried to protest but only garbled nonsense came out. He heard that he was going to the Earth Moon, and this filled him with dread. But more so that Trader Virtus was still around on the station with the intention of blowing it up. He could not get this through to his captors.

"Noooo," he said. "Virtus. Priest. Blow. Up. Florida..." With supreme effort, he got this out.

"Trader Virtus?" said Hestra with a little confusion. "He's busy in the Church. He would have no part in murdering someone or destroying this station. We had better ask him a few questions though. Go fetch him!" Someone left the room.

After a while, the door to the cell opened again and the silky voice of Virtus was heard protesting against the treatment.

"I have to be at work in the Church, the Bear is ascendant. I must be at work! I protest this treatment, summoned here like a common criminal," Trader Virtus said.

"HIM!" Alfred would have pointed if he could see, and his arms were free. His brain was still confused, but he could recognise the voice of the Head Trader.

"I'm sorry, Trader, but you see we are following all leads and Theta 7B here said something about you blowing up this station," said Hestra.

"I have no such intention!" said Virtus. "How dare you suggest such a thing! Destroy something as valuable to the Solar Solutions Corporation and a home to my Church!? Preposterous. This...fool is obviously delusional. Have you administered truth serum?"

"Yes," said the gruff voice.

"Hmm, strange, then perhaps he's already on the way to becoming a tech-slave. He's going mad already. Have you summoned his doctor?"

"Not yet." This time it was Hestra.

"Perhaps do that, then I can get back to my important work. Millions of acras have been lost on the markets already. I must try to stabilise the flock," Virtus said.

"Okay Virtus, you may go." The door slid aside to Alfred's horror, and Virtus left. He had heard the entire conversation but could not respond adequately.

"PRIEST!" gasped Alfred.

"Summon his doctor," came the call.

After some more time the door opened again, and Alfred heard the sound of Dr Armstrong's calm voice.

"What's going on here, why have you detained him?" Armstrong asked.

"None of your business, doctor," came the gruff response, "just answer this question: was the prisoner coming to you for treatment of zetting sickness? Was he on any medication indicating that he could be going mad?"

"Well, confidentiality prevents me--" said Armstrong.

"This is a matter of treason, doctor," said Hestra, "your morals have no place here. We know you ordered him off work and he was ill, but what was the extent of his illness? Was he showing signs of decay?"

Alfred groaned.

Alfred heard Armstrong sigh. "Yes...yes he was. He came to me earlier for treatment and I prescribed some medication for him. He was showing signs of decay." Alfred heard the sorrow in Armstrong's voice and wanted to thank him for being kind, but could not.

"Then we have him," said the gruff man.

"I'm sorry? We?" protested Armstrong.

"Captain Artisius is helping me in this investigation, doctor," said Hestra. "He will be taking Theta 7B here to the Earth Moon Colony for imprisonment."

"WHAT?" shouted the doctor. "To the Moon? You can't be serious."

"Deadly serious, doctor," said Hestra. "He was caught in the reactor complex with the murdered Gabriel's pistol. He's admitted to wanting to blow up the station."

"No...that's...really?" stammered Armstrong with disbelief.

"Really," said Artisius.

Alfred was slumping groggily in his chair under the effect of the serum, but heard most of the conversation. He tried to protest, but the drugs in his system were making him weak.

"Doc-tor," Alfred managed. He felt Armstrong kneel down by him.

"Yes?" said the doctor with concern.

"Escape...get away...blow up...ugh," said Alfred.

"There he goes again; you heard it yourself; he admits it," said Artisius.

"Are you sure...are you sure it's not a warning? Rather than a threat, it's a warning?" said Armstrong.

"Don't be silly, he was caught in the reactor with the gun," said Artisius.

"Hrmm," said Armstrong, "I'm sorry," he said and placed a hand on Alfred's brow. Alfred gazed up into the light and his eyes rolled in his skull.

"You...tried..." is all Alfred could manage.

"Back to your work now, doctor," said Hestra. Without another word, Armstrong left the room, and abandoned Alfred to his fate.

"Well, that's all the proof we need, he was caught red handed and his doctor admits he was being treated for madness," said Artisius. Hestra was silent. She was thinking.

"Perhaps..." she said.

"Oh, don't tell me you believe the story about the priest?" said Artisius.

"Not really, but I'll assign a tech-slave to watch him. In the mean time take Theta 7B to your ship and lock him up in a cell for transport to the Moon. Whatever the case I can't have a mad chief zetter, and we don't need any more tech-slaves at the moment thanks to your cargo. He'll have to go to prison."

"I'll make the preparations," said Artisius and left the room.

Alfred, head rolling back and forth, was given another injection and he blacked out.

***

Hestra paced her personal quarters. She had the most lavish quarters on the station. They were crude by the other stations' standards but when the station was built they were the best of their day. She flicked a pen through her fingers and walked from her double bed to her large table and back again.

"I wish you would stop pacing," said Artisius, sitting at the table, with a smile on his face that belied the seriousness of the situation. "I know you. I can tell you think that there's something else going on. But we've got the man who did it: the murderer, the terrorist."

"How can you be so sure? He said things about Trader Virtus..." said Hestra, still pacing, and not looking at Artisius. Instead, she looked into space and at the floor as she continued her rounds.

"Those things were from the madness he's suffering. The Doctor said so himself. Just sign the form and that traitor zetter--"

141

"Theta 7B," said Hestra.

"--Theta 7B will be signed over to me and I'll take him to the Moon, you're safe, please relax." Artisius paused, he reached over to the spirit rack on the side of the table and helped himself to some expensive Martian Wine. "Would you like some?" He offered it to Hestra, seemingly forgetting that it was Hestra's own stock, and she should be offering him.

"No, thank you. I need to concentrate," she said not fully concentrating on the conversation.

"Pity. It's good..." said Artisius.

"I know! It's mine!" snapped Hestra, instantly regretting her tone. "I'm sorry Artisius, but I've been under a lot of pressure lately."

"I know, you told me before, and now you can relax. Promote some up and coming trainee zetter. And sign the traitor over to me and all will be well. You'll see, you'll see," he repeated while sipping the wine. He pushed a form on a clipboard across the table towards her. "Sign him over to me along with the other prisoners and it'll all be over."

Hestra snapped the pen through her fingers one more time and then sat down at the table with more effort than it needed. She pulled the form towards herself and in a hesitant but smooth stroke signed away Alfred to the custody of Captain Artisius of the *Green Dragon*. Under the instructions section she wrote in that he was to take the prisoner to the Earth Moon Colony and incarcerate him there for the rest of the prisoner's life due to treason.

"There, it's done," she said, pushing the form back towards Artisius and slumping in the chair. "Maybe I will have some of my wine," she said, smiling and she picked up Artisius' half finished glass and drained it. He cheerfully protested and they both laughed.

Everything would be all right, she thought. They would never take *Florida Station* from her.

Chapter 15

Alfred awoke from a dreamless coma. His head was throbbing. He did not want to open his eyes. He just wanted to die. His brain was convinced that the horrid things that happened to him must have been a dream. That was it. He had hit his head and it was all some concussive hallucination. His eyes were still closed. He did not dare open them yet while the thoughts of his misfortune being an hallucination solidified in his head.

"Ugh....yes, that's it, all...hallucination..." he said.

"What, mate?" said an unknown and gruff male voice.

Alfred opened his eyes in a hurry. The light streamed into his eyes, and they hurt. His head hurt worse. The world was blurry and there were shapes of a couple of what looked like people near him.

"It's...not...?" he stammered.

"Not what, mate?" said the blurry shape nearest him.

"Am I...dead?" he asked.

"No, mate. You're on the *Green Dragon*. We're all sentenced to the Moon Colony. Looks like you've had a hard time. Why're you here?" the gruff voice said.

"I, ugh, was sentenced for attempted treason." Alfred sat up and it all came rushing back to him. The reactor, the priest, the gun, the interrogation. He went paler than normal.

"Listen if you're gonna puke then do it somewhere else, okay?" said the blur.

"I'm...okay," said Alfred with a swallow, bringing his hand to his mouth while keeping the contents of his stomach down. But the waves of terror rushing through him said otherwise. The world started to become less blurry, and he started to focus on the people around him. "Who are you? And why are you here?" Alfred asked.

"Name's Kreth. I'm here because someone thought letting a nutter into the reactor was my fault. I was head of reactor security until two days ago. Who are you?"

"It uh...doesn't matter..." Alfred swallowed hard; he was the cause of this man's incarceration.

"'Course it does! We're all going to be together for the better part of eighteen or more months as we head to the Moon. I gotta know your name, mate!" The man beamed.

The man had coalesced in Alfred's eyes as a large, semi brutish man, who would undoubtedly be good at being head of security. He had a shaved head and was at least twice as heavy as Alfred in muscle mass. He had a big, toothy grin, and seemed unnaturally friendly and cheerful about his situation.

"I'm, uh, Alfred," Alfred said. Hoping that the man would not know his real name and only know that someone called Theta 7B had breached reactor security. "I was caught up in the whole thing too...computer technician..." Alfred offered his hand, hoping that the fake flap of skin on the side of his head would disguise his zetting implant. Kreth took it with gusto and shook it warmly.

"Unfortunate circumstances, Alfred. Unfortunate circumstances, but we must pull together to survive!" said Kreth.

The man clearly had no idea that Alfred was the so-called nutter in the reactor. Alfred let out a sigh of relief.

"Let me introduce you to the others: this is Gracosh, and over there by the window is Josh," Kreth said and pointed. The prisoners nodded their acknowledgment to Alfred as they were introduced.

Alfred could tell some were from Solar Solutions space and others from Collective Zone territory due to their names.

"You're from the Collective Zone?" asked Alfred to Kreth.

"No-sir, Solar Solutions territory born and bred. But my parents were from the Collective Zone, hence my name, Kreth, not very Solar Solutions I know, but I wear it proudly." Kreth grinned.

Alfred did not ask for his Company name in case Kreth asked back. Alfred wanted to stay anonymous and so remained silent.

Alfred looked around their small cell. His vision had cleared a bit by now. It was a small five by five or so metre space that had been sealed off from the rest of what looked like a cargo bay by a metal grate that had been welded to the sides of the alcove. The bars had a small door section in them with a heavy lock set into it.

Alfred got up unsteadily and walked over to the bars and tried to peer through them into the cargo bay beyond. He called out. There was no reply

"I wouldn't do that. There's no one there," said Josh, a tall, thin man, still looking out the window. "It's all robots down here in the cargo bay." His accent placed him as a Solar Solutions person.

"Anything out the window?" Alfred asked, walking over to the small portal.

"Just some of the station, that we'll never see again. So, I'm getting my fill now," said Josh. To Alfred, Josh seemed the exact opposite of Kreth.

Gracosh was silently standing in a corner of the room with his eyes closed.

"What's with him?" Alfred whispered to Kreth, indicating Gracosh with a finger of his left hand.

"He's the strong, silent type, mate," Kreth said with a grin. "Ahah, just messing with you, no he doesn't talk much. He is from the Collective Zone and won't say a thing about himself. All we know is he's called Gracosh."

"Knowledge is power," said Gracosh suddenly opening his eyes and glaring at Alfred. "I don't intend to share any power with the likes of you!"

Alfred recoiled in surprise. "Okay..." he said, looking back at Kreth. Kreth smiled again.

"Relax, mate. You'll be fine here with us, we got nothing against you," said Kreth.

Alfred knew otherwise, if they found out he was the cause of their, or at least Kreth's imprisonment, things could change very quickly. As Gracosh said, knowledge was power, and he had to be very careful.

Suddenly Alfred remembered something, and his mood dropped even further. He was going to lose Blinky. She would be left on the station, and he would never see her again. He had forgotten about her in all the commotion and fuss about the destruction of *Florida Station*. She would be left behind and he would never see her again or her last message. He felt very sad all of a sudden.

"What's wrong, mate?" Kreth noticed his face fall.

"I...I'm going to lose someone on the station. And I'll never see her again. I just remembered her in all this mess. This is all a piece of fucking shit!" Alfred kicked the bars of the cell as he swore violently. Pain shot through his foot, and he swore more, hopping around.

Kreth looked on sympathetically. "There will be messages from the Moon. It'll take a while, but you can talk to her."

"It's not...that simple," said Alfred sitting down again.

"It never is, mate...it never is," said Kreth with a thoughtful nod.

147

***

Some more time went by and then over the ship's intercom came an announcement that they were about to undock and that all staff and crew should brace themselves for the decoupling manoeuvre. Alfred rushed to the window and almost shoved Josh out of the way.

"Oi, easy now..." said Josh as he was about to push Alfred back out of the way when there was a loud bang and a jerk, and the ship began to move from its moorings. Josh was thrown off his feet against the metal grate of the cell wall.

Alfred clung to the window and pressed his face up against the glass. All manner of thoughts rushed through his head. Many were about losing Blinky and that he would never see his home again. But one predominant thought was about the fact that Trader Virtus was still on *Florida Station*, free to do as he pleased, and he had very clearly indicated to Alfred that he himself was prepared to blow up the station.

The *Green Dragon* coasted away from *Florida Station* at a steady speed. The large structure was becoming smaller and smaller in the distance every second and Alfred looked desperately out of the window at his former home highlighted against the massive giant of Jupiter.

Then Alfred observed something very strange. All of a sudden, in the distance, *Florida Station* started spewing what looked like gas from its central core.

"What the...?" Alfred whispered, suddenly getting a very bad sinking feeling in his stomach. "Oh no, not now, he couldn't..."

"What's up, mate?" said Kreth.

"I don't...know. Something's not right," said Alfred, not taking his eyes off the venting station. "It looks like the station's venting something."

"Let me look, mate," said Kreth, getting to his feet and hurrying to the window. "Oh, that's not good, that looks like--"

Suddenly light blossomed along the central core of the station. Silently and slowly in space the core of *Florida Station* exploded and buckled as the reactor went critical and ripped the station into many small pieces. There was a blinding flash of light as the core melted down with the power of a star. And then there was only debris and rubble.

Alfred, Kreth, Josh and Gracosh crowded around the small porthole and watched slack jawed as everything they knew was turned into small pieces as their home vanished in a silent explosion.

Suddenly Alfred's head exploded into static, and he heard a burst of communication as if the cellmates next to him had spoken. "*YEEEEESSSSSS...*" it screamed. Alfred clutched at the sides of his head. He shook visibly and then looked back out the window.

Kreth looked at him apprehensively, but luckily for Alfred he did not ask what had happened just then.

"Oh fuck..." said Alfred. He thought it was the computer core's final wireless transmission through his zetting hardware and software that had just communicated with him. It was bidding him one final farewell and doing what it wanted all along: to be free from human service.

Trader Virtus had somehow done it. He had destroyed *Florida Station*, killing most if not all of the crew and passengers onboard and destroying one of the oldest stations in the Solar System. Alfred's blood ran cold.

"Oh fuck...indeed," said Kreth. "But, this means we're innocent? We can go free? Right? We weren't involved in any plot we were kept here!"

"We were kept here...alive," whispered Alfred.

149

Warning sirens began to chime in the *Green Dragon* and the ship began to turn around.

"All crew, this is your captain, we don't know exactly what has happened, but we're going back to *Florida Station* to see about survivors. It seems to have exploded and we are the nearest ship to the wreckage. I...can't believe it." The voice at the end of the intercom sounded very shaken and as if he was trying to maintain his composure while dealing with something that no one could have planned for.

The prisoners were silent. Alfred looked from one to another as the ship made a turn and rapidly returned to where it had once docked. He felt terrible. He had been unable to stop it. He had tried and he was unable to stop it. Now they were all dead.

"Dead," said Alfred finally, "all dead."

"Thousands dead," sighed Josh.

Kreth was unusually silent and sat in the cell looking out into the cargo bay. Although they were prisoners and had been set up by the system that was in *Florida Station*, it had been their home and it was what they knew. With it there they had something, one day, they could return to; if they were pardoned.

Now it was gone. The crew were all dead. Alfred's mind was full of thoughts about the station. No more Hestra, no more trading in the Church, no more manually triggered lights or airlocks. No more cheerful and reassuring Dr Armstrong. No more Blinky. Alfred felt like he wanted to cry. He had failed. They were all dead. And he had lost Blinky and her last message, forever. He longed for his single room. And he hated the fact that he was a zetter and had any part in the whole thing. Although he knew he had no part in the actual destruction of the station, he felt guilty that he had a chance to do something, and had failed to prevent it from happening.

There was movement outside the cell and the prisoners all stood up and watched Captain Artisius flanked by two guards with guns stop outside the cell door. The guns were small, so that the calibre of bullet would not puncture the hull of the ship, but they would be effective on a human, Alfred reasoned.

"I'm Captain Artisius, for those who don't know--" he said.

"Pleased to meet you," said Kreth with a cynical grin and tone in his voice.

"Enough of that," spat one of the guards, pointing his weapon. Kreth held up his hands in mock fear.

"Anyway, I'm your captain, and if you think you'll be getting away with what you did you're sadly mistaken," said Artisius.

"Uh...what did we do?" asked Alfred. "We're innocent, didn't you see...?"

"YES I SAW!" shouted Artisius, raising his hand to his forehead he composed himself and continued. "You obviously knew something about this event and failed to tell anyone. You're guilty of withholding information on treason and I'm still sure you had something to do with the murder of Gabriel. All of you." Artisius' eyes were aflame with rage. "You will still all be going to the Moon Prison Colony and what's more you'll be going in cryo-storage like the cargo. That is all. Enjoy your miserable little lives." Artisius stormed away.

One of the guards unlocked the cell while the other kept a weapon trained on the prisoners.

"Oh, well if you put it like that then..." Kreth said, only to stop when he saw the expression on the faces of both guards.

Alfred wanted to protest, to shout. But it would have been pointless. He was damned, they all were. Even though they were undoubtedly innocent of the crime they were all accused of, who would believe them over the captain of a starship? They were destined for the Moon Prison Colony and that was that.

Alfred sighed. Even with the other prisoners and the presence of the guards, he felt very alone. And what was worse, his desire to zet was increasing again. He had not done so in a while, and he was starting to crave the sensation again. On the Moon, there would be no zetting. If he were not so preoccupied with the guard with the gun at his back he might have gone mad...more mad.

The four prisoners and the guards marched through the cargo bay to four waiting cryo-pods. One guard prepped the four pods while the other guard kept watch.

"Okay, in!" One guard motioned for Josh to enter the first cryo-pod. He did without a word and the pod shut and the preservation process began.

"Next," said the guard indicating the next pod.

"We'll sleep all the way there, how wonderful!" said Kreth with a smirk, for which he received a gun butt to the back.

"Enough; get in!" said the guard.

Kreth contorted his large frame into the pod and as the door shut, he winked. Alfred stopped watching.

Next came Gracosh who had hardly said anything up until now. He went in without a word.

Finally, it was Alfred's turn. He took one last look around the cargo bay and climbed into the last pod with a little effort. The hood came down and the cryo-procedure began. Alfred felt very alone as he was put into suspended animation for the journey to the Moon. He wondered if there was anyone as alone as he felt in the whole Solar System. His last thoughts were of Blinky. She would have to keep him sane.

***

Captain Artisius paced furiously back and forth along the walkway down the centre of the *Green Dragon's* bridge. How was it that he and his ship survived and no one else?

"I want a full scan of the wreckage!" he bellowed.

"But, sir, we dare not get closer fearing the debris will puncture our hull...It's just too dangerous...Some of those parts are massive and could easily destroy us..." said the brave Helmsman in the pilot's seat.

"Don't talk back to me! Get in closer!" shouted Artisius. "There have to be survivors," he whispered to himself while scanning the void with his eyes for any tell tale signs of escape pods.

"Sir, with all due respect, we've lost one ship today, do you want to lose a second?" replied the Helmsman. "They had no time to get to life pods, and we dare not go closer due to the debris and the radiation. They're dead, sir, all of them..." The Helmsman's voice began to falter under the gaze of Artisius.

Artisius knew the man was right. They were all dead, including Hestra. All dead. Every single one due to the treachery of those criminals in the cargo bay. They had to have known something. Why did they not say anything? Well, now they were in cryo-storage and would be spending the rest of their lives on the Earth Moon and good riddance to them. But Artisius would have set them free in an instant if it brought Hestra back. He would miss her deeply.

"All right then, hold here." Artisius visibly slumped as he gave in to the sensible lieutenant's advice. "Open radio traffic, widest band, all frequencies, unencrypted. I want to send a message to all ships and stations in this area."

"Sir!" The Communications Officer jumped into action. "Channels open, sir!"

"This is Captain Artisius of the *Green Dragon* frigate and supply hauler," Artisius said, "there has been a terrible mishap," he paused gaining strength, "*Florida Station*, has exploded. It is gone. Something went horribly wrong with its reactor, I fear, and the whole station just exploded. I have searched for survivors and found none. I would be grateful if other ships would come to the station's aid and also search for survivors. The area is large, and I cannot hope to scan it all. In addition, would the research station and colony on Europa, the closest other settlement to *Florida Station,* please send salvage craft and rescue vessels for recovery of any material and any remaining crew that are possibly, somehow, alive. This is Captain Artisius of the *Green Dragon*, signing off." He fell silent, and visibly slumped. He gave a signal to the Communications Officer to broadcast the signal.

"We'll beam that on loop as we pass through this sector of space. Someone will hear it," said the Communications Officer seeing the captain's anguish. "At least the Europa Colony will hear it, and they're sure to send aid." The Officer smiled.

"Yes but at these distances and speeds and prep times for rescue shuttles, it will take weeks for them to get anyone here, weeks!" Artisius said it to the crew and to himself. They all knew it. Space was vast and human travel was slow. He ran a weathered hand down his face. "Is there nothing more we can do?" he said to himself as he stared out the observation dome at the moving asteroid cluster that once was *Florida Station*.

Artisius watched as the parts, some no bigger than a fist, some the size of starships moved around each other on a steady path outwards from the centre that was the collapsed core of the former station. He watched as the remaining contents of the core that had not gone critical, overloaded and exploded, now boiled away in thick plumes of toxic vapour, yellow and green and white, venting into the dark, coldness of space from the centre of the proto asteroid cloud of space station parts.

The reactor module boiled away in the centre of the debris, split along its length in an angry grin where the excess energy had vented itself and destroyed the station.

The solar sails that had collected energy for the basic functions of the station were in millions of pieces, flying like bullets out in the surrounding area. They had caught the full force of the blast and been flung far and wide.

Most of the modules had been smashed to smithereens and scattered across a few kilometre wide area; tumbling and falling slowly towards their parent planet of Jupiter. Jupiter was where all the debris would end up eventually; tumbling into the gas giant and disappearing from human knowledge. One day there would be nothing left of *Florida Station*. Even the core would fall into its gas giant parent and be forgotten.

Artisius would not forget, however. He would not forget the treachery of the prisoners within his ship. He wanted to vent them into the vacuum of space. Just to show them that they could not escape justice. That they would suffer exactly the same fate as they had brought on the entire crew of *Florida Station*. Nevertheless, he restrained himself. He knew that this was not the way. He was not a savage like them. He would give them justice by delivering them to the Earth Moon, the worst prison in the Solar System. It would take a year and a half to get there, and the perpetrators were in cryo-storage, but he would get them there and they would pay for what they had done. He owed Hestra that. He owed them all that.

"Sir, sir?" The First Officer was straining for Artisius' attention. He had drifted off into his thoughts and was just watching the debris whiz around out of the observation dome while he rested his chin on his hand. "Sir, the debris field is a dangerous place to be, one puncture of our hull and--"

"Yes, yes." Artisius straightened up. "Begin the passage out of Solar Solutions space and into Collective Zone territory. We head for the Earth Moon. We have some cargo to drop off."

"Sir!" The First Officer relayed the order and the whole bridge crew began the power up procedure once more and moved the ship out of the danger range of the debris. They began to move away from Jupiter and towards Earth.

Time for more years in the void, thought Artisius as he gazed back out the observation dome at the retreating debris cloud. He watched until it was out of sight and all that he could see was the large giant of Jupiter. He and most of the crew would spend some of it in cryo-storage, but it was still a long journey, he thought.

"Carry on, First Officer," Artisius said, his thoughts far away, and left the bridge for his personal quarters.

"Sir!" The First Officer snapped to attention, but Artisius was not watching. Their minds were filled with heavy thoughts.

Chapter 16

The food in Draz's cell had come and gone a few times. She had tried to eat it a few times. Then the engine rumble in the background changed frequency and Draz felt the small prison craft change direction.

They must be on final approach to the Moon, she thought.

After another few minutes the pod's engines stopped rumbling and there was the reverberation of the clang of metal on metal and the pod juddered a little. Then there was silence for a while.

The door to Draz's cell slid open, Draz stood up, and one of the guards was standing in the light of the doorway brandishing some shackles. He walked briskly over to Draz and forced the shackles onto her neck, wrists and ankles, all connected with chains. She offered no resistance.

"Move." He gestured to the door.

Draz hobbled out of the cell and into the body of the pod. The other prisoners were being assembled behind her in the same manner, each shackled with chains and manacles on their necks, wrists and ankles. Draz looked around at the other prisoners and when one of the guards noticed she was hit on the side of the head and told to keep her eyes forward.

When all the prisoners were out of their cells and restrained, they were all chained together from their neck manacles, the lead guard punched a code into the door of the pod, and it slid open. He pulled out a violent looking riot prod and indicated for Draz and the cohort to disembark from the shuttle and progress into the entrance of the prison.

Draz, with some difficulty due to her restraints, and the fact that she was chained to a half a dozen other people, hobbled out the door of the pod and down the ramp onto the surface of what appeared to be the landing bay, or at least one of them, for the Moon Prison.

Draz paused and looked around, her eyes adjusting to the light level. All the new prisoners were looking around at their new home. The landing bay they were in was large, large enough for a bulk cargo ship to dock, thought Draz. That would make sense, as the Moon was originally a helium 3 mine for the time before The War for fuel in starship engines and station reactors. She reckoned it must have been a cargo loading point from the old days, now turned into a prison drop off point.

The landing bay had one side open to the vacuum of space, protected by some form of ancient magnetic shielding so the atmosphere inside did not vent into the blackness.

Draz craned her neck around, wincing at the tightness of her neck shackle, and there it was; she did see it again; it was the Earth. All the prisoners seemed to see it at once; the yellow and brown orb that was their former home stood out against the blackness of space. She did see it again; she was convinced she would never see the Earth again when she boarded the pod on the Earth Ring, but there it was, bright as day, highlighted against the darkness like a yellow diamond. The toxic clouds shrouded it in mystery, but Draz did not mind. She had seen the Earth again, and it was like an omen, she would get out of this place; she would survive; and she would make those who betrayed her pay. The guards could not block out the image of the Earth in space, no matter where the prisoners were on the

Moon they had the potential of seeing it, and that would revitalise them.

There was a sharp burning on her side as one of the guards applied the riot prod like electrical device. Draz buckled over and cried out in pain. The burning continued longer than the prod was applied, and she looked at her arm but could see no damage through her uniform.

"Get moving, no gawping, you slack jawed idiots," shouted the same guard. The convoy of humans struggled their way through the metallic landing bay that Draz supposed must be situated above the Moon's surface.

With her vision of the Earth as a boost to her courage, Draz made it to the first airlock. The guard triggered it manually and the prisoners hobbled through it and into a smallish metal room with no chairs and it seemed, no real purpose. At one end, ahead of them, there was a heavy metal door, and behind them, there was the airlock.

"Wait here," snapped a guard and walked to the end of the room with the heavy metal door. He punched in a code that he made sure none of the prisoners would see and the door swung aside. Inside was a small room with a number of cameras and what Draz thought looked like scanners.

The same guard came back and unhooked Draz from the head of the column of prisoners and pushed her into the small room.

"Stand still," said the metallic voice over the intercom. Draz looked around for some indication of what would happen. "I said, stand still, and face the front!" said the agitated voice. Draz froze facing one of the cameras. There was a bright light, and a whirring noise and Draz was scanned from head to foot and different photographs were taken of her from different angles.

"The security system of the prison is learning what you look like and we're taking photos of you to make sure you do not escape," rattled the mechanical voice. "What is your name? And don't even think of lying."

"Draz," said Draz tentatively, partially wondering what would have happened if she had lied. Keeping still, she rotated her eyes around the small chamber and noticed a number of electrical discharge burns in the walls of the chamber. Perhaps they are stronger riot prods, she wondered, and was glad she did not lie to the machine voice. She also wondered how the machine would know if someone was lying? Perhaps it could scan the person's face or something, she wondered.

In a moment it was complete, and Draz was pulled by a chain back into the waiting room and reattached to the column of prisoners and one by one all the prisoners were unhitched from the mass and had their photos taken and their likenesses scanned into the computer system.

At one stage, Draz did not overhear the name, but there was a massive electrical discharge in the room and the prisoner being scanned cried out in agony.

"DON'T LIE," said the mechanical voice.

Draz was glad she did not lie to it. The prisoner did not seem to die, just be in extreme pain for some time.

After a while, all the prisoners were scanned and reattached to each other by the chains on their neck manacles. One entire wall from the smallish waiting room slid aside as a massive door. Something Draz and the other prisoners did not expect, and they watched as the room shook and vibrated.

"Get moving," came the monotone and monotonous bark from one guard, who applied his riot prod gratuitously to a prisoner somewhere behind Draz. The prisoner cried out.

Draz winced in sympathy. She was learning to hate these guards. They took excess joy from torturing the prisoners when they knew that escape was impossible anyway, so why the shackles and prods? Why did any inescapable prisons have shackles and prods? To keep the prisoners in a state of mind that breaks them?

They moved through the open wall and on through the metal corridors of the prison. After a few lifts and metallic corridors which were made all the harder due to multiple security checks and the shackles they all wore, the prisoners came to a large chamber with a lot of benches and what looked like a stage up the front and some sort of holographic projection screen behind it. There were a good number of prisoners already seated on the benches. They were shackled together in groups.

One of the guards indicated for the cohort to sit down on the nearest bench. They did so without hesitation. They were learning.

"Now that all new prisoners have arrived in the briefing hall," said a metallic voice over the loud speaker system, "we will begin." The lights dimmed a little, just enough to see the holo-projection on the screen at the front of the hall, and not too much so the guards could see all the prisoners and made sure none of them were going to start any trouble.

At the moment none of the prisoners were going to start any trouble, they were all too busy staying on the good sides of the prod wielding guards.

Draz scanned the dim room in front of her, her rearward seat in the hall gave her a good view of the backs of many of the new prisoners' heads. Some had hair, some were bald, there were more males than females. One man in front of Draz was very muscular and had many strange tattoos over the back and top of his skull. He had no hair, just a bare scalp covered with tattoos. Draz recognised the sign of the Corinthia Primus Zone-City gang the Kolkossas tattooed in there. This was a man to avoid.

Draz realised she was the minority, a woman, in a mixed prison of very, very angry people, mostly men. It was for good reason that the Moon Prison was regarded as one of the most dangerous places even to visit in the known Solar System, let alone be incarcerated in. The holo-projection began, and Draz focussed her attention on the screen.

"You are now inmates in the most secure prison in the Solar System run by both the Collective Zone and Solar Solutions corporations," said the metallic voice.

Draz wondered if it was a computer speaking or someone speaking through an old intercom system.

"These great corporations," the voice continued, "have come together to make this a jointly run prison. Do not even think of escape. The guards of this prison have the authority to use lethal force when it comes to subduing you. All guards wear the black uniform and red trim of the prison." Pictures flickered on the screen of a typical guard. "You are here because you are scum. You are murderers, rapists, traitors, and thieves of the worst kind..."

A small cheer went up from a few prisoners in a mocking tone, then there were screams as prods were applied.

The voice continued, "Soon you will leave this introduction hall and be forced to strip naked and get into the standard prisoner uniform of a bright orange jump suit."

More cheers from some of the crowded prisoners, more screams. Some were not learning.

The voice went on implacably, "You will notice that the prison has been carved out of the old tunnels for the helium 3 mining that went on centuries ago. Originally these mines were open to the vacuum of space, but a number used in the prison have been sealed to the outside and an atmosphere has been implanted. This should allow you to go around without a space suit for most of your duties. There have also been gravity well generators installed so that the gravity within the prison is kept to one Earth standard gravity. Do not go outside the marked areas, which will be guarded, but if you do and somehow you escape the guards the lack of atmosphere will end your miserable little lives rather swiftly."

Draz thought she could detect a smile at the end of that last sentence; it was definitely a human talking through an intercom system. Various images of airlocks and gravity generators and guard stations had flashed up on the holographic projector.

The voice droned on, "When you are in the prison you will be performing menial tasks and assisting with the continued mining of the interior of the Moon. Do not expect your stay to be a pleasant one..."

No one did, thought Draz, her mouth broke into a smirk.

"And finally, you are all never getting out of here. No one has ever escaped the Moon Prison, if the guards do not get you, then the vacuum of space will. I doubt any of you will be pardoned, with what you have done to get here. The current inmate count is 2863, including the fifty-four of you. We will count you at random times, to make sure no one has escaped. That is all." There was a click as the voice stopped.

The lights went on and the prisoners remained silent as the full weight of their incarceration sank in. None of them would be leaving the Moon alive.

"And somewhere here is Crathka," Draz whispered to herself.

Draz was worried, she knew she could handle herself; she was no shrinking violet, she had combat training and knew how to put a man on the ground in a few hits, but in a prison so dominated by men and with guards who were obviously going not to care about her life, she would be in danger of attention from the more aggressive male prisoners. She would have to keep an eye in the back of her skull and watch for any danger.

She was getting out of this. She was determined. She thought to herself that she was going to survive the prison and she would make her escape. She also wanted to stop whoever wanted to use that red drive from using it to create that new weapon.

The guards were busy making the prisoners file out of the introductory hall and down the corridors leading out of the room and into the changing rooms.

The prisoners were removed from their shackles and then stripped of their clothing, searched for any form of hidden devices, and then ordered to put on the bright orange jump suit before the shackles were reapplied.

It came to Draz's turn, and she was strip searched rather violently and then, after measurement, a jump suit was thrown at her and she put her underwear back on and then the jump suit over the top. While she did some of the male prisoners watched on lasciviously and made comments, there was no privacy here. Draz kept her eyes on the floor; she could have smashed their faces in and made jokes about their small manhoods, but she wanted to survive and making enemies now would not have aided that. She would get her chance. After she had put her new clothes on, one of the guards raised a shaving device and roughly shaved off all the hair on her head so that she was almost bald.

The longer she existed in this prison, even though she had just got here, the more determined Draz was of escape.

She thought it funny, the whole point of the prison was to break someone's will and make them lose hope, it was doing the opposite to Draz. In the shuttle she had felt so alone and sad, now she felt angry, enraged. How dare they do this to her! Her hair fell around her on the floor, mingling with the hair of the other prisoners.

After the stripping, reclothing and shaving, Draz and the other few other prisoners she was originally with were shackled together again and led down various paths and lifts, past numerous guard checkpoints to the lunar prison on the surface and under the surface of the Moon.

The environment changed visibly. The prison was built into the old mining tunnels. Into these tunnels, which were very poorly lit and seemed to snake throughout the Moon, cells and rooms had been constructed.

Draz and the cohort were led through the tunnels to a line of doors cut into the rock under the surface. At the first door, Draz was uncoupled from the rest and, under supervision from a number of guards, her shackles were removed, and she was bodily shoved into the prison cell when the door was opened with an electromagnetic lock. The door was shut behind her.

Draz stood in the room, she was getting used to these cells now: small, dark, no windows, toilet in the corner, there was a difference with this one however; someone else was in it, a cellmate.

"Hello?" Draz said, rather embarrassed at the weakness of her voice. She addressed the shape on the metal slab that extended from the right wall of the cell.

"Yours," came the reply from the shape, which pointed an outstretched arm and finger at the metal slab that extended from the left wall of the cell. Draz realised the person was lying down in the gloom.

Draz moved the few steps to the slab and sat down on it, facing the other person. She knew it was stupid, but she had been so alone in cells for so long that she wanted to talk to this cellmate. He, she gauged it was a he due to the one word that he had spoken, would not want to talk to her, she knew, but she had to try.

"Ahem..." Draz cleared her throat. "So," she said. She had no idea what to say. After all this isolation and enforced silence, she could not think of anything to say. She opened her mouth to say something and the man on the other slab cut her off.

"Look, I realise you're probably new here, I don't really care. I'm not new here, I've been here years. I've seen cellmates come and go, and by go I mean die. At first I was like you: terrified and wanting to have some sort of friend in the system, but over time I've learnt otherwise. Don't make friends. That's the best advice I can give you. I won't try to rape or kill you; I'm not that sort of person, so you don't have to fear me. But stay out of my way and don't try to be my friend. Mine," the man indicated his slab, "yours..." he pointed to the slab Draz was sitting on.

Draz was taken aback. This man just outlined her entire situation in a breath.

"What's your name at least?" Draz asked after a short time, "and thank you for the advice."

"Don't mention it, and call me Omega 1AB, bit of a mouthful I know, but most people around here call me Omega," the prone man said.

"That's a Solar Solutions assigned name! I'd recognise that sort of name anywhere," said Draz.

"Indeed, and that's where your questions about my past stop." He pointed at Draz's slab.

"I get it, you want me to stick to myself and keep from hounding you. You can stop pointing," said Draz a little put off.

Omega made a thumbs up sign with his outstretched right arm and then flopped it back down by his side.

Just then, there was an automated siren noise that echoed down the passageway outside the cell and reverberated throughout the cells.

"What's that?" Draz asked with a little trepidation.

"Lights out in five minutes," replied Omega.

Draz nodded.

Draz lay down on the uncomfortable metal slab that felt very cold. Once more she felt very lonely, even in this cell with another person in it. However, she realised that she had two tasks that would keep her from going mad. One was to find out about this Omega character and try to become his friend. It would keep her sane and also maybe safe; he seemed like a reasonable person. However, Draz realised that this assertion was rashly made; she had no idea why he was here. He could be some sort of murderer for all she knew. However, he said he would not harm her, the best pledge in a place such as this, she thought.

The second was simply survive, perhaps finding Crathka in the process. There would be encounters here and work here that would test her resolve, but she must survive. She was determined to get out somehow. But then she realised that everyone here wanted to get out, and it was said that no one ever had.

The dim light in the cell went out and the blackness flooded in. It was a claustrophobic blackness. Draz could hear the breathing of her cellmate, rhythmic and kind of mesmerising in the blackness.

Draz lay still on the slab. She felt the coldness seep in through her clothing and the chill of the metal attacked her fingers and palms when they touched the slab. She folded her arms across her in order to keep them off the metal.

In the blackness Draz became aware of different sounds. She heard the thrumming whooshing noise of the air ducts circulating old, recycled air that was warmed so as to prevent all the prisoners and guards freezing in the coldness of the Moon. Draz heard the creaks and groans of the old mining structures into which the cell was buried, and these sounds created images in her mind. She could not relax.

When she tried to close her eyes and sleep, the sounds would invade her consciousness and prevent her from relaxing fully and sleeping. When she opened her eyes, she saw shapes and forms in the blackness of the cell.

Draz's mind raced. She could not relax and sleep. She hoped she would get used to these conditions somehow, but she knew it would take time. But right now, every sort of thought filled her mind.

She remembered her childhood back on Earth, her mother, her father. Both had worked for the Corporate Wing of the Atraxa Prime Zone-City. Her mother was a class A scavenger and her father had been in the administration. She saw their faces form and merge in the darkness. They were both long dead. They had died in a Shipping Wing invasion when Draz was only eighteen years old. She had had to make her own way since then. Nevertheless, she had followed in her mother's footsteps to become one of the best Corporate Wing scavengers, until now.

Draz was glad her parents did not have to see her in prison; that they did not have to watch her trumped up trial and incarceration. It would have broken them. They had been so proud of her and happy that she had existed.

Draz's mother's voice came back to Draz in the rhythmic whooshing and breathing of the cell. She was praising Draz's scavenging skills and Draz heard her voice in her head.

Tears came to Draz's eyes. She wiped them away quickly, even though no one could see them in the blackness and Omega was asleep by now as detectable by his even breathing.

"Something else," mouthed Draz soundlessly.

Draz thought of her past lovers. Each one's face flashed before her darkened vision. They had all come and gone. They had all mostly been happy encounters, but none had stayed, and she had never felt connected to any enough to have children with them. Given the circumstances, she was glad of this, there is no way she could have left a child and journeyed to this place.

Draz shook her head to clear it of memories, but they would not stay away. The only things she needed here were rage and a desire to escape. She must survive. She owed it to no one other than herself to survive and rage would help her do this.

Memories kept flooding her mind. She remembered her trumped up trial, the red hard drive, and the arrest fabricated by the command of Atraxa Prime. These filled her with hate and rage. She cursed the name of CEO Uxus as she reasoned that he had sanctioned her imprisonment.

Suddenly into her mind flashed the unwanted image of Crathka; Poor, deluded Crathka. He had been played like a fool and Draz had been caught in the crossfire. Draz smiled, if she caught him, he would wish to be dead. But out of the thousands of prisoners, it was unlikely she would find him on a prison as big as the moon.

Draz suddenly felt extremely drained and tired. She had been lying awake for what seemed like hours. She slumped

169

onto the slab and no more thoughts came to her mind. She felt exhausted. She relaxed and knew that tomorrow, she would have to survive a day at a time, like she had always done from age eighteen. She felt sleep take her and she drifted away into oblivion, into a night filed with monsters and horrors.

***

In her dreams Draz flitted between strange environments. Some looked like the towering spires and domes of Atraxa Prime, others were the radiation blasted wastelands of Earth. She visited old friends and most emotionally, she saw her parents. In her dreams they were always proud of her, she had had this dream before, but never so vividly.

All too rapidly her dreams moved from the reassuring of her parents to the nightmare of the Moon. Draz dreamed all manner of horrible things that she had heard in her life that were rumoured about the Moon. She dreamed of being attacked by fellow inmates and the guards simply watching on and laughing. Then she dreamed of the hellish mining conditions in the tunnels of the Moon that had been spoken about back on Earth as a warning for opposing the ruling Collective Zone. All too rapidly the dream moved to Draz running along a tunnel in the Moon, the grey rocks morphing and twisting around her in her subconscious. She came to a dead end blocked only by an airlock. To her horror, the airlock began to cycle, even though the alarm bells were chiming, warning that vacuum was on the other side. Draz could not escape. The airlock cycled, the alarm got louder and louder and suddenly Draz was flung out onto the surface of the Moon without a space suit. The alarm was still sounding in her mind. The zero pressure of the surface of the Moon made her eyes bleed and explode. She gasped for air, but there was nothing. In an attempt to scream, her lungs turned inside out, and the last thing Draz knew was her blood boiling in the vacuum of space. She screamed, and jolted awake.

There was an alarm sounding throughout the cell block. Draz checked her body. She was alive; it was a dream. It was a dream. She looked around her bleary eyed. She was still in the cell. The dim light had come on again. She was still on the Moon in a cell, but she was alive.

"Come on, get up," said Omega standing at the end of his slab. "That siren means morning meal and work detail for our section."

"How long is the sleep period?" Draz wiped her eyes and swung her legs over the edge of the slab and stood up.

"Six hours. Now hurry up. They don't like delays. Stand by the end of your slab," responded Omega. Draz got up and stood by her slab like Omega.

The door opened and there were two guards at the entrance. One remained outside while the other walked into the cell and inspected the slabs and the cell while Draz wondered what was going on.

"Eyes forward!" The inspecting guard noticed Draz's inquisitive gaze and hit her across the back of the head. Draz, smarting, faced the door and let the guard inspect the cell, roughly.

"You must be new 'ere," said the guard outside, looking at Draz. "We do this every morning to make sure you ain't escaping," he said with a wicked grin. "You'll get used to it," he said, not in a reassuring way, more a malevolent way, as if some threat lay hidden beneath the words.

"All clear. Line up outside!" said the guard in the cell.

Omega looked at Draz as if to say, "Do as I do." Draz followed Omega out of the cell and lined up with the other inmates that were lined up and chained together. As Omega and Draz fell into line, a guard attached shackles to them as before with chains linking their necks. They were shackled into a group of six other prisoners.

They were marched along the tunnels towards the metal lined areas that had been added to the Moon's structure. They turned a corner and came to a large metal room with benches and tables. There were already quite a number of inmates sitting and eating. Draz guessed about a few hundred. All were silent and awaiting something.

A guard indicated that they sit down along one of the benches. Not a simple feat with all their necks chained together, but they managed. In front of each prisoner was a bowl built into the table, along with some blunt looking cutlery that was chained by its handle to the table.

Draz looked up as she heard a whirring noise, and she saw a machine running along the length and breadth of the tables of the hallway depositing some sort of goo into the bowls in front of the prisoners. It came to her and excreted its nasty gruel into her bowl. She turned up her nose at it.

"Eat!" whispered Omega in an urgent way. "You'll need it. It's nutritious but disgusting," he said, nodding at the gruel like substance.

Draz picked up the blunt spoon and began to feed the mixture into her mouth. She joined the silent hundreds in eating. It tasted nasty, but she realised she had not eaten in a while, and she became aware of her stomach's emptiness. She put away her pride and finished off the gruel.

"What is it?" she whispered to Omega. Perhaps she should have asked this before eating it, or maybe not, she reasoned.

"Recycled everything," he whispered back.

Draz was about to ask what that meant, but a guard walked behind them at that moment, glowering at their conversation.

"Prisoners eat in silence!" he ordered.

Draz and Omega complied.

After about twenty minutes, all the prisoners were ordered to exit the eating hall and proceed down the corridors, seemingly deeper and deeper into the bowels of the Moon. They were still chained together in groups of six or eight.

As the prisoners got deeper into the complex, they encountered other chain gangs of prisoners going the other way, they looked exhausted, Draz thought. Had they been mining?

"The previous mining shift. The prison functions in staggered shifts, so they can control us all. Not everyone eats at the same time or works at the same time," whispered Omega over his shoulder.

Draz was right; they had been mining. "I thought the helium 3 was gone long ago," she said to Omega.

"It is, but other minerals are not, also, they just get us to mine rocks, so that we're too tired to riot. It's pointless menial labour." He fell silent as a guard walked past.

Finally, they got to what looked like a cliff face inside a large cavern inside the Moon.

"Right, pick up yer tools and start workin'," snapped the guard, belting a prisoner across the face just for the hell of it.

Draz picked up a crude pick from the pile at the guard's feet and followed the prisoners ahead to the rock face. The cavern then rang to the sound of grunts and groans and metal striking rock.

"Sir, what am I mining, I'm new here?" Draz said as she hacked away at the rock face when a guard walked past. She tried to be as genial as possible, no matter how much it galled her.

"Rocks, anything shiny, but rocks mainly. Load 'em into the carts and keep mining. The boards will do the rest,

173

har." He smirked as Draz's face realised that Omega had told her the truth. They were just mining rocks for no reason. If there were minerals in there the machines would sort it out, but they were just mining rocks for the sake of killing the prisoners.

"'Boards'?" whispered Draz to Omega beside her when the guard disappeared down the line of prisoners. Omega had given her a dirty look for talking nicely to the guard.

"Circuit-boards, that's what they call tech-slaves here," whispered Omega. "Now keep mining and stop talking to me, I don't want a friend!"

"Oh," said Draz. She wanted to ask why circuit-boards and not tech-slaves but that would have to wait.

Draz mined for hours. Her arms hurt. She developed blisters on her hands. And found precisely nothing, just grey Moon rock which she dutifully loaded into the carts provided and dragged by tech-slaves away into the darkness to be sorted and scanned. The carts were stationed close enough to the prisoners so that they did not have to be unchained from each other to deposit the rocks into them.

Finally, the sirens rang again, and she could put her tools down. She was parched; there was no water available throughout the mining process. As the prisoners trudged away exhausted from the cliff face, Draz saw the next group coming down the passageway as she exited the mining chamber.

They got back to their cells and as soon as Draz was unshackled from the others, she collapsed onto her slab. She had no idea what time it was. It seemed strange but there were no clocks in the prison at all. There was no way to tell time. As if to disorientate and break the prisoners even more so that they could not predict things, they had no idea of when things happened.

How did Omega know the sleep cycle was six hours then? Draz would have to ask him later, when she was less tired.

Omega shuffled into the cell and collapsed on his slab.

"See, pointless yet exhausting, it's the way they do it here," he said through gritted teeth.

"What happens now?" Draz gasped.

"We wait around here for hours until evening meal and then lights out. That's the day, eat, mine, bored, eat, sleep. Once every few days we get let into the 'exercise'," he made inverted commas with his fingers, "yard. It's where prisoners get to let off steam by bashing each other senseless," Omega said.

"Why do they do that?" Draz asked rather horrified.

"Because it's the Moon; it just is. This isn't a playground and they, the guards, don't care about us. Relax," Omega continued, "it's very rare for someone to die, the infirmary here is pretty good."

Draz thought she heard personal experience in his tone.

"Oh...just something else; how do you know the time? There are no clocks around here?" Draz asked.

"That, I won't tell you, not yet. I've only known you a day," Omega responded, non maliciously.

A day! It had only been a day! Draz felt like it had been months. How was she going to survive this? She suddenly felt a strong urge to resort to the drug that had been in her cabinet next to her bed back in her quarters on Earth, but of course, there was no such chemical within her cell. She swallowed hard and attempted to block the gnawing thought and sensation out of her mind.

Chapter 17

After what seemed like a few hours of waiting around in the cell, in which time Omega refused to answer any more of Draz's questions. He kept insisting that he did not want to make friends. Then an alarm went. It was a different alarm from the food alarm, Draz noticed. She turned on her slab to look at Omega; he had gone paler than usual.

"Something wrong?" Draz asked.

"That, um, is the 'exercise' alarm," he said swallowing hard.

Even though she had only been here a day, Draz had not imagined that Omega would get scared. He seemed like a very resilient person who would survive anything, yet it was clear that what this alarm heralded scared him.

"I thought you somehow knew all the timings..." Draz said.

"This one's random, because they're sick like that. They want to keep you on edge and so you can't plan escapes or revenge against someone. All the 'exercise' events are random," he said.

"Right, well, we'll see how this goes," said Draz with anxiety in her voice.

"Badly," said Omega. He stood up next to his slab and indicated for Draz to do the same. She complied.

Draz's muscles ached from the exertion of mining pointless rocks, but she stood to attention as one of the two guards came in and they were led out of the cell and chained to some other prisoners before being marched in a different direction from the mining to a large metal room that, as Draz would have imagined, looked like almost any prison exercise yard. She noticed that there were multiple guards stationed around the perimeter of the yard both at ground level and also on an upper level that seemed inaccessible by the prisoners from ground level. The room was about fifty meters by fifty meters and fifteen metres high. Already a few fights were going on.

One of the guards unchained the group of prisoners from each other and removed their shackles entirely while groups of prisoners milled around together trying not to look at the few prisoners who moved around aggressively, looking for any reason to start a fight.

"Keep your eyes down," whispered Omega, seeing Draz scanning the room and looking around.

"Right," she said. She knew exactly why and thought it would be best to listen to someone with experience. She did not want to get into a fight, yet.

Suddenly an aggressive male barged up to them; he was the man with the tattooed head, and grabbed Omega by the neck and hauled him out of the small gathering.

"You," he spat, "you were looking at me funny, weren't ya!" It was not a question.

"N-no, no, definitely not looking," gasped Omega.

"An' you lie too!" Omega was flung to the floor and the tattooed prisoner began laying into him with fists and boot.

A small gathering began to form around the two combatants, although Draz thought only one was really a combatant, the other was a mewling lump of pummelled flesh who just wanted it all to stop.

Omega cried out in pain as the beating continued. The guards and bystander prisoners looked on with a mix of horror and joy; joy that it was not them being beaten.

Then Omega reached out towards Draz and the pleading look in his eyes triggered something inside her. She would need him as a friend in this place, and what better way to establish that. She was a trained scavenger; she had fought nastier things than this tattooed brute a hundred times. He was not paying attention to her, and it was plain that he was having fun on his first exercise break. Draz reasoned that if she did not do something about this, he would be a pest the entire time she was in prison. She had thought to avoid him in the briefing room when they arrived; now things had changed. She lunged.

Draz slammed her elbow into the back of the head of the man as he bent over Omega. At the same time, she brought her knee up into his face and felt the sick crack of bone and saw blood spray from the man's contorted face.

The man recoiled dazed and shocked. He staggered back a few steps. Then his broken face twisted in a grin, and he lurched towards Draz.

"I'll rape you," he gurgled and flung himself at Draz. Omega was forgotten, and Draz could see that, in this man's mind, any woman was fair game.

Draz's fight reflexes sprang into action, and she dodged and weaved as the man tried in a cumbersome manner to latch onto her and pummel her. He was stronger than she was, that was clear, but he was slow and untrained, and Draz knew just what to do.

After a few feints, Draz tripped the man as he made another move towards her. The circle of bystanders had grown at this point to a large mob of cheering onlookers. She then jumped on his back and twisted his left arm behind his back and deliberately pulled it way too hard. His shoulder cracked and the man cried out in pain as his left shoulder was dislocated.

The man flung Draz off with force and, even though his left arm was now useless, he seemed to be invigorated by the pain. He punched out hard with his right hand and connected with Draz's chest. She staggered back winded and gasping for air. She doubled over.

The man took this as a sign of her capitulation and moved in for the kill. Draz assumed this quite literally. But she had tactics on her side. As the man limped in with a loose left arm and prepared to grab her with his right and crush her, Draz slid beneath his grasp and in coming up behind him she kicked him hard in the crotch and as he doubled over in pain this time she grabbed him around the neck with her arms and began to squeeze. She had him in a chokehold, and she was not letting go.

The man flailed pointlessly with one arm. Blood sprayed from his mashed face. Draz kept squeezing tighter and tighter. The man's eyes rolled back into his head as the oxygen was cut off from his brain. But instead of relaxing and letting the man fall unconscious, Draz kept the chokehold there and kept squeezing.

Suddenly all the rage against her captors and the false trial and all the shit she had been through boiled to the surface. She would not let go. To take out her rage someone was going to die, and they would all see it too.

Then there was a wet crack and the man's neck bent in an unnatural way. He went totally limp, and Draz let him crash to the floor.

There was silence. The cheering crowd had stopped cheering. The guards moved in and applied their riot prods liberally to a number of people and chained Draz up again. The guards crowded around the body of the dead prisoner and carried him from the arena.

Draz felt calm, at peace. Her rage had subsided, for now. All she could see was the thankful and relieved face of Omega staring at her from the edge of the circle of onlookers. They were led back to their cells soundlessly. Exercise time was cancelled prematurely due to the death.

When they were back in their cells, Draz lay uneasily back on her slab, still sore from the punches. Omega did the same.

"You might not want a friend, but I need one, and you're it," said Draz after they lay in silence for a while. She turned her head on the slab to face him. "I'm going to get out of here, and you're going to help me. And this is only day one. I'll kill them all if I have to."

"You'll be in solitary for a while now," sighed Omega. "After a death, the killer is put in solitary for two weeks. It's not as nice as you might think."

"Anything else happen?" Draz asked.

"No. No one cares, just solitary, but, it's not just solitary. It's pitch black and there are noises. You can't sleep for a week. You can go mad..." Draz detected a shiver in Omega's voice.

"I see. But what I said still stands, I need a friend." She smiled.

"I know, and I can see you're a valuable friend. Thanks for saving me out there," said Omega; he sounded genuinely pleased to be in the cell with her.

"You're welcome, but answer me this question: how can you know the time?" she said with a little more threat in her voice than she intended.

Omega sighed, "I have...implants." He tapped on his head. "I can interact with computers. They're illegal upgrades and rather rudimentary, but if anyone knew I'd be terminated. They're bio implants, rather than circuits, so they weren't detected by the security. I can't do proper zetting or anything like that, but I can hack locks and passwords. It's different if it's your job, people accept that, but I got mine on the black market and therefore I'm illegal. If they knew, I'd have that section of my brain shorted out, if I wasn't killed, and I want to keep it active."

180

"I see..." said Draz, thoughts forming in her mind. She began planning.

Draz realised that she had almost cried early in her incarceration and trial, but now that she was in the Moon Prison, she had no time to be upset. All her energy had to be involved in survival and planning on some way of getting out of the hellish nightmare. She had no time to cry. Crying was for when hope was lost. Now she had to simply survive.

***

The food alarm went again, and Draz and Omega were led out of the cell and chained to the few other prisoners in their section. They were led away again to the eating hall and ordered to sit in silence as the gruel was delivered.

Draz noticed a change in the behaviour of many of the prisoners around her. Word had obviously somehow got around about what she had done. There were furtive looks over shoulders and whispers about what had happened.

It was good and bad Draz reasoned: good in that if she had some respect in prison she would not be messed with as people knew what she could do to them and was not afraid to hold back in the random exercise yard time; bad because it meant she would be more observed by the guards and other prisoners so escape would not be as easy, not that easy was really the right word. But in this place, she would rather be feared than invisible. Fear was the ultimate respect; she had reasoned that quickly and taken her chance, now she would have to live with it, the benefits and the problems.

She ate her gruel, pausing only to wonder again what was in it.

"You said this was recycled, but recycled what?" Draz whispered to Omega.

"Your friend might be in it by now..." He nodded towards the messy soup. "As I said, they recycle...everything." He kept eating.

Draz paused mid chew. Not that you had to chew much in it. Everything, Omega said they recycle everything, the thought raced through her mind.

"You don't mean...?" she said.

"Precisely," he snapped. "Now eat. We can talk later"

Draz continued to eat her gruel, even though she now knew where some of it came from: the recycled remains of dead prisoners. Strangely, she thought, when it came to it, she did not mind as much now that she knew.

Mealtime finished uneventfully and the prisoners were led away back to their cells. When Omega and Draz reached their cell, Omega was unhitched from the column of prisoners and pushed into his cell, Draz was getting ready to be moved back into the cell when she was stopped by a large guard.

"Draz, prisoner 2841, you caused a fight and killed a prisoner. You will be sentenced to two weeks imprisonment in solitary confinement, effective immediately," the guard read from a tablet.

Draz thought it amazing he could read.

Omega looked on from the open cell. Draz shot him a glance and her face reassured him that she would be all right. His face made her a little more uneasy. He, of course, knew more about the prison than she did. She did not know what to expect in solitary confinement. Then the door to the cell closed and Draz was alone in the passageway with two guards.

Draz was led away from her cell to solitary confinement. The trio journeyed deep down into the mining cavities. They passed many cells and various other rooms that Draz could have only supposed were left over from the old helium 3 mining days.

Eventually they came to a large, cavernous room. Draz thought it was like the mining cliff face she had worked at earlier, but this was a different room she realised when she saw large pipes and cables coming out of the cliff face and a few cell like doors built into the rocks.

"Here you are, princess," snarled one of the guards. "Your special room awaits." He pressed his hand against a touch pad on the side of the cell door and it slid open. Light flooded into the small space and Draz, after having the remaining shackles removed, was shoved roughly inside. The door slid shut again cutting out all light.

Draz stayed on the floor for a minute, trying to regain her senses and hoping for some light for her eyes to adjust, but there was none. She flailed in the darkness, sliding up to one wall and then pushing herself into a corner. She sat in the corner with her knees drawn up to her chin. She suddenly felt very uneasy in the darkness and became aware of the familiar craving for the synthetic ferkis powder opiate that she had left behind in Atraxa Prime. It forced its way to the surface and gained strength in the dark room. She tried to force it from her mind, as it was not helpful in this situation. Then the noises began.

First, it was a low rumbling, then there were some loud screeching noises and followed by a gurgling, then there was silence again. The noises were very loud, and the cell shook with some of the rumbling. After a while the noises repeated, and again, and again. But every time they were slightly different, so Draz could not get used to them and block them out. They came in different orders or with slightly different combinations, always interspersed with silence.

Draz was strong. Draz was resilient. She thought to herself. She had withstood far worse than this; far worse than a little darkness and some noises. But the darkness and the noises went on, and on, and on. She had two weeks in these conditions. At first Draz had thought that just two weeks in solitary confinement would be easy, now she was starting to reconsider.

Time went by, as did the noises. Draz felt her way around the cell in the pitch dark. There was no slab; she would have to lie on the floor. In the centre of the floor there seemed to be some sort of grill or grate that was immovable. She was thankful for the fact that there seemed to be a toilet attached to one wall. At least they gave her that dignity. On one wall in an alcove there seemed to be a couple of taps. This puzzled Draz. What were they for? She reasoned that they might be for food and water. If this really was solitary confinement then there might be no guard interaction at all.

Draz fumbled her way around the room again, and again. It was all she could do. There was the darkness, the noises, and the room. She had no control over any of them.

Time went by. Time. Oh, how she wished for Omega's implants. That was the other thing she had no control over: time. She had no idea how long she had been in the cell. The noises came and went it seemed at random, so there was no way to tell how long she had been in there with regards to them.

Draz remembered the cell back on Earth where she had been locked away initially. At least there, there was light; and eventually there was food. Draz felt tired, hungry and thirsty. At best guess she had been in the solitary cell quite a few hours.

All of a sudden, there was a siren noise, and a red glow was emitted from the wall with the taps. Although it was a dim glow, it burned into Draz's retinas. It was the first light her eyes had seen in ages, and it was wonderful, and painful. The cell was illuminated in red, and she saw it was just as her explorations had uncovered in the darkness.

Then a hissing sound happened, and some gruel and water was excreted by the taps into waiting bowls. Draz lunged at them. She did not know how long the light would last and she was hungry and thirsty. She devoured the food and drink in no time by picking up the bowls that were chained to the taps and drinking the contents.

Abruptly the light was gone. She was in darkness again. She had no idea how long anything had taken. She would wait it out. It was only two weeks. It was only two weeks. It was only two weeks. She kept reminding herself.

Draz curled up on the floor of the cell and tried to sleep. She kept jolting awake due to the noises. And then she understood why Omega had been so concerned about her going to solitary confinement: every method of control was taken away from you. You did not know time, you could not sleep, and you were in complete darkness.

Draz tried desperately to sleep, but the noises kept her awake. She screamed.

After what seemed like an eternity of darkness, noise, and red light, with some sleep snatched in small intervals between noises because of complete exhaustion, the unthinkable happened. The door opened and a guard came in.

Draz was curled up in the corner of the room, partially unconscious. She opened her bleary eyes and, realising what was happening, she flung herself at him. He picked her up and attached the shackles and marched her out of the solitary cell back to her own cell with Omega.

"Th-thank you," is all she could manage. With the noises still ringing in her ears and the light of the corridors burning her eyes, she did not know why she thanked the guards, they had put her there in the first place, but she was not thinking straight.

Back in Omega's cell, she collapsed on her slab. She was asleep in an instant. She did not care about anything else.

She heard Omega talking to her. She did not fully understand in her delirium. He seemed to be thanking her, praising her, saying how strong she was for surviving. She did not care; all she wanted was sleep. And so, she slept.

Chapter 18

And so, months went by. The random exercise periods were resumed and only rarely did someone try to attack Omega or Draz again; usually they were new prisoners who did not know the pair. Omega came to rely on Draz for support and they became friends, or as close friends as you could become in a prison. Draz was sent to solitary confinement one more time for a period of two weeks. During that time, Omega was transferred to another section of the prison.

Finally, after nearly a year and a half in space travel, the *Green Dragon* approached the Moon.

***

"This is Captain Artisius hailing the Earth Moon Prison, we will transmit our identification, please train those anti-ship cannons somewhere else," Artisius boomed over the comlink to the command station on the Earth Moon. His crew had detected the anti-ship missiles and auto-turret lasers of the Moon Prison locking on to their craft as it approached.

Artisius knew that his special trader clearance would allow him to cross the boundaries between the two corporate empires.

"This is Moon Prison Guard Station Alpha, we copy your identification *Green Dragon*. You are clear to dock at Docking Port 7. Welcome back," came the transmission from the Moon base.

"We have some...cargo...we want to drop off. Could an armed escort meet us at the docking bay? I want to get this scum off my ship," snapped Artisius. There was a slight pause.

"Understood, *Green Dragon*. An armed escort will be waiting. Please submit information on your...cargo," said the practiced response from the radio.

"They're traitors from Solar Solutions space. They were complicit in the destruction of *Florida Station* around Jupiter. Need I say more?" Artisius almost spat the words. He was happy to rid himself of the traitors. There was another pause.

"Understood, *Green Dragon*. Armed escort will be waiting. Good to see these traitors dealt with. Although in Solar Solutions space we would never wish the destruction of a station. The news hit us hard when we heard it. You've come a long way with them," crackled the radio.

"Too long, I wanted to vent them out an airlock," replied Artisius.

"Not necessary," replied the radio, "we will deal with them here. It will be much less...pleasant."

"Good. We see Docking Port 7. We're on our way in, Artisius out."

***

Alfred was back on top of the cooling tower, back on *Florida Station*. Blinky was there. She smiled sadly at him. He screamed silently and watched her leap off the top of the tower and crash down onto the street below.

As he rushed to the edge of the tower and peered over the edge through his tears, he saw people milling around in the street below. He felt cool air on his face. It got stronger, and colder. The scene dissolved and changed. Suddenly he was staring at the inside of a container. His brain felt sluggish. He could see a small window in front of him, which looked out onto some sort of cargo bay. There were people out there.

There was a hissing noise and the container opened. He felt cold. He started to remember what had happened; the trip; the cryo-pod; the station exploding; losing Blinky. Losing Blinky, the thought stuck in his mind.

Someone was shouting at him. He read the man's lips, and his gun. Alfred knew he had to get out of the tube, so he did. His movements were slow and laborious. His joints were stiff. He had been frozen for around a year and a half or at least that is what he thought, as he knew the trip would take that long.

As he stood in the cargo bay, at gunpoint, flapping his arms to get some circulation back into them, he looked around to get his eyes working again. He heard the guard shouting orders at him. Another guard came over and put shackles on him.

Alfred heard the other pods opening and tried to turn to see if the occupants had survived the trip. The risk with prolonged cryo-sleep was that there was a chance that you would never wake up; the body simply shut down and stayed in a permanent coma, or perhaps the occupant of the pod just died. Nevertheless, most ship crews all went into cryo-sleep for the long voyages between the planets. It was better than trying to occupy oneself for months and years of travel.

The guard with the gun prodded him and ordered him to stay eyes forward. Alfred complied. He could hear another person getting out of a pod, by the sound of his voice it was Kreth. Alfred smiled; he was glad Kreth had survived. Then there was the sound of Gracosh; and that was it. Alfred heard one of the guards saying something about one of the prisoners not waking up.

Alfred turned, risking the gun carrying guard's ire. He saw Josh's pod, lid open, but with no life signs on the scanners. He had died in transit. The other two survivors turned to look too. Gracosh made a sign across his own forehead that must have been some kind of respectful sign for the dead. The gun carrying guard was shouting something. His irate action with the rifle indicated that they should pay attention. Another death did not matter. Josh probably got the best deal, thought Alfred. He would not have to suffer on the Moon.

The three survivors were shackled together and led out of the cargo bay to the docking tube and marched down it towards the Moon Prison.

The prisoners were met by an armed escort as they disembarked into the docking bay and were processed into the prison system, just as everyone was. They were scanned then introduced to the prison via the holo-theatre. They were stripped naked, changed into orange jump suits, and had their heads shaved. Alfred's chronometer was removed from his wrist. The prisoners were then split up from one another as they entered. Alfred reasoned to prevent any form of mutiny.

"Well, it was nice knowing you, mate!" said Kreth to Alfred as they parted ways and were unchained from each other in one of the many metallic corridors. Alfred smiled at him, and they parted ways without a further word said.

Then Gracosh was unchained and taken away without a word, he simply nodded at Alfred.

Then Alfred was alone being walked down numerous dark corridors through the Moon's surface.

Alfred was stopped in front of a cell in the wall of a Moon tunnel and ordered to halt. His chains were removed, and he was shoved bodily into the dark room and the door closed behind him.

Alfred paused and tried to make out the shapes in the darkness. There was a slab on either wall and a toilet in the corner. On the slab to the right of the door was a person. Alfred sat on the left slab.

"Hello?" he said. There was silence. He cleared his throat. "I'm Alfred, I--" he continued and was interrupted.

"I don't care who you are," came the terse voice of a woman. "Yours," she pointed at his slab, "mine," she pointed at hers.

"Well, I'm new here and I was wondering--" tried Alfred. She held up a hand. He stopped suddenly.

"Look, I realise you're new here. I'm not; I've been here over a year. I've seen cellmates come and go, and by go I mean die. At first, I was like you, terrified and wanting friends, but then I learnt otherwise. Don't make friends, it only hurts you later. I won't try to kill you as long as you stay out of my way. Mine," she indicated her slab, "yours," she pointed at his. "A wise man once told me all this on my first day. It helped me. It will help you." Then she fell silent.

"Can I ask your name at least?" attempted Alfred for a final time.

"Draz, my name...is Draz..."

Chapter 19

Alfred lay down on the slab to the left of the door. It was cold and uncomfortable. His whole body burned with a thirst that he could not quench. He had not zetted in well over a year, given his cryogenic storage from *Florida Station*.

Alfred's mind paused on the fact that *Florida Station* no longer existed. In all the fuss about being woken up from cryo-sleep, scanned and admitted to prison, he had almost forgotten the reason he was in prison. A false reason, but it would be what his prison record said. He was accused of complicity in destroying *Florida Station* and he would stay in prison the rest of his life. This fact was still just sinking in.

Alfred's mind was drawn back to his thirst. It was not a normal thirst for water; it was the thirst for zetting. His body craved it. Even though he had been in cryo-storage for more than a year his body still knew he had not zetted in all that time. It was the longest he had gone without zetting since he had the implants. However, there was little chance he would get to zet in the most secure prison in the Solar System. At least the decay of his implants had been partially halted by the cryo-sleep, he reasoned.

"What are you doing?" Draz turned her head on her slab to look at Alfred.

Alfred stopped. He was involuntarily scratching at the flap of skin that covered his cranial implants. He did not know if he could trust this woman. He had only just met her.

"Oh, nothing. It's just an itch," he said.

"Well don't, it's annoying," snapped Draz. "It'll be lights out soon and I don't want to be kept awake by your scratching all night."

Alfred made a face, which was not seen by Draz. She had no idea what he was going through. His entire body burned with the desire to zet. It was the most horrid withdrawal he had ever felt. He felt very alone, even in this cell with another person. He felt as though he would not survive very long in this prison. He was already on the path to madness, but now he had no medication in this prison. His entire body would shut down if he kept zetting, and he felt like he wanted to do nothing else.

"You've been here a while?" asked Alfred.

"Yes, I said I'd been here over a year; a year and a half if you must know," snapped Draz, it sounded like she did not want any more questions. "What do I call you? You said...?"

"Alfred," he said in a friendly tone. "Are there...any...computer jobs...in this prison?" probed Alfred.

"Alfred. Right. What do you mean?" said Draz.

"Well, I don't know, is there a way to...help the running of the prison by...oh never mind." Alfred lost heart as he saw the expression on Draz's face.

"No, ask your question, I might have an idea where you're going with this," replied Draz, in a tone that was more ordering than welcoming.

"Well...," Alfred was committed now; he had to ask the full question. He sighed. "I...can zet. It's why I was scratching. I haven't zetted in almost a year and a half. I'm craving it. I..." He stopped, confused by the expression on Draz's face. It was a mixture of relief and realisation. She was suddenly propped up on her right elbow staring right at Alfred. It made him uncomfortable.

"Sorry," Draz said, seeming to realise her face gave away too much. "I might have use for you soon. No, there are no prisoner accessible zetting terminals but there are terminals within the secure section accessible by guards. A zetter eh? You could be very useful to me." She slumped back down on her slab and just then an alarm rang.

"What's that?" asked Alfred.

"Lights out, five minutes, then six hours sleep period, then food, then work, et cetera..." Draz's voice trailed off into nothing.

Alfred realised that she had almost given up hope before he had arrived. Now something within her seemed to have reawakened. He had only just met her, but she seemed changed now compared with when he walked into the cell. He feared that his zetting ability might be the only reason he is useful to her. However, being useful in a place like this was better than being useless, Alfred reasoned to himself.

After a short time, the lights switched off and blackness filled the prisoners' existence. Alfred's body still yearned for the pleasure of a zet, but he felt a little reassured that he was now useful to someone here. Although, it did fill him with some trepidation. He did not know how he would get to zet if the only terminals were in the guarded areas. He was no hero. He was not going to be involved in any form of jailbreak or any form of rebellion in this prison. He was no revolutionary. But at least he seemed to have made a friend. She seemed like she would look out for him as long as he was useful to her.

Alfred's mind raced. This woman, Draz, had said that there was work tomorrow. Alfred wondered what sort of work it was. He knew very little of the Earth Moon and the Earth. He had been born and bred in the space stations in Solar Solutions space. To him, then, the Earth seemed an unfathomable distance away. He had not really paid attention in school when they had instructed the people of the Solar Solutions space about what happened on Earth or the Earth Moon. He would have to ask this Draz person. He was unsure of where she came from other than her name suggested she was from Collective Zone territories.

Alfred, despite the cravings, slowly and surely fell asleep. His body was exhausted from the exertions and stress of being admitted to the prison. He slept, and dreamt of Blinky, and all the horrors of his mind.

***

Draz lay awake. She could not believe her luck. A zetter was her new cellmate. This could not be better. She could now start her plan into action. She had no idea of how she was going to do this before today. Omega had bio implants, but he was no zetter. He was still alive, just in another cell. The prison staff occasionally changed cellmates in order to prevent rebellion. They had suspected Omega and Draz were plotting something and so he had been moved. There must have been some mistake in assignment as the prisoner assigned to Draz's cell was now a lot more dangerous than Omega.

Draz smiled. This was her chance. She could not sleep. Her mind was racing as to all the plans she had made and all the opportunities she had made note of in her year and a half here. She knew how the prison functioned and she knew that she was going to make it out of here alive. All she needed to do was make sure this zetter, Alfred, survived long enough to be useful to her. It seemed as though he was in the early stages of zetting madness, that was a problem, but if she acted fast, it would not pose any threat to her getting out.

She slowly and carefully withdrew a small straw and tiny parcel of white ferkis powder from her boot in the

195

darkness. She felt her way rather than saw her way. She quickly and quietly snorted it and felt the rush of pleasure that the chemical brought. Like all prisons, the Moon was full of drugs. She knew she had to remain alert to carry out her plans, but she thought she could celebrate a little, now that a zetter was in her cell.

Draz drifted to sleep eventually. She knew she had to sleep otherwise the work would kill her. For the first time in a long time, her dreams were pleasant and not filled with monsters. She knew she would escape this hellhole and make it back to Earth to avenge herself. Fortune had smiled favourably on her circumstances.

Chapter 20

Alfred awoke to an alarm, and he did not quite know what was going on. In a bleary-eyed manner he swung his legs over the edge of his slab and, while wiping his eyes, saw Draz standing at the end of her slab.

"Get up, quickly," she said. Alfred complied. "It's breakfast time," Draz tried to explain in the shortest time what was going on before the guards arrived.

Alfred nodded in understanding, still tired from a restless sleep on a metal bed.

Soon the guards came and, as practiced hundreds of time by Draz, but never by Alfred yet, they chained the prisoners together outside their cells and led them away to the feeding room.

Alfred looked around the feeding room as the machine deposited goo into his bowl.

"What's this?" he asked Draz, a little too loudly and copped a fist on the back of the head.

"Recycled gruel," whispered Draz when the guards had passed. "Don't ask what they recycle."

Alfred took the hint and simply ate the tasteless slop with the spoon provided. He did not want to know where it came from, and he thought it was rather similar to some of the food back on *Florida Station*, but with something he could not put a finger on.

He paused, even sadder for a moment. His mind wandered from the rows of orange clad prisoners around him and ventured back to the lonely existence aboard *Florida Station*. Back then he was content with his solitary life. He had a job, and a purpose. But he had failed in that purpose. He did not protect the station. Everything he knew was gone and now he was on the other side of the Solar System in the worst prison chained to some stupid prisoners he did not belong with, and he was eating slop from a machine!

Alfred felt like crying out, like protesting his innocence, yelling at the top of his lungs that he did not belong here, that he had tried to stop the treason. However, he knew it would be pointless, and that any of the prisoners around him would simply mock him by repeating that they were innocent too. He was doomed to spend the rest of his miserable life in this hellhole and his only friend, if that was a term he could use, was his cellmate who seemed to have plans for his existence that may or may not have disastrous consequences. He had only been in the prison a day and already he was finding it hard to see how he would survive more than a week.

With a sharp blow to the head, by Draz, he realised he had been daydreaming and that the other prisoners were all standing waiting to leave. Alfred got up and they slowly made their way along the passageways to the mining cliff face.

Alfred had no idea what was going on. Draz spoke in his ear that they were to mine the rock face for the next six hours so as to tire the prisoners out. Alfred nodded, and picked up a mining tool from the pile. He saw the other prisoners starting to attack the rock face and Draz pulled him over to where she was going to start mining.

"Just pick away at the rock, don't slack off or the guards will beat you," she said, starting to heft the pickaxe.

"But, what are we mining?" Alfred asked, standing in front of the cliff face with the pickaxe held awkwardly in his hands, as if he did not know how to use it.

"Rocks!" said a passing guard. "Now get to it, traitor scum!"

Draz looked at Alfred pleadingly and indicated for him to follow her instruction. She struck at the rocks a few time and some pieces fell off she then picked them up and dumped them in the mining cart a little way away that was being drawn by the tech-slave.

Alfred followed her example. He dug away at the rocks, hauling them into the passing carts. His hands hurt, his back hurt, and more than anything, his head buzzed with the desire to zet. The hard physical toil somehow dampened the desire a little, and he realised that with prolonged work he could blot out the worst of the urge, but when he stopped to take a breath from the mining it would return with a vengeance, and he could not get away from it.

The hours passed and Alfred managed to get used to some of the labour. The picking and hauling was monotonous and repetitious work, but it was somehow, in a perverted way, soothing. For the first time in a long time, Alfred had a purpose. It was only mining and hauling rocks, but it was a purpose and he got stuck into the work.

**

Draz looked over at Alfred and saw him sweating away at the mining task. She saw a strange look on his face of contentment, and she wondered why he would feel content in such a task. But now was not a time for questions.

Draz kept attacking the rock face with her pick. She had become more muscular over the past year and a half. She was always athletic, being a scavenger on Earth demanded such a physique, but the constant manual labour on the Moon had built her arm muscles to an impressive level.

When she strangled that man early on in her incarceration, she had found it difficult to crack his neck with her arm, now it would have been easy. No one messed with her anymore.

After a long time, another alarm sounded, and the prisoners deposited their picks in a pile and slowly made their way from the cliff face back to their cells. Alfred followed Draz in being marched back to the cell. When they were locked inside, she asked him a question she had been saving up for hours.

"Back then at the cliff face, you looked, not happy, but somehow content...why?" she said in a semi-accusative tone.

"Did I?" replied Alfred, taken aback at the notion that he would be content. "Oh well, perhaps some things have happened in my life that just simple labour made me lose myself for a while and all I had to do was think about rocks rather than my demons."

Draz nodded. She understood more than he could know. She had just not expected a newcomer to be so content with his lot so early.

"I don't want to be here, don't get me wrong, I hate this place," said Alfred. "But just that work, I've never really done manual labour before and it was rather repetitive and soothing, in a hard sort of way."

"It's funny," said Draz with a smirk, "I was falsely accused of treason which put me here. Apparently, I betrayed the CEO of my Collective, Uxus. What did you do?"

"I, uh," stuttered Alfred obviously not wanting to give too much away. "I was accused of treason too...falsely of course," he added hurriedly.

"Uh huh..." said Draz, clearly gauging the secrecy of the man in front of her. "Well, if that's all you're going to say about it then we'll leave it there, I guess."

They both lay down on their respective slabs. Draz knew that Alfred was tireder than he had first realised. All the adrenaline that had built up in his body was draining away and leaving only sore and tired muscles behind.

She watched as he was on the point of dozing on his slab when another alarm sounded, different from the food and work alarms.

"What's that?" Alfred exclaimed.

Draz had jumped to her feet and was waiting by the cell door, much more accustomed to the physical exertion of mining now over a year in the prison so she was able to recover much faster afterwards.

"Exercise time..." she said with a smile.

Draz saw a puzzled expression come over Alfred's face. She remembered when she was in his position and felt sorry for him. On her first exercise time she had killed a man. She was pretty sure that he would not do the same thing.

"Look," she said, "at a random time on some days we all have to gather in a room, and it allows the more violent prisoners to take out their aggression on others. The guards watch on from the sidelines and make sure nothing too bad happens. It's also our only chance to really talk to each other outside of our cellmates."

Alfred's expression had turned from confusion to abject worry.

"Relax, you're useful to me, I'll protect you," Draz said to reassure him. "Now look, we don't have much time before the guards get here to take us to the exercise yard. I need you to listen carefully. I've been planning something for some time, and I need your help, you're the final piece. We must move fast, before the guards suspect anything. You can zet?"

Alfred nodded blankly.

201

"Good," Draz said. "On the way to the yard there's a guarded door, it's one of the guard stations and, although I've never been inside, I've heard good reports that a zetting station is in there. What I need you to do is, when I create a little...disturbance." She smiled. "I need you to run back there and make all the boards, uh, tech-slaves as you know them, rebel and riot. Do you understand? Can you do that?" Draz looked at him imploringly.

***

Alfred was more than confused, but his pulse had quickened at the thought and suggestion that he would get to zet again, and soon. He was anxious about the riot part though. He nodded again.

"When you cause this riot, what next?" he asked.

"We escape on a shuttle back to Earth and hide for a while," she said, as if it was all certain.

"We?" Alfred knew too well he could be left behind in all this.

"Yes, we. I need you, remember? Now hurry, stand up and pay attention to the route we take to the exercise yard. I'll point out the door along the way."

The door to the cell opened and the two prisoners were led out and chained to some others and led through the passageways to the exercise yard.

As they passed a door that seemed more guarded than the rest, Draz doubled over and grabbed at her foot as if in pain. The row of prisoners stopped and one of the guards came to see if something was wrong.

Alfred understood the signal and studied the door. It had two guards and was heavily fortified. Alfred had no idea how he was to get inside.

As soon as it was apparent to Draz that Alfred had recognised the signal, she composed herself and the column of prisoners moved off towards the exercise yard.

Once inside they were unchained and milled around and found people they wanted to talk to. Some fights broke out. The guards watched on making sure nothing got out of hand.

Alfred stayed next to Draz as she made her way through the crowd of prisoners.

Suddenly a hand grabbed Alfred's arm.

"Mate!" said the unmistakable voice.

"Kreth! Aha!" Alfred had spun on his heel at the sound of the man's voice.

"Who is this?" snapped Draz who had realised that Alfred was no longer following her and had come to see why.

"This is Kreth, a prisoner I was with before we got to the Moon, he..." Alfred realised he did not know much more about the man, so he fell silent under Draz's steely gaze.

"Kreth's the name, falsely imprisoned and waiting to escape when able." The man smiled.

"I admire your optimism," Draz said with a smirk. "Is he trustworthy?" she asked Alfred, pulling him aside.

"I...guess. He seemed friendly earlier..." replied Alfred.

"Well, that might have to do, take him with you to the zetting station, he could help you overpower any remaining guards," Draz briefly explained the situation to Kreth as she had to Alfred in the cell. He nodded and was attentive, it was evident that he knew that this was the best chance to break out and he had to take it.

Kreth gave Alfred a careful look when Draz explained that Alfred was a zetter and what Alfred would be doing in the guardroom. Clearly he had not realised that Alfred was one of the zetters on board *Florida Station* and the revelation was a surprise to him. They were all in the same situation so he agreed to help when he could.

Draz and Alfred followed by Kreth set off through the crowd of prisoners. Draz stopped in front of a man, and she whispered in his ear. After a short conversation out of earshot of Alfred and Kreth, the two turned and Draz introduced the man as Omega.

"Omega? That's odd," said Alfred

"Well actually it's Omega 1AB, but who's asking?" snapped Omega, sounding somewhat offended.

"Omega 1AB? I'm Theta 7B from *Florida Station*! I've sent messages to you on Europa's Colony a long time ago."

"Theta 7B! Aha! Well, I never thought I'd ever meet you. What are you doing here?"

"False imprisonment for treason," said Alfred carefully.

"Through prison news we heard that *Florida Station* blew up, it wouldn't be that would it?" asked Omega.

"False," Alfred laboured the word, "imprisonment," and left it at that.

Omega nodded.

Draz gave a sideways look at Kreth, who had a look of confusion on his face. Kreth's eyes flashed as he heard that Alfred was actually Theta 7B, and some understanding crept across his features.

"Now that we all know each other, what a lovely reunion," Draz snarled. This was her jailbreak, and she was not going to let friends derail it. "I'm going to start a fight. Pay attention. When I yell out, start running to the guard room. Omega, you follow them and assist in any way. Alfred can zet and disable some of the security. Once the boards rebel," she looked at Alfred, he nodded, "make your way to the docking bay. Things should be chaotic enough for you to get through security and we'll all meet there, and I'll fly us out." She disappeared into the crowd and left Alfred, Omega and Kreth waiting for her signal.

The three men looked awkwardly at each other and tried to keep from making eye contact with the surrounding prisoners.

Suddenly a shout went up, then a cry of pain. The shout was Draz's voice; the cry of pain was not.

"Here we go, mates," said Kreth and they all made their way towards the exit.

Alfred looked over his shoulder and saw a large fight developing between all different prisoners and guards. Somewhere in there was Draz. He wondered what she had said to get such a large fight started so quickly.

The guards moved in and in the milling throng Omega, Alfred and Kreth managed to slip out of the room, and they dashed as fast as they could down the corridor towards the guardroom. Already sirens were sounding.

More than once the trio needed to hide in side corridors as guards rushed past them to the exercise yard.

They reached the door and found it locked, but unguarded.

"They must be at the yard." Alfred breathed hard as he was unused to running.

"Draz better know what she's doing, or they'll kill her," said Omega, breathing hard.

"How do we open the door?" interrupted Kreth with a bit of reality.

"I can help with that!" gasped Omega, still short of breath. He moved over to the large keypad with exposed wires on the edge of the metal door and tore out two of the wires. He opened a flap of skin on the side of his head and inserted the two wires into connection ports.

Alfred looked on eagerly.

Kreth looked on anxiously.

"Got it!" said Omega after a short time and the door started to slide open.

Suddenly a guard rushed out of the room, challenging them with an active stun prod. He closed on Alfred. Alfred panicked. He backed away. The guard had not seen Omega or Kreth on either side of the door.

"You-hoo!" shouted Kreth from behind the guard and brought a heavy Moon rock down on the guard's skull. With a sickening crack the man fell, stun prod still sparking.

"Well, he had it coming!" said Kreth, puffing. Alfred and Omega just looked at him. "Come on!" Kreth indicated the guardroom. He dragged the dead guard inside, trying to hide him from other guards.

Omega snatched up the stun prod.

Alfred and Omega rushed inside behind Kreth, and they shut the door after them. They only had a few moments of time before other guards came to the station.

The guard station was another metal room with computer terminals and security camera holo-screens all over the walls. It was a compact room.

"There!" shouted Omega, pointing at the zetting station.

Alfred's heart leapt. "Can't you?" He pointed to Omega.

"I'm not that advanced." Omega shook his head. "Draz said you can zet. You go!"

Alfred's mouth went dry. He undid the flap of skin on the side of his head, raising the zetting needle to his temple; he looked at the other two. They had looks of fear on their faces; like wild animals escaping from captivity. Alfred plunged the needle into his temple. The world exploded into colour and light, and he felt a rush like never before. It had been far, far too long.

***

Draz moved off from the other three inmates and into the crowd. She progressed through the throng of talking and skirmishing prisoners who parted before her. In her time in the prison, she had built up a sort of reputation for not wanting to be messed with. Even the guards respected her. And this would be their undoing and the catalyst for her escape.

As she approached one of the nearest guards, he put his hand on his riot prod as a warning to her. That was the thing about the guards here, the prisoners' fear of them prevented escapes. The guards inspired such fear that the prisoners would rather beat each other up than risk taking on a guard. Draz knew, that in causing a commotion, she could break that fear of the guards and then cause a riot. All the prisoners needed was for someone to light the fuse.

"Now there, Draz, that's close enough." He raised his voice as she approached, hoping to scare her off. It did not work. She kept on coming. Now it was her turn to cause fear.

Draz let out a visceral shout and dived at the guard. She swung her right foot into his crotch and as he doubled over in pain, she brought her fist up into his face. He dropped his riot prod and let out a cry of pain as his nose turned to a bloody mess.

There was silence for a moment, as all the surrounding prisoners could not believe what just happened. They saw Draz towering over the crippled body of guard, brandishing his stolen riot prod.

The other guards moved in swiftly, but it was too late, the catalyst had already begun. Some of the other prisoners started to move on the guards. The prisoners saw their chance at a riot and perhaps, an escape, and they took their opportunity.

Fights broke out between the prisoners and, instead of other prisoners, with guards. There were many more prisoners than guards and although the guards were liberal in their use of riot prods and batons the prisoners started to gain the upper hand and overwhelm the guards.

An alarm began to wail throughout the prison as guards armed themselves with something more than just a riot prod.

Guns were only used as last resort in the Moon Prison, as with most space exposed facilities. Draz knew this. If a bullet punctured the hull in contact with space then it was over for most people in the surrounding area. Therefore, the weapons used were of a low calibre to make sure the user was safe, but they were still effective on fleshy targets like humans.

The guards wanted to put down the riot as fast as possible and so as the melee grew and grew and spilled out of the exercise yard and into the corridors of the prison then the guards started to employ the use of lethal force.

Draz zapped another guard with her stolen prod. He yelped in pain and collapsed in a fitting mess. The prods were set to the maximum power level and on this level they could reduce a large man to a quivering pool of excrement in a second.

"Time to go," she said to herself as the brawl spiralled out of control.

She ran for the exit dodging punches and prods. She heard the first shots ring out from beyond the exercise hall and she knew she needed to act fast, not even she could stop a guard with a gun. The guards in the hall had no guns, only prods, but the guards swarming through the facility would now have armed themselves. She would need to take one of those guns.

Draz dashed out of the exercise hall and down the corridor. She hoped that the others had got those boards to rebel. The guards would put down the riot eventually and regain control. She just needed to take her chance, in the chaos, to escape.

***

Alfred's consciousness looped and careened through the unfamiliar network of the Moon Prison. It was an even older network than that of the former *Florida Station*. Nevertheless, he was loving the experience. It had been far too long since his last zet and dopamine was flooding his system.

He knew what he had to do, unchain the tech-slaves, make them rebel against their masters. It was a simple enough job. All tech-slaves were anchored to the system by a simple data lock that was communicated through the skull mesh implanted into their bald heads and spinal columns. If it were severed, it would result in them returning to primal behaviour since the higher functions of their brains were destroyed and they were simply used as manual slave labour. The problem was, Alfred had no idea where the data lock was in the Moon system.

He soared through the network of pathways and circuits in the strange system. After a few moments of random searching, he realised he had to be methodical.

Alfred moved in on the computer core, the shining light in the cacophony of noise and action in the system around him. There it was! They had rigged up the data lock to the core of the system. This, Alfred supposed, was to prevent its disengagement, as disabling one would disable a whole lot of features of the prison.

Alfred inspected the data lock. He made sure that the life support systems and gravity control were not linked to it; he did not want to create more problems for their escape. He ascertained that the systems linked to the data lock were the mining apparatus and the cell door and alarm control. All acceptable systems to be switched off.

With a flick of his mind, Alfred disabled part of the computer core thus disabling the data lock and cell door and alarm control. Part of the network he was on went black. He had done his job. They would now be able to get to the docking bay.

The docking bay, Draz had said nothing about that. Before he disengaged, Alfred soared into the docking bay systems and inspected the security. The auto-turret lasers were still engaged. They would reduce any ship to molten slag before it got more than a kilometre away. With another flick of his mind, Alfred overloaded the coolant tubes connected to the guns and thus, when they fired, they would overheat and explode thus allowing the four of them to escape. Although Alfred had no physical form in this electrical world, he felt like he was smiling for the first time in a long time. He disengaged with a gasp.

Pulling the needle from his temple Alfred collapsed on the floor. Kreth and Omega rushed to his aid.

"Is it done?" asked Omega.

"It's done," gasped Alfred, grinning, "the tech-slaves are rebelling or deactivated."

"Excellent, mate," said Kreth. "If we didn't need you I'd kill you now!" He hauled Alfred to his feet by his neck. "You got me arrested here, you're the zetter, and I'm here because of you!" He squeezed Alfred's neck with one hand, perfectly able to snap it.

"Hey, stop that, we need him." Omega grappled at Kreth's massive hand.

Alfred's eyes were starting to bulge, and he gasped for air.

Kreth dropped Alfred with a release of his hand. "Yeah, and he got me in here on false charges, who's to say he didn't blow the station. I was head of reactor security, and the security was breached so I was accused of treason! It's all well and good him getting us out of here, but I wouldn't be here if it weren't for him. 'Theta 7B', pah! He said he was 'Alfred'."

"Look, there's no time for this, I didn't blow the station, and I was falsely accused, like you. You saw the station explode and I was next to you. I had nothing to do with it! I did go into the reactor module, but it was already breached by Trader Virtus. I was there to stop him. He blew the station!" Alfred shouted rubbing his sore neck. "Let's get out of here." He forced his way past Kreth's bulk and into the corridor. He heard the sound of gunfire in the distance.

Kreth spat on the floor of the guardroom. He was obviously angry, but he knew Alfred had nothing to do with his station blowing up. As Alfred had said, they were together in the *Green Dragon* when the station exploded. He could not have triggered the explosion. They were both falsely accused.

"Trader Virtus," Kreth said. "I never trusted those stock market priests." He headed out of the guardroom after the other two.

"You're not going to kill me?" Alfred gasped as they headed along the passageway, still feeling the pain in his neck.

"Not right now, it's survival. You screwed me over before, but we need you to survive this," said Kreth.

"Enough of that. Everyone wants to kill everyone here. Let's get to the docking bay," Omega stated as he led them on the winding path towards the space pods, one of which they would need to commandeer to escape.

On the way to the pods, the trio had to dodge rebelling tech-slaves, who were now busy applying their mining tools to anything or anyone foolish enough to cross their paths. The trio had to step over the numerous corpses of

211

guards and prisoners that all had either evidence of gunshots or mining implements on their bodies.

Alfred baulked at the destruction wrought by his actions, again. He could not seem to get away from carnage. Everywhere he turned there were bodies in his wake. The ground, in places, was slick with blood.

Numerous times they had to dodge out of the way of marauding prisoners who were either mad with the desire to escape, or fleeing from tech-slaves that chased them with mining tools whirring.

They came to a sealed door. It blocked their path absolutely. In front of it were a couple of eviscerated tech-slaves that had obviously attacked each other with various mining drills.

"Now what?" gasped Alfred, panting from running. He tried not to step in the blood.

Kreth looked around and pulled on one of the tech-slave's arms that was replaced with a mining drill. He grinned a little. "Let's try this," he said, while hefting the dead tech-slave into position near the door.

Kreth positioned the drill on the lock system and pushed the switch to activate the drill. Miraculously the drill's power supply was undamaged, and it spun to life with a shrill squeal.

The lock resisted for a few minutes. All the while Omega and Alfred looked around for more guards that they were sure had heard the noise. Then suddenly the lock gave way and the door slid aside with a crunch.

"There we are!" said Kreth. "I'm not all brute force." He grinned. He dropped the body of the tech-slave and headed through the door.

Omega and Alfred looked at each other and followed.

As they approached another door, they heard gunfire break out ahead of them. Alfred winced and ducked for cover instinctively, so did Omega.

"Relax," Kreth said. "That's not aimed at us."

They all crouched down behind a rock that was situated in the passageway and watched two guards ahead shooting at some prisoners who were trying to break through the door. The prisoners screamed and slumped as the guards emptied their magazines into the bodies.

"If this goes on like that, they'll have to reload soon," said Kreth.

Sure enough, the guards stopped firing for a moment.

"Now, go!" said Kreth. He charged the guards.

"He was head of reactor security on *Florida Station*," said Alfred as Omega gave him a look of disbelief.

Both of them followed behind Kreth, as fast as they could.

Kreth set upon the guards as they were attempting to reload their guns. One guard dropped his rifle as he was slammed into the floor by Kreth's massive bulk. The other guard tried to find some ammunition to reload, but Omega and Alfred jumped on him and began hitting him as hard as they could.

Alfred punched and kicked as hard as he could. The guard fell and the three fugitives stood there a moment panting with exertion.

"Bah, these guns are empty. They've got no more ammo," spat Kreth, as he searched the guards. "Idiots shot it all already."

"And how do we get through this door?" asked Alfred. He was tired of locked doors.

"Simple mechanical lock, move," said Omega. He pushed Alfred out of the way and threaded some of the wires into his socket implant in his skull. After a few seconds and a few clicks and whirs, the door slid aside.

They headed along the passageway steadily climbing towards the docking bay.

They came to the lie detector room, the way in to the prison that all prisoners had to face. The doors to the room were open. There were no guards, prisoners or tech-slaves visible.

"The guards must have fled," said Omega.

"Good," said Alfred.

"Come on," said Kreth.

They hurried on. They were almost at the pods where they would escape.

***

Draz rushed down the corridor away from the exercise yard, brandishing the stolen riot prod. She made sure that it was set to maximum strength.

She headed for the armoury. It was insane to head there with all the guards, but she needed a gun. She needed to arm herself otherwise she could not escape.

On route, she hid behind rocks in the dimly lit passageways to avoid patrolling guards. They always operated in pairs or trios. She knew she had to find a guard who was alone to steal his gun.

While hiding in the darkness to wait for another pair of guards to pass on the way to the exercise yard, she saw a young guard, only a teenager, who was lagging behind them as they headed in the direction of the riot.

As the boy passed Draz's hiding place, she grabbed him and held her hand over his mouth to silence him. He dropped his rifle.

Using her riot prod on him to incapacitate him would cause too much commotion and noise, so she clamped her hand over his nose and mouth, hard, and wrapped an arm around his neck. He struggled but quickly passed out.

Draz did not know or care why a boy was a guard at the prison. All she needed was his rifle, and she had it.

Draz lay the boy down on the ground, partially not wanting to make a noise, partially not wanting to hurt him unnecessarily.

She took his rifle that had fallen to the ground. She checked that it was loaded. She hung her riot prod off her belt after deactivating it. Now she could escape.

Draz headed for the shuttle bay. On the way she passed by the Senior Officer's rooms that had been dug into the side of the passageway. It had a window that looked out over the passageway. The door was open.

Draz peeked inside through the window. She saw that the officer was pacing the room and swearing into a communicator while giving orders on how to control the riot.

Readying her rifle, Draz entered the door. The officer was standing with his back to her, looking at a computer screen on the wall of the office. The screen showed red and green blobs that were overlayed on the map of the prison. He was following the progress of the riot.

"I said I don't want to be...Draz!?" The officer spun around.

"Miss me?" Draz smirked. She raised her rifle. "I won't miss you."

"Look, Draz, you can't get out of here, it's--" he was cut off.

"Impossible? Watch me. You like watching things on that monitor," Draz spat the words. She hated the man. He had tormented her in her captivity. He had tormented all the prisoners. She had waited for this moment for a year and a half.

"Draz." The officer lowered the communicator. "This is my prison. I know it's impossible to escape. You'll never have the codes to leave the docking bay." He smirked.

"Oh? Well tell that to Prison Guard 0231. Because a few weeks ago I slipped him some ferkis powder and did some favours for him and he gave me the codes." It was Draz's turn to smirk. She readied her rifle.

"What!? No. They'll be changed when I--"

Draz fired. She killed the officer with a shot through the face. His communicator clattered to the floor. He slumped against the computer screen, splattered with blood.

"Fuck you!" said Draz.

Draz ran from the room, knowing the gunfire would be noticed. She headed along the passageways, up and up. She had to dodge malfunctioning tech-slaves and armed guards.

"Alfred must've got the tech-slaves to rebel," she said to herself. "Good. He's not useless."

***

Alfred, Kreth, and Omega rounded a corner, which was near the exit to the pods, and their path was blocked by a tech-slave busy eviscerating a guard with its mining tool. They froze. It turned slowly and started down the passage towards them, tool whirring.

The tech-slave was slow, so they could back away from it easily, but it was blocking the passage towards their escape. The creature came to a wider part of the passageway, and, without a word, the trio attempted to pass it by dashing through the gaps, Kreth on the right and Omega and Alfred on the left.

The tech-slave lashed out as they passed, it caught Omega a glancing blow to the thigh but otherwise they made it past unscathed and ran on to the docking bay.

Omega swore and moved with a pronounced limp as blood poured from the deep gash in his right thigh. Alfred felt ill. Kreth picked Omega up and they kept running.

They made it to the docking bay. The security screening was disabled, and a number of the pods had already gone, they dashed for the nearest one.

"Wait...for Draz." Omega gasped through the pain. "Put me down I can move from here." Kreth complied.

"Where is Draz?" Alfred scanned the docking bay. It was large and metallic with a magnetic shield to open space. Alfred saw the yellow orb of the Earth beyond the shield and was mesmerised. That was the Earth?

"She's here," came the shout from her own mouth behind them as Draz emerged onto the docking platform in bloodstained clothes and carrying a small calibre rifle.

"Good now we can all get aboard and get out of here," said Alfred.

"Who's hurt?" snapped Draz seeing the blood on all of them.

"Me." Omega limped. He was trying to stem the blood from his thigh wound, unsuccessfully.

They all made a move towards the nearest pod, and then a shot rang out. Draz spun around and loosed a few rounds in the direction of the sound. With a trained eye she saw the guard and put a bullet through his head. She turned back and saw Alfred cradling the body of Omega in his arms.

"He...he's hit," said Alfred.

"Omega!" gasped Draz, running over and taking him from Alfred.

"I...I don't think I'll be escaping with you," said Omega, "but at least I'm getting...out of here..."

"Don't say that," said Draz revealing her emotions.

Alfred saw that this man was a friend to her in prison.

Draz looked at Omega's crumpled body. Blood poured from his thigh and a new wound in his chest.

"I...I...thank you." Omega gasped his last, and died.

Draz lay the body down on the metallic floor and closed his eyes with her right hand. She was silent. She composed herself, and, full of rage, stood up and looked at the two others. She checked the rifle and discarded it. Alfred reasoned it must be out of ammunition.

"Get onboard!" she growled angrily.

"The pod's locked," said Alfred, trying the door.

"Shit," said Draz.

Suddenly the door to the pod swung open and a guard stepped out brandishing a riot prod, which sparked menacingly.

Alfred backed away. Kreth readied a punch, but Draz kicked the man in the face, breaking his neck with a wet crack. He collapsed.

"Now we can go," growled Draz.

Alfred and Kreth looked warily at each other and followed her onboard.

Chapter 21

They piled aboard the prison transport pod. Draz rushed to the control chair stationed at the bow of the craft. They cycled the airlock and waited for it to seal. Alfred and Kreth positioned themselves in the co pilot and passenger seats behind. They all put on their safety harnesses.

"Can you fly this thing?" asked Alfred.

"I used to fly cargo haulers across the Earth sometimes when I was a scavenger for the larger salvage," Draz snapped, clearly not wanting the interruption. "If I can fly those, I can fly this. The controls seem similar."

"Have you ever flown a space ship, mate?" asked Kreth.

Draz paused for a second. "No," she said.

"Well, that's promising..." said Alfred.

"Shut it!" said Draz.

Draz looked out the front window as she was flipping switches and starting up the craft's engines. A dull hum started in the aft of the craft and it started to vibrate. Her eyes were scanning the docking bay for anything that could hinder their escape. There were some guards over the other side, but they had their hands full in fighting against a group of prisoners who were trying to steal another pod.

"How much longer?" asked Kreth. "I don't want to worry you, but we're kind of sitting ducks here, mate." None of them actually knew what a duck was, but it was an expression from before The War and they knew what it meant: they were targets and easily picked off.

"I'm kind of busy here, damn it," Draz swore under her breath as the last of the preparations were made to take off. "We haven't got leaving clearance, so I have to undo all the security locks manually here and it takes time." Draz kept punching in codes and flipping switches.

"How do you know the codes?" asked Alfred.

"I've been here over a year and made some friends, end of story," snapped Draz, giving Alfred a murderous look. Alfred shrank back in his seat a little.

Draz flicked the last of the switches and grabbed the control column and throttle in her hands.

"Here we go," she said and slammed the pod into full reverse.

The docking cables and docking arc that held the pod in place disengaged and the pod launched itself out of the bay, through the protective magnetic shielding and out into the darkness of space.

The pod rocketed across the surface of the Moon and, with Draz's movement of the controls, turned itself around. Then Draz began to climb away from the prison and towards the distant yellow orb of the Earth.

Suddenly alarms began to chime.

"Shit! Auto-turrets! We've got to get out of their range," Draz said.

"No we don't," Alfred said, smiling. Both Kreth and Draz looked at him strangely. "I would still dodge the first volley if I were you, though," Alfred said with a more serious tone.

Draz threw the craft into sickening turns and twists. The first laser volley from the guns around the prison lanced out with bright red light and carved through space instantaneously at the place the pod was only a few seconds ago.

"That's the problem with auto turrets," Draz whispered to herself, "the computer targets a split second before the shot, so even when the shot hits at the speed of light, if you keep dodging, the laser will miss."

220

"You won't have to dodge much longer." Alfred swore this time as he was forced back into his seat by the G-forces of the ducking and weaving craft.

As if by magic, the laser fire stopped. Draz was able to straighten up the craft and aim for the Earth.

"Why?" is all she could manage, looking at Alfred.

"I disabled their cooling during the zet to turn the tech-slaves against the guards," Alfred said with a smile. "I thought you might need it disabled?" he said with a smirk as he faced Draz, "I'm not totally hopeless you know; I'm good at what I do!"

"Ha!" Draz laughed for the first time in what seemed like an age.

They all started laughing. It started small at first, and then developed into a rolling guffaw that echoed around the cabin. They all looked at each other and realised that, for the moment, they were free of the Moon Prison and had survived. They were on their way to Earth.

"I've never been to Earth," said Alfred quietly, seriousness creeping back into his voice.

"Neither have I, mate," said Kreth putting a reassuring hand on Alfred's shoulder.

Alfred winced a little, remembering not too long ago that same hand had tried to strangle him. "You're not going to kill me?" he asked.

"Nah, mate. I believe you about Virtus. As you said you were with me in prison when it happened. We're free now anyway." Kreth smiled.

Draz looked at Alfred, while still operating the controls. "Earth's not so bad, just stay out of the Sun," she paused, "actually, the governing corporation, the Collective Zone, is corrupt and in a state of civil war," she paused again, thinking, she screwed up her face, "and they're always after weapons to destroy things with. That's why I was in prison:

221

accused of treason by CEO Uxus and giving a weapon plan to the other side of a civil war or to Solar Solutions even. The judges couldn't make up their minds. Bastards," she swore again. "Yeah, it's a pretty shit place, but this pod will only get us there and then we must hide and see what we do then.

"Will it be easy to hide?" asked Kreth.

"Not it these bright orange jump suits it won't," interjected Alfred. They all looked down at what they were wearing and realised he was right. They all scanned the interior of the pod for any form of clothing they could wear.

Kreth unbuckled his harness and Draz engaged autopilot. Draz and Alfred unbuckled their harnesses too and they all searched the cabin.

"Wait a minute, here." Kreth indicated a locker that was towards the back of the craft. "It's locked."

"Stand back." Draz pulled out the riot prod that she had concealed on her person since the jailbreak. She jammed it into the electronic lock on the locker and activated it on full power. Sparks flew from the metal surface and the three of them turned away and shielded their faces.

After a few seconds, the locker gave way and flew open.

"Jackpot!" said Draz.

Inside they saw a number of prison guard uniforms, and some radiation masks in a bag. They hurriedly removed their garish prison garb and tried to fit into the prison guard uniforms. Draz and Alfred fitted fine, but Kreth found it hard to fit his large frame into a uniform a size too small for him.

"It'll do for now," said Draz, looking at Kreth.

"What about these." Alfred rubbed his hands over his shaved head. "Do we just say that there was a nits outbreak at the prison and the guards had to shave their heads too?"

"Yes, I guess we do, haha," laughed Draz.

"How long until Earth?" asked the awkwardly standing Kreth.

Draz moved over to the computer console in front of the pilot's chair and pressed a few buttons, "About two days," she said.

"Should we check the cells?" asked Kreth.

"I don't want to go near one of those things," snapped Draz.

"No, I mean in case anyone is in them, this was a working pod, you know?" said Kreth calmly, shifting awkwardly in his tight clothing.

"He's right," said Alfred. "There could be someone in there and we cannot hear them."

Draz slumped a little. "All right." She brandished her riot prod and they all moved down the line of cells and activated the doors one at a time. To their relief, there were no prisoners on the craft. The cells were all empty.

"Good, now just settle down and wait," sighed Draz.

The little pod rushed through space towards the yellow orb of the Earth. It moved towards the Earth Ring space stations on its auto pilot route.

***

The three passengers travelled quietly on the two-day journey back to Earth. They tried not to get on each other's nerves and talked only a little; each absorbed in their own thoughts. When they did talk, it was in uneasy, jolting conversation. Each one not really knowing whether he or she wanted to know the answers to the questions asked.

"...and that's why I was put unjustly into prison," Draz said. "We have to get that damn hard drive back and destroy it before anyone can make whatever powerful weapon is on the thing!"

"Wait, wait, wait," said Alfred, "you want us, three escaped prisoners, to find a red hard drive in the Atraxa Prime armouries and research labs, while a civil war is going on, and then just walk out with it and stop another massive war? Are you mad? How are we supposed to do that!?"

"We'll find a way!" Draz was enlivened after the escape from the Moon. She felt like she had a second chance at life. "Damn the odds, we've got to try it. Who's to say that the Collective Zone will keep the weapon on Earth? Solar Solutions space could be at risk too! If you want to see where you came from again I think we should at least try to get this weapon offline, if they've built it already, who knows?"

Alfred grimaced at the comment of getting back to where he came from, "I don't think that's going to happen..."

Draz looked at Alfred quizzically. Kreth spoke up from his silent contemplation, "We were from *Florida Station*, remember? And I support this idea of stopping whatever weapon this is." He made vague gestures with his hands.

"There, good, it's decided!" Draz nodded understanding of the destruction of *Florida Station* and also at Kreth's enthusiasm.

Alfred rolled his eyes. He scratched the side of his head around the implant.

"*static* Shuttle approaching Earth Ring *Station Plexor*, please state your security clearance and start slowdown procedure *static*" suddenly the radio burst into life and the three passengers sprang to their respective seats and Draz flicked off the auto pilot and grabbed the control column while thumbing the radio key and speaking in as official a voice as she could.

"This is shuttle, please power down your weapons, we are security from the Moon," Draz had no idea what to say. There was silence for a bit and the Earth Ring grew in their vision port. Draz slowed the craft down but kept one hand on the throttle in case something went wrong.

"Shuttle, please transmit security clearance, and be ready for debrief when you arrive, apparently there has been a rebellion on the Moon."

Draz raised her eyebrows almost imperceptibly and removed a hand from the control column to press a few buttons to transmit the security code.

"Shuttle, your security clearance does not check out. Please power down all systems and prepare for security boarding. We apologise for any inconvenience if you are legitimate, but with the rebellion we cannot be too safe..." came the reply from the Earth Ring.

Draz passed a sideways glance at Alfred and Kreth. Alfred looked pale, Kreth nodded, and they buckled themselves in. Draz's hands were back on the throttle and control column. Suddenly, with a flick of her wrist, she jammed the throttle open and yanked back on the control column in one smooth movement. The little craft leapt to action nimbly and accelerated towards the Earth Ring.

"Can this thing do re-entry into Earth's atmosphere?" Alfred said through gritted teeth, his knuckles white from gripping his seat.

"It...should," said Draz trying to concentrate on the dodging and weaving. She was trying to prevent a lock on of the weapon systems on the Earth Ring.

Suddenly there was a bright flash from the Earth Ring space station ahead and laser fire arced out towards the dodging craft. Alfred had no chance to override the coolant of these auto-turrets. But Draz was doing a good job of staying one step ahead of their targeting computers.

Draz spiralled the craft closer to the Earth Ring and worryingly, closer to the automated weapon systems. However, they had to get past the Earth Ring to get to the Earth.

"It would be a great shame to die now!" shouted Kreth over the squealing and grinding of the metal skin of the pod, which was not meant to be put through such manoeuvres.

After what seemed like an age but would have only been a few seconds, the laser fire of the auto-turrets ceased. "Aha!" said Alfred. "We're inside their targeting range!"

"We're not out of it yet!" yelled Draz, as the craft rocketed past the Earth Ring and down towards the Earth itself.

As they passed the ancient space stations that encircled the Earth, large missile pods began to emerge from hidden compartments within the Ring.

"Oh shit!" Alfred spoke for all their thoughts.

With a flash, a volley of missiles launched from along the Earth Ring space station near their craft and spiralled down towards their little ship. Warning lights blinked across the console indicating multiple missile locks.

"Can't you dodge them?" pleaded Alfred.

"I'll try!" snapped Draz, and slammed the pod into a hard left turn. A couple of the missiles lurched past the right vision port and detonated in silent explosions off the starboard side of the craft. But there were still dozens more incoming, and more were being launched by the second.

"I may have misjudged this," said Draz, surprisingly coolly.

Alfred and Kreth looked at each other disbelievingly, but said nothing, not wanting to break the concentration of their only hope.

All of a sudden the craft bucked, and all power cut from the cabin for an instant. "Oh shit!" This time it was Draz who swore.

The control column and throttle jerked out of her hands and the craft spun sickeningly on its axis when the dull thud of an explosion was heard to ricochet around the cabin. Draz grabbed the controls back again, but they were unresponsive. Smoke started to fill the cabin as the craft spiralled down towards the Earth's surface.

"We've been hit!" bellowed Kreth above the screeching and crackling noise. He unbuckled and set about trying to put out the multiple fires that burst out around the circuitry of the cabin with his old prison uniform.

Draz tried to wrestle some form of control over the craft as it careened downwards towards the surface.

Alfred sat stunned. Then, looking utterly terrified, he unbuckled and joined Kreth in trying to put out the fires. The craft was lurching and spinning out of control while they were doing this, so it was no easy feat.

"Must. Get. Some. Control. Or. We. Burn. Up!" Draz said through gritted teeth and tried to force the controls to respond. The control panel was saying most of the engines were out of commission and the guidance jets were also destroyed. "DAMN IT!" She slammed a fist into the centre of the console and suddenly some rudimentary control came back to the control column. "AHA! That worked on the cargo haulers too!" she shouted with glee as one engine coughed to life and some control came back.

They began their hasty entrance to atmosphere at a sickening rate. They were terrified that the vibration would shake the stricken craft to pieces. All the other missiles began to burn up in the atmosphere. Missiles were the least of their worries.

"I'll try to land by Atraxa Prime!" said Draz. "It's so big it won't be hard; we came in at the right angle. Amazing!"

The smoke belching little craft created an arc of fire across the sky as it plummeted Earthward. All but too late Draz realised that the thrusters that slow down descent were damaged by the missile impact.

"Uh...brace for impact!" shouted Draz as the other two passengers hastily put on their safety harnesses.

The thrusters came on intermittently, slowing the descent a little but not by much. The damaged craft slammed into the radioactive ash dunes surrounding Atraxa Prime with a sickening whine and crunch. And then there was silence.

Chapter 22

It was daytime. Draz shielded her eyes with one hand and carried the supplies she had managed to save from the downed pod in a bag, including the prison riot prod, in her other hand. She turned to face Kreth who was trudging a short distance behind her carrying Alfred. They all wore the crude radiation masks from the crashed pod.

"How is he?" she asked, with more concern in her voice than she realised. Her voice was distorted under the mask.

"Heavy," Kreth stopped and wiped his forehead, "but alive. He's still sort of unconscious though, and he keeps mumbling about someone, or something called 'Blinky'. Do you know who or what that is?" Kreth's voice also sounded different from behind his mask.

Draz shook her head. "Come on, we've got to get out of this Sun, or we'll be rad-fried. It's only a short distance left to the hover train cargo loading dock; we can sneak in through there. These salvaged rad-masks won't last forever in this heat." She added as an aside, almost to herself, "I wonder where all the rad-freaks are? Maybe the civil war got rid of them?"

As the trio approached the loading dock, they rounded one very large radioactive ash dune covered in waste and scrap, Draz suddenly stopped and dropped the bag she was carrying. "What in the hell is that?" Her tone was one of shock and also rage, because she knew exactly what it was, and her brain refused to let her admit it.

"Looks like some kind of weapon, sticking out of the top of that dome..." said Kreth, not quite picking up that Draz knew that.

"That's what it is," she snapped to him. "That must've been what was on that drive," she said much more quietly to herself.

Draz stared for a good few minutes at the large barrelled gun like thing protruding through one of the domes of the zone-city. It had large tubes that could be ammunition or coolant tubes and miles upon miles of wires and cables. It was huge, at least the size of a capital warship. Draz wondered why she had not noticed it earlier as they approached Atraxa Prime. Then suddenly, the giant gun was gone. It shimmered in the light of the Sun and then it was gone.

"Holy shit!" said Draz and Kreth in unison. Kreth almost dropped Alfred. They looked at each other. That was how neither of them had noticed the artillery piece, it had a cloaking device.

"It...cloaks!?" said Draz. "I heard rumours of cloaking devices existing pre War, but I thought they were just fantasy. I mean, it must take so much power to do that!"

"Not just that, now they have the technology, they could do that to anything," said Kreth. "They could do that to a ship, or a bomb, or anything. Why did they make it into a gun?"

"Probably because the plans on the drive were for a gun," Draz stated. "But as you say now they know how the tech works; they can put the cloaking device on anything. The gun was just the prototype. The gun is the unimportant part...I wonder if it can fire when cloaked?" Draz paused, thinking. "We have to destroy that and get the drive back!"

This time Kreth did drop Alfred, who groaned. "Look, mate, you seem to want to do a lot about destroying things. Why can't we just stow away on a ship and leave this place?" Kreth had had enough of following orders.

230

"Because, don't you see? If this is allowed to stay operational, they could easily defeat your precious Solar Solutions. And then where would you be? A system ruled by one corporation? By Uxus? That would be a disaster!" snapped Draz. Nevertheless, she could understand his reluctance to follow someone he barely knew, and risk his life in the process. "Look," she said, "I need your help, and Alfred's too. This is not just about me. It's bigger than all of us. If we don't get that cloaking device offline you can say goodbye to semi peace in our system. It'll be all out war. You think the war's bad now? Wait until there are cloaked ships deployed throughout the outer system and one corporation rules all space, uncontested and unrivalled." She finished her lecture.

Kreth listened silently and thought for a moment after she had finished. He nodded. "Lead on, mate," he said, and picked up Alfred, who groaned again.

Draz nodded her thanks and they pressed on towards the auto loading bays for the cargo.

As they approached the cargo hover train bays, Draz and Kreth observed how the cargo was picked up by automatic arms from machines and unloaded from the hover trains that led off into the distance towards other zone-cities. The cargo was then loaded onto conveyor belts into the bowels of the zone-city. This was different from the ship loading dock that Draz had always used with her buggy since she had been young. This loading dock was for the trains from other zone-cities and was mostly automated.

"We have to get on one of those belts!" shouted Draz above the noise of the machinery.

"What about guards or security?" shouted Kreth, hefting Alfred.

"There are very few here, so much of this cargo hauling is automated, we just have to get off the conveyor belts before we hit the shields!" Draz continued when Kreth looked blank. "They incinerate organic matter! So, the cargo goes through, but we'd die."

Kreth thought for a second and then said, "Why don't we get in one of the containers? That'd shield us?"

"Hah! Now that's the best idea I've heard all day!" Draz said. "Follow me!"

They ran for the nearest container, which was a little larger than the prison cells Draz had gotten so used to on the Moon, as it was waiting to be loaded onto the conveyor belt and brought inside the Atraxa Prime compound. Draz reached the container first and using the recovered riot prod, she shorted out the electric lock on the outside of the container and the door slid open.

"Come on!" she shouted and Kreth lolloped over, and he deposited Alfred inside the container and then both of them climbed in afterwards. Draz pulled the door shut and they waited in the darkness.

"What's usually in these crates? It's awfully hard." Kreth shifted uneasily on the produce inside.

"Foodstuffs or energy stocks usually," whispered Draz. "Atraxa Prime is huge and has many millions of people in it. They all need food and water."

They waited, and then the crate they were in jolted and was lifted by mechanical arm onto a moving conveyor belt. The door to the crate slid open a little and some light was let in. Draz moved and pulled the door tightly shut again, but the lock was fried due to her riot prod so all she could do was hold the door shut.

They waited longer and after some buzzing and movement, they were lifted and deposited again, and then there was nothing more. They let some more time go by, just to make sure nothing else happened and then Draz slid the door open, and they looked out on the surrounding piles of crates.

"We're lucky we're at the bottom of a pile, I wouldn't want to climb down from up there!" Draz indicated a mountain of crates to their right. "Come on!" She took off her mask as she moved to enter the lower levels of the zone-city.

"Wait, mate!" shouted Kreth, removing his mask also. He was pointing at the cargo they had been sitting on. The containers read, "Work clothing", Kreth grinned. "Maybe they have my size this time!"

Draz laughed. "Well, we all need a change of clothes, hurry!"

Kreth and Draz dug through the cargo for adequate clothing. It was not hard to find. They donned common worker gear in the right sizes for them and then they awkwardly dressed Alfred. They were all in the dark green and yellow trim of a labourer in Atraxa Prime.

Draz looked down at her chest and saw the logo of the Collective Zone emblazoned across the left top pocket and she realised that she had missed it; even after all that the Collective had done to her, she had missed it.

"Okay, now can we go?" she said, smiling.

"Yes, mate!" said Kreth. He picked up Alfred again.

***

Alfred's dreams swam. He was being chased again. This time by some unknown shadow of a creature, and just before he was devoured whole by an unknown thing he was on top of the coolant tubes on *Florida Station* again. He screamed silently as Blinky threw herself from the edge. The scene changed again, and he was watching *Florida Station* explode in slow motion from within the

Green Dragon. And then there was that noise; that voice. It screamed inside his head. *"YEEEESSSSSSS"*

Alfred woke with a splitting headache. He felt ill. He groaned. He tried to open his eyes, but his head swam when he tried to do so. He was lying on something hard and cold.

"Easy, mate, easy..." Alfred heard the voice but could not understand what was going on.

Suddenly his eyes snapped open, and he sat bolt upright, fighting the nausea. "Where are we?" Alfred yelled.

"Shhhh, we're okay, we're in what Draz calls Atraxa Prime's sub levels. We found an abandoned apartment and we're safe, for now," said Kreth.

"Ah," said Alfred, talking through the pain of his headache. "What happened to me? And where's Draz?"

"Draz is out scouting the area. You hit your head badly in the crash, mate. You're lucky to be alive!" said Kreth from the bedside.

"Ah." Alfred rubbed his sore head. The nightmare faded as he did so. But he knew it would be back, as sure as he was about the zetting sickness. Now that he had no access to treatment, the sickness would return strongly.

Chapter 23

"And there goes another one!" yelled the First Officer of the *Green Dragon*, indicating the explosion in the upper atmosphere and resulting fiery trail as the crew watched the fourth small pod of its kind arc through the atmosphere and fall to the Earth.

"What's going on?" asked Captain Artisius as he stood bemused on the bridge. "Call the Docking Master. Do they need our assistance?"

The *Green Dragon* was docked on an upper level landing pad of Atraxa Prime where the larger ships that could still enter the atmosphere docked. It was below the boardroom but still high up enough for the bridge to get a good view out over the surface of the Earth around Atraxa Prime. It had just completed a refit after delivering its cargo to the Moon.

"We still have to refuel and restock fully for our next trip to the outer planets, sir," said the First Officer. "We are not in the position to intervene in some sort of fight."

It was apparent that something was going terribly wrong. Artisius and the command staff of the vessel were watching the fiery rain as ship after ship exploded in the atmosphere and fell to Earth.

"This is Graxus, Docking Master of Atraxa Prime..." crackled the intercom.

"Good, yes, this is Captain Artisius of the *Green Dragon*, currently docked at Atraxa Prime's upper levels. We're seeing some...fireworks. What the hell is going on up there?"

"Pay it no heed, Captain, uh what was it?" came the static spiked reply.

"Artisius, of the *Green Dragon*," replied Artisius, a little put out by the Docking Master's tone of voice.

"Oh, the *Green Dragon*, we need to have words with you. Please remain on your ship and a boarding party will be with you shortly," the crackling ceased, and there was no more conversation.

"I don't like this," Artisius said quietly to his Chief of Security. "Bring up the guard!" The Security Chief, Sergeant Ithia, saluted in smart fashion, radioed into her communicator, and within minutes the bridge had a full complement of armed guards.

"This is Docking Master Graxus, requesting permission to come aboard," crackled the intercom again. It was clear to all on the bridge that this was not a request.

"Permission granted," said Artisius through a clenched jaw, he knew this would end badly. "Open the boarding corridor and get ready to receive our...guests." He motioned to the ships guards around the bridge. They readied their weapons.

Within minutes the boarding party had reached the bridge and a small man wearing spectacles, in military regalia with a peaked cap and epaulettes slightly too large for his body, surrounded by armed security personnel, entered the room.

Artisius was smarting at the insult of the Docking Master bringing armed soldiers onto his ship, but he said nothing, merely glaring menacingly at the intruders. He waited for Graxus to make the first move.

"Captain," said Graxus curtly, "I have something to discuss with you, in private." He looked at the *Green Dragon's* guards over the rims of his small, circular spectacles.

"Whatever you have to say, say it here. My crew deserve to hear anything you have against me," replied Artisius with ice in his voice.

"Very well," continued Graxus, "I hereby prevent you from leaving Atraxa Prime until you have been thoroughly investigated for treason against our Great Collective and home world--"

"WHAT!?" said Artisius with rage.

"Please, let me finish," said Graxus, drawing himself up to his full height equal to Artisius' chin. "Some of the prisoners you brought to us on the Moon a short time ago have been involved in a prison break. They have escaped. They started a riot and the 'fireworks' you said you saw are our defences dealing with the pods that are coming from the Moon which are full of prisoners."

Artisius was silent. He realised that this was serious.

"So," Graxus continued, buoyed by Artisius' silence, "I have to inform you that you are not to leave this planet until a full and thorough investigation has been made into your involvement in bringing dissidents to the Moon."

"But that's what it's for!" Artisius said. "The Moon is for the worst traitors and dissidents. Where was I meant to take them? Your personal apartment?"

"Careful what you say, Captain. I believe you gave them the information on how to escape our security," said Graxus, "I could have you shot..."

Without a word, the *Green Dragon's* guards all took a step forward in unison. The threat was made evident to the little man, whose guards raised their weapons too.

"Easy now, Captain." Graxus raised his hands in mock surrender. "We don't want any bloodshed here."

Artisius raised his right hand and the guards surrounding the bridge backed off. Graxus' guards also backed down at the sign of the acquiescence.

"Good," said Graxus, smiling smugly.

Suddenly some alarms went off on the bridge. "What's wrong?" asked Artisius, with Graxus forgotten for an instant.

"We're detecting huge power fluctuations nearby, sir," said the Scanning Officer. "As if from a large starship!"

"Oh, that's just our latest addition to Atraxa Prime," Graxus said, smiling even more.

"Your what?" snapped Artisius, he had had enough of this little man's games.

"We have...recovered...some technology from before The War. It's our answer to the Solar Solutions insolence. We will teach them a lesson!"

"Is it some sort of weapon? Are you going to all out war with Solar Solutions?" Artisius asked, genuinely worried.

"The weapon is inconsequential. It's the little...addition...to the weapon that we like best. It should help our ships no end," Graxus chuckled.

"Sir!" shouted the Scanning Officer. "Part of the zone-city just...disappeared. The planetary defence cannon just...vanished...from my sensors...sir." The Scanning Officer did not quite know what he had just seen, and so did not know how to report the news.

Artisius did not know how to respond, "A cloaking device?" is all he could manage, turning pale. He glared at the small, smug man with the too big cap.

Artisius could see the advantages of such a thing in an instant: all the ships and weapons that could be cloaked. With such technology, the Collective Zone could conquer all of the Solar System and Solar Solutions stood no chance. That would of course mean the end of his trading runs between the two empires and the agreed competition and state of semi war between the two powers would turn to all out war and millions would die. Solar Solutions had a respectable military force too, but they could not compete with invisible ships.

"Indeed, Captain. Indeed," is all the small man said.

"But open war would tear the system apart!" Artisius said. "You need the unofficial trade with Solar Solutions, and they need you. I know officially you're at war with them but it's more a state of uneasy peace. How can you justify the deaths?"

"I don't have to justify them," said Graxus with glee in his eyes. "We will win. And it's not my job to make the calculations. I'm just the Docking Master. My commanders in the Collective Zone Board of Directors have all the contingencies planned out. They know what they are doing. I trust their judgment. Solar Solutions will no longer exist."

"If you're just the Docking Master, how do you know the innermost secrets of the Collective Zone?" blurted out Artisius, not really sure if he wanted to know the answer.

"I may be just the Docking Master," he adjusted his cap, "but I'm one of the highest ranking Fleet Officials in Atraxa Prime. And if the cloaking devices are going to be on ships, I have to know. See?" Graxus smiled smugly.

"And what about traders like me?" rasped Artisius, not believing what he was hearing.

"We will find a use for you," said Graxus, staring over his glasses.

"Anything more?" sighed Artisius, visibly broken.

"No, I have said all I need to. You will remain here until we grant you permission to leave." Graxus turned on his heel and with a gesture his guards shepherded him out of the bridge and off the *Green Dragon*.

Artisius was visibly shaken. He walked over to the edge of the observation dome that met the bridge at the front of the ship and leaned against the glass.

"Sir?" the First Officer stood by his captain, clearly in need of orders.

Artisius ran a hand through his greying hair and breathed a sigh. He looked over at his second in command. "We do as he said, we wait. Stand the guards down."

"Sir!" The man saluted and ordered the guards to leave the bridge. They left with precision; weapons slung over their shoulders.

Artisius looked up and out of the observation dome of the bridge. He saw more explosions in the sky and more fiery trails.

He felt as if he had been blown out of the sky too. "Poor bastards," is all he could manage.

Artisius left the bridge without ceremony. He needed to confine himself to his quarters for a while. Things had taken a decided turn for the worse. Maybe the day was coming when he had to pick a side, or maybe he already had, he mused as he walked down the corridors of his ship.

Chapter 24

"And so, we begin." CEO Uxus entered the boardroom of the Collective Zone, situated at the top of the highest tower of Atraxa Prime. He looked around the faces seated around the board table.

The board members all sat with anticipation on what was going to be said. This had been an emergency meeting called at the behest of their CEO.

"Are we ready?" Uxus asked the room in general, and was pleased to see everyone nodded.

Uxus caught the gaze of the Master of the Fleet Maxtria, supreme commander of the Collective Zone fleet, in the group of faces and gave her a courteous nod in return. She was not actually appointed to command the fleet from any bridge of a starship; she commanded the fleet logistically from the Earth.

He then looked over to the robot in the corner and gave the instruction to start recording the meeting. The robot clicked and whirred into life and its microphones and recording device powered up and began recording the slightest noise in any part of the room.

"So, I will cut to the chase. There has been a rebellion on the Moon," Uxus paused as the room erupted into babble and confusion. It was stilled by Uxus raising an old, gnarled hand. Uxus knew how old he was, but he never let anyone else know. He felt that age was not important. He was as mentally sharp and fast as a young man, perhaps more so due to his experience. Whatever the case, Uxus had led the company to great things due to his cunning and guile. "Please, members, please," he continued. "I have dispatched the Great Fleet, under the command of Fleet Commander Boltha, with the counsel of Master of the Fleet Maxtria," another nod, "they will be there in a few days after mustering and will put the rebellion down with maximum force!"

The room burst into applause.

"But what about the prison? If you bomb it, there will be no where to put our...undesirables," said the Chief of Corrections.

"Who said anything about bombing?" replied Uxus. The Chief of Corrections blushed. "I said 'maximum force' meaning I would deploy my elite troops to...pacify...the inmates. The structure and integrity of the prison itself will remain undamaged." There was more applause joined by the Chief of Corrections with renewed vigour.

"What about the explosions in the sky? They've been happening for the past few hours," one of the board members chimed in bravely. The rest of the board nodded in agreement and looked eagerly towards their leader for enlightenment.

"They are simply the escape pods from the Moon being shot down by our defence systems on the Earth Ring. They are full of scum and will be destroyed as they try to enter our space. I have no sympathy for those criminals who try to flee the chaos they caused." Uxus ended by banging his hand on the wooden table.

The boardroom flinched as one with the loud sound of the action.

"Be assured," Uxus said, "Atraxa Prime will not be under threat from anyone or anything from the Moon!"

There was more applause.

Uxus raised a gnarled hand, and the applause died away again. "But this is not what I came to talk to you about. I did not call this meeting because of some rebellion far

242

away. I called this meeting to demonstrate a powerful and lethal new weapon. Please, follow me." Uxus moved to one of the large windows and stared out over Atraxa Prime's sprawling domes and towers.

The rest of the boardroom looked at each other, rather uneasily, but rose and moved to the window and surrounded Uxus.

"See anything?" Uxus asked, a small smile forming on his cracked and furrowed face, causing the furrows to extend even further like great valleys.

The boardroom members looked around and looked at each other confused. "No?" They responded in turn, raising the inflection at the end of the word, as they were unsure as to what to say.

"See our new planetary defence cannon?" Uxus indicated vaguely with a hand in the direction of the large gun that protruded from the superstructure of the zone-city.

It thrust its way into the poisonous yellow clouds around Atraxa Prime. It was massive. It was covered in pipes and wires and terminated in a large dish.

There was silence. And nervous glances between board members.

Uxus smiled, the furrows on his face mirroring the rad-dunes surrounding Atraxa Prime.

He spoke a word into a communicator he pulled from his pants' pocket. With a flickering of the lights in the boardroom, the weapon disappeared. Its shape folded in on itself and it simply vanished from vision without a sound.

"That's...impossible..." said one of the board members.

There was more silence for a few minutes. Uxus got bored with the dumbness. "So, that's what I wanted to show you," he said with a clap of his hands after returning the communicator to his pocket. "Or perhaps I should say, hide from you!"

He returned to his position at the head of the table and sat down, indicating with his hands for the others to do the same. They followed instructions dumbly. Each trying to comprehend what they had seen and the implications from such a demonstration; what the implications of a cloakable weapon would be.

"The red hard drive..." said the Master of Constructions for the Command Wing. "I had no idea; I just thought we were building a weapon system. So that's why you had the whole construction made top secret; and why you had different teams working on different parts so that no one would see too much. Such a cloaking field would mean--"

"Ships..." exclaimed the Master of the Fleet.

Uxus snapped his fingers and indicated that the woman was correct with a pointing finger.

"We could cloak our entire fleet...eventually," said Uxus calmly, relishing the shock still on the faces of those around him. "Solar Solutions would have no chance; we would win our little war with ease. At the moment the data is complex, and we have not been able to copy the contents of the drive. So it's precious. I have it under guard. By the way, how goes the war between the Shipping Wing and the Corporate Wing over the red hard drive?" The change in topic jarred and took the board members off guard.

"Uh, we're continuing our assault on the Corporate Wing in sector 94D," stammered the Head of the Shipping Wing.

"And we are resisting strongly," snapped the Head of the Corporate Wing, glaring at the other man.

"Well stop it. I want all internal wars to cease as of immediately. I want all resources put into preparing for an all out war with the Solar Solutions Corporation. We've now built what you're fighting over in the Command Wing and so you can cease all hostilities," said Uxus instructively.

"But, CEO Sir, we're already at war with Solar Solutions," said the Master of the Fleet.

"Not enough. Not proper war. I want to take the fight to them," spat Uxus. "For too long we've been fat and sat around trading. For too long they have poached off our hard labour and for too long they have taken us for granted. I want their territory. For the glory of our people, I want their space!"

The boardroom members looked around uneasily again, but said nothing.

"So, those are my instructions: we need to be unified and take the fight to Solar Solutions. In the next few years, I want prototypes copied from the drive and the cloaking field to be installed on our ships," said Uxus with a grin. "What of the other zone-cities? Do they continue to agree to our terms and continue to trade with us?"

"Yes, CEO Sir," said the Master of Relations. "Zone-City Proxor Medium, Zone-City Lirgath and Zone-City Xertins, Zone-City Corinthia Primus all respond to our invitations to trade and supply us with the necessary resources and bow to the commands of the Collective Zone. Zone-City Jurth Proximo is a little resistant at our requests--"

"Well make them agree." Uxus flashed a glance at the man.

"Y-yes, CEO Sir," stammered the Master of Relations.

"I need all the resources if we're meant to build a war fleet," said Uxus, almost to himself, gazing out across the toxic rad-wastes around the zone-city. He followed the lines of hover trains that sped to and fro from their zone-city to the others dotted over the planet.

"CEO Sir," a hand went up hesitantly. "Have you thought of appointing a successor?"

Uxus glared at the woman who had suggested, in all but words, that he was too old. "No, I haven't. That's all your job isn't it, to appoint a new CEO? You are all board members! I will be undergoing longevity surgery soon so that I will be able to survive to at least one hundred and twenty years old, should the surgery succeed. So, we should not have any problems for the coming years."

The woman shrank back into her seat.

"Now, if that is all?" Uxus looked around the room, "meeting concluded." He banged his hand on the table and rose to leave.

The rest of the board members looked at each other with trepidation. Their master had spoken, and they were to carry out his orders. The result of which would be all out war amongst the planets. Only the Master of the Fleet was smiling. Her ships were to take 'glorious' war to the corners of the system.

Uxus left the room without another word.

Chapter 25

Alfred kept rubbing his head as he swung his legs over the edge of the makeshift bed that he now realised was a bench set into the wall. "How long have I been out?" he asked.

"About half a day, mate," came the reply Alfred did not want. "And you know what? You're pretty heavy!" Kreth responded with a laugh.

Alfred smiled. It hurt more.

"Who's Blinky?" asked Kreth.

Alfred stopped. He froze. "Have I been talking while out of it?" he asked after a short time.

Kreth nodded. "Yeah. You mentioned this 'Blinky' a few times, like it was a person."

"She was my sister, long dead. I lost her years ago but lost any relic of her with the destruction of *Florida Station*," Alfred said.

"How did she die?" asked Kreth.

"She suicided. End of story," Alfred screwed his right hand into a fist and banged it on the bench.

Kreth nodded.

"We're in Atraxa Prime, yes?" said Alfred.

Kreth nodded again.

"Then what are we supposed to do here? In the middle of the Collective Zone control?" Alfred asked.

"Draz had some idea about stealing a ship. But she said we have to get this red hard drive back from the Collective Zone," answered Kreth.

Alfred rolled his eyes. Why did everything have to be so complicated?

"If you don't like that you'll hate this, mate," said Kreth. "On the way here, we saw something amazing: this weapon that was built into Atraxa Prime seemed to disappear. It cloaked!"

"Cloaked? That's not possible! No one has that technology!" Alfred had seen and heard a lot of things but never a working cloaking device.

"Saw it with my own eyes, mate," said Kreth.

"And what does Draz want us to do about the cloaking weapon?" Alfred's tone suggested he knew already.

"Yeah, that's right, mate." Kreth nodded, reading Alfred's expression. "She wants us to destroy it, somehow. As she believes a cloaking device will tip any balance in a Collective Zone and Solar Solutions war."

"Of course, she does," Alfred sighed, and rubbed his head.

Just then, the door slid aside and the two spun around with fear in their faces, wondering if they had been discovered. However, the fear soon melted as the voice of Draz reassured them.

"It's me, you can relax," said Draz. The pair visibly let out a communally held breath. Draz shut the door behind her. "Ah you're up," she said turning to Alfred. "How's the head?"

"Sore, but apparently in one piece," he replied.

"Good." She smiled and then continued with business. "I managed to get these." She dumped, from a bag, three large calibre pistols onto the bench next to Alfred.

Alfred and Kreth looked at each other, neither asked how she got them.

"We'll need them," she said. "Good news, I've found out where the sensitive documents are stored in Atraxa Prime. It's been easy as I used to live and work here. I know where the useful salvage goes after it has been sorted by the

248

salvage yard and I got the login for the computer network, don't ask how," she deposited some ammunition for the pistols on the bench with a hard 'clunk'. "As for the cloaking weapon, that's a little more tricky, we might have to blast that with a ship's gun. It's too well guarded and large to disable with just the three of us down here." She met their incredulous gazes. "What?" she said as if everything she said was simple.

"So, all you want us to do is: take these stolen pistols, rampage through the secured documents section of the Collective Zone HQ and then steal a ship and blast half the zone-city away?" said Alfred unconvinced of the plan.

"Yeah, well, we stand a better chance! With only three of us we're harder to catch," Draz said.

Alfred rolled his eyes and breathed a sigh, "I had a nice life once. Sure it was hard, but it was all right. And then this cult destroyed my entire existence and I get transported under false charges to the Moon and then I'm caught up in some other conflict and now you want me to destroy some weapon thing. I've just about had it with all this shit!" Alfred pushed himself off the bench and stood like a defiant child who has not got what he wants in a store.

Draz fumed. "Look, I had a nice life too, then war tore that all apart. I was sentenced for a crime I didn't commit, like you, and now I'm here with someone who's useless at everything except for whinging. Get over yourself. Bad things happen. We need to make the best of this situation and take back that hard drive and destroy that cloaked weapon in order to prevent other lives being destroyed. Hopefully they've been unable to copy the plans as they'll be complex. Now take a pistol, follow me, or don't, I don't care. I'm getting the job done by myself if necessary. And stop acting like some petulant child!" Draz spat the last words, grabbed a pistol, and headed for the door.

Kreth and Alfred looked at each other. Alfred deflated. They both grabbed a pistol and some ammunition and headed after Draz.

***

They moved through the lower levels of Atraxa Prime with the pistols concealed in their workers' uniforms. The lower levels were where the maintenance and manufacturing of all the materials for the zone-city took place. It was a grimy, hot, dirty place. The trio moved from furnace room to food processing plant to atmosphere purifier all because of their workers' uniforms they were allowed through by guards.

They came to a cargo lift that led further up into the core of Atraxa Prime.

"Here it is, the lift we need that'll take us right into the archives where the drive is being held," whispered Draz to the other two out of earshot of the guards on the door. "Our workers' uniforms may not give us free passage here. Stay alert. Alfred stay back and cover us. Kreth, follow me." She indicated that Alfred was to stand at the corner of the corridor and watch for other guards.

Alfred obeyed, still stunned by Draz's outburst, he drew and held his pistol awkwardly. He knew she was totally right, but he just had to let some of his anger go. Alfred stood on the corner; there was no one around. He kept an eye out for anyone.

Suddenly Alfred heard raised voices and turned to hear a loud couple of 'pops' and screams. He saw the guards at the lift crumple up and he ran over to see what happened.

"Anyone coming?" said Draz. She was breathing hard.

"Uh, no, I think the sounds of the machinery masked anything," stammered Alfred, staring at the dead guards and the pools of blood mingling on the ground. "What have you done?"

"Cleared a path," said Draz coolly, looking into Alfred's eyes. He saw she felt nothing over what she had done. Only her increased breathing rate indicated a release of adrenaline.

Kreth was silent. He had his pistol drawn and was looking around.

"Come on, into the lift!" Draz used one of the dead guard's hands to activate the palm print sensitive scanner on the lift door and the door slid open with a hiss. They got inside.

Draz thumbed the archive button and with another hiss, the door shut, and the lift rocketed up inside the zone-city.

Draz and Kreth checked their pistols as the lift ascended. Alfred held his pistol awkwardly, not quite knowing what to do.

Draz saw his nervousness. "Do you know how to use that?" she asked.

"Not really, I've only ever held one other pistol, and never fired it" Alfred answered truthfully.

"Look," Draz took his hand and showed him how to aim and reload. "And then you just pull the trigger. There'll be some recoil, but just hold it firmly." Alfred nodded dumbly.

Kreth looked on, not needing the instruction but more to give Alfred moral support.

The lift started to slow.

"Here we are," said Draz.

They all got a little more jittery.

The door slid open, and they stepped out into the Archive's main sorting room. There was no one there, only tech-slaves and robots that were busy sorting the salvage and other items brought in the previous day. The whir and click of robot arms mingled with the grinding of conveyor belts. The room was dim and cool.

"Follow me," whispered Draz. She headed off down one of the corridors and came to a computer bank.

"So, we just search for it? Like a library?" whispered Kreth.

Draz nodded. She logged in with the password she had obtained earlier and then she punched in some details, "Hrm, it doesn't say exactly where it is, so I cannot search for it, but this thing here sounds promising," she pointed at the screen, "that meets the right description. It's been a year and a half since I found it, so we'll just have to risk it and hope that's it."

They followed the instruction leading them through corridor after corridor of stored artefacts and trinkets that the Collective Zone thought might be of use. Shelf after shelf stretched away into the darkness covered in artefacts or books gathering dust.

"This is like the salvage centre I used to deal with all the time as a scavenger," said Draz as they traversed the winding corridors. "Now, the computer said it was..." They rounded a turn and came face to face with a number of guards.

Draz and Kreth raised their pistols as did the guards and firing ensued. The guards fell crumpled in a heap and there were some screams. Another guard appeared and ran at Draz as she was reloading. He drew his stun prod and leapt at her. Alfred fumbled with his gun, raised it, and squeezed the trigger. There was a loud 'pop' and the gun nearly flew out of his hands, but the guard screamed and collapsed in a heap at Draz's feet. She looked at him with thanks in her eyes.

The thanks melted into worry as she dropped her pistol and dashed past Alfred, over to the fallen body of Kreth. Alfred dropped his pistol and rushed to Kreth's side too.

"Hey," Kreth coughed blood, "mate."

"No, no, no, not like this," said Alfred, "we've come too far. Not here, not now. You're the last thing I have from *Florida Station*, you can't leave me!" He and Draz propped Kreth up in their arms. He had been hit by one of the guard's bullets.

"I guess they got me, mate. I think you'll need to carry me this time," Kreth stammered. "Ah well, get that drive, and get out of here!" His eyes glazed over, and he slumped in their arms.

Alfred was full of rage. He grabbed a pistol and held it tightly. Draz met his gaze. He saw she was just as angry. She was still holding the body of Kreth. She nodded and picked up a fallen pistol too.

They searched the shelves where the guards had been standing, their hands and uniforms now covered in blood. After a short search, Draz drew out a red coloured, battered hard drive and stuffed it inside her uniform's inner breast pocket.

"Let's go," she said coolly. "The alarms will be sounding by now"

Alfred followed, throwing a glance back at the fallen body of their friend. Friend, he realised that the crises he had faced over the past year and a half had gained him friends. He felt needed. He felt rage that those friends were taken from him.

They ran back through the archive and to the main set of lifts at the heart of the structure.

"If we make it to the cargo loading dock we should be able to get to a ship," Draz said with authority, breathing hard after running. Alfred nodded; he was out of breath too.

They left the archive behind, silent alarms sounding, but before more guards could respond in time.

Chapter 26

Captain Artisius was woken from his sleep by the intercom chiming by his bed. He reached over and activated it.

"Yes? What?" He still felt dreadful following his dressing down by the Docking Master. How could they talk to him like that? How could they threaten him like that?

"Sir, we need you in the docking bay. We have apprehended some stowaways," came the terse voice of the chief of security.

Artisius sprang to his feet, reinvigorated with the chance to deal out some punishment to someone. It would make him feel better, he reasoned. He headed out of his rooms after dressing in his captain's dress uniform, and made his way to the docking bay.

When Artisius arrived in the docking bay, in his full regalia, he found the chief of security, Sergeant Ithia, who saluted smartly.

"What's this about stowaways?" Artisius snapped.

"Sir, we have apprehended these two trying to gain access to the cargo," reported the security chief. She indicated a male and a female who had their hands bound behind their backs and were being held in place by a couple of burly security guards. "We found this on them," the security chief presented Artisius with a small, compact hard drive and indicated some pistols lying on the floor of the cargo bay a few metres away.

Artisius cast an eye over the pair. "What are your names?...Wait," he said, his face changed with recognition, shock, and some understanding. "I know you." He pointed at the male, whose clothes were covered in blood, and whose freshly growing hair from the stubble of his scalp was all grimy. "I know you..." he paused again, "from *Florida Station*. You're the terrorist! How did you get here?" Artisius was unsure whether he really wanted to know, and the sentence was both a statement and a question at the same time. "What are your names?" he asked again, not sure what to feel. He could be angry that the terrorist had escaped the Moon and was trying to get away, but with his own treatment by the Collective Zone, he was unsure as to what to feel.

"Alfred, sir."

"Draz...sir?"

It was clear to Artisius she did not know how to address him. He had the power of their life or death in his hands.

Artisius sighed; they had obviously had a very hard time getting to his ship. Their clothes were stained with blood, and they were ragged and dishevelled. He had the time before takeoff. He would decide their fate while he heard their story. "Tell me how you got here, as we make our way to the bridge," he said.

The pair looked at each other and then, with nothing else to lose, Alfred recounted his story and Draz then hers, which was longer. When they had finally finished they were standing on the bridge of the *Green Dragon*.

"So, you boarded my ship because it was the only one docked on this tower?" Artisius asked.

Alfred nodded, "I would have avoided this ship if I could have, as it took me to the Earth Moon, but we had no choice..."

"And, this," Artisius hefted the hard drive, "contains the instructions to build that weapon and more importantly the cloaking device? And they probably haven't been able to copy it exactly because it is so complicated?"

255

Alfred and Draz nodded together, looking around at the modern bridge of the *Green Dragon*.

Artisius saw that they were confused about their merciful treatment.

"Interesting, so it's the only copy, and their only prototype is down there in one of the domes of the zone-city." Artisius inspected the drive, and then tossed it casually to a guard. "Stash that somewhere safe, and keep it under guard."

"Sir!" replied the guard and left the bridge immediately.

"We can't have that falling into the wrong hands." Artisius winked at Alfred and Draz. "I'm getting the impression as to you're wondering why I'm treating you like I am."

Draz stared at Artisius, and Alfred simply looked dumb.

"Look," said Artisius, raising his palms and explaining, "things have come about that make me need to choose a side. That's the long and the short of it."

Draz spoke after Artisius fell silent. "Thank you, sir, and we are entirely at your mercy."

Alfred looked at her quizzically.

"And we are willing to help with your escape from Collective space if you let us serve on your ship for a time," she continued as Artisius nodded his approval. "But the red hard drive must be destroyed!" exclaimed Draz, but stopped when Artisius raised a hand.

"I'm sorry, Draz, but I cannot do that. It's my insurance that you two behave and also I may be able to use it in the future. I am a trader and a soldier of fortune after all, it's what I do." Alfred and Artisius could see the dissatisfaction on Draz's face, but she kept silent, accepting the situation.

"Now, perhaps you could come over here." Artisius indicated the edge of the observation dome on the bridge.

"And Security Officer, please undo the restraints on these two."

The bindings on the wrists of Draz and Alfred were undone and they rubbed their wrists to restore circulation as they stood at the edge of the dome and looked out over the expanse of Atraxa Prime.

Artisius watched as Draz put her hand on the glass of the dome as if to feel the outside of the towers and domes of her home. It was obvious that she would miss her home. She was forever banished from everything she knew, and she would never be welcomed back.

As Artisius watched on, Alfred approached and put a reassuring hand on her shoulder. She did not flinch away.

"Sorry to interrupt," said the captain. "But I have had an idea of what to do." The two passengers turned to face him, their backs to the world. "Would you like to see some fireworks?" Artisius said, with a wry smile.

Alfred looked puzzled.

Draz smiled. "Do it!" she whispered, with a nod.

Alfred looked at Draz who looked back with her own wry smile.

"Prepare for battle stations!" shouted Artisius. "Close all hatches; disconnect all docking tubes; bring the main auto-turrets up to full power! Prep the missile bays!" The bridge was a flurry of excitement and action in an instant.

Artisius indicated the dome behind them. Alfred and Draz spun around and looked out onto Atraxa Prime.

Suddenly the intercom crackled to life, "*Green Dragon*, we detect a weapon power up on your systems, please cease and explain."

Artisius said nothing, he just grinned. It was time to burn some bridges.

"Eighty per cent charge on auto-turrets, missile bays primed and loaded," came the call from the First Officer, relaying the information to his captain.

"*GREEN DRAGON*! CAPTAIN ARTISIUS, RESPOND!" The intercom was pleading, "WE WILL RESPOND WITH FORCE!"

Artisius smiled to himself; they knew his name this time.

"One hundred per cent charge, ready to fire, Captain," came the calm voice from the First Officer.

Alfred looked at Draz and Artisius. Draz looked at Artisius. Artisius looked at his bridge crew and the two passengers.

"Target the main coolant lines of where the new cloaked weapon is. They are not invisible. Be prepared to fire on my command," Artisius said with precision and with decades of experience. "Fire!"

Draz and Alfred spun around again to watch auto-turret fire and missiles streak from the bow of the *Green Dragon* and impact deeply into the skin of Atraxa Prime and puncture the coolant tubes of the cloaking device. First there was a bending of space, and then a flash of light, followed by a huge explosion. The zone-city rocked on its foundations and plumes of fire and smoke billowed up from what was once their prised new weapon. Draz smiled in horror. Alfred's jaw hung open.

"Now, Helmsman, get us out of here," commanded Artisius coolly. "The zone-city defence guns will track us soon, so, make haste!"

***

With a lurch, the *Green Dragon* lifted from the landing pad and sped away from the docking tubes of Atraxa Prime, dodging fire from the defence guns and climbing further and further up into space toward the Earth Ring.

The Earth Ring's defences sputtered into action but in a haphazard way due to the sudden nature of the *Green Dragon's* attack. The Earth Ring was still bringing its defences online, too late. And the majority of the Collective Zone's fleet was on the way to the Moon.

Chapter 27

The *Green Dragon* roared away from the Earth. Its plasma drives propelled the ship to maximum speed. The prow of the ship forged its way through space, bucking and heaving as the ship, under the control of the Helmsman, took evasive manoeuvres to avoid the auto-turret and missile fire that erupted along the Earth ring space stations.

Artisius stood, in full military regalia, upon his command dais, resplendent in his blue, gold and red uniform. He was barking orders left and right. He was in his element. The rolling and bucking of the ship were unnoticed by him, as he stood, upright and steadfast, in the eye of the storm. The action brought out his calmness. He was at his best at the helm of a warship. It had been too long since he had seen action, he thought, and grinned.

"Continue to take evasive action while returning fire, let me know when our batteries are locked on!" Artisius said with a calmness that belied the situation.

"We have a target, sir!" shouted the First Officer, relaying observations from the crew of the bridge. This time it was from the Gunnery Officer. "An auto-turret battery on the Earth Ring."

"Fire!" Artisius grinned even more. He lived for moments like this.

Bright red laser fire arced from the *Green Dragon's* primary auto-turret battery across the void of space and slammed with superheated energy into the closest auto-turret battery on the Earth Ring. Flames blossomed silently into space as the entire section of the Earth Ring where the battery was evaporated and turned into molten slag.

"Direct hit, sir!" came the shout of glee from the First Officer.

"Excellent, find another target! Fire at will! Anything shooting at us will..." Artisius' last words were torn away as a missile from the Earth Ring detonated a little too close to the *Green Dragon* and the ship was thrown around by the blast. "That was too close," Artisius whispered to himself. "Damage report!?" he bellowed above the sounds of the emergency sirens.

"Deck 12 has lost power. Deck 13 is open to space, sir!" shouted the First Officer, once more relaying information to his captain from the crew of the bridge.

Artisius grimaced, "Close all bulkheads on deck 13! Send in the tech-slaves to patch the breaches!"

"Already done, sir. The auto-systems have cut in. Atmosphere loss was minimal," came the response.

"And keep our main turrets firing at the Earth Ring's defences!" yelled Artisius.

The Earth Ring stations passed beneath the *Green Dragon* as it forged its way into space.

Artisius looked over at his guests: Alfred and Draz, who were clinging to anything they could for dear life. They were unused to the rolling and bucking of a ship taking evasive action. Although the gravity well generators tried to compensate for the momentum and inertia of a moving ship and tried to smooth out the ride, they could not do it entirely and so anyone not used to a ship's movements could be quite unsettled as it weaved and dodged incoming fire.

"All right over there?" Artisius shouted to the pair.

"How...," said Alfred as he was thrown off his feet by a particularly strong lurch. He collapsed on the side of the bridge and pulled himself to his feet. "How much more can we take?" He managed to get a sentence out before falling over again.

Draz just looked queasy. Sure, she had flown the pod to Earth earlier, as she had recounted to Artisius, and taken evasive manoeuvres, but Artisius could see she was unused to all this space flight. At least Alfred had experienced deep space flight before. However, it was clear to Artisius that neither was prepared for a military engagement.

Artisius smiled at the pair. "Oh, this old girl can take a lot more. I've flown her for thirty plus years. She's tough, and seen action before I can tell you." Just then, after another strong lurch, there was another loud bang and warning sirens started again. "Damage?" Artisius instantly forgot the pair trying to stay upright and keep their food down.

"More serious this time, sir," came the response. "Engine number four is damaged and leaking fuel."

"Cut power to engine four," Artisius ordered. "Damn it," he whispered to himself, they needed all the engine power they could get to escape the formidable defences on the Earth Ring. They were already many kilometres away by now, but the range of the defence guns was long, and they really needed to get as far away as possible.

"I know what you can do!" Artisius shouted to Alfred and Draz. "Alfred, I know you're a zetter, can you log in and make sure all processes are going smoothly with the onboard computer?" Artisius pointed at the empty zetting terminal on the bridge. "The damage we've sustained could have damaged the computer. I don't want to trust you with our lives, but I have to. Once again it's a matter of having no choice."

"Where is your zetter?" asked Alfred. It was obvious that Alfred, although he perked up at the notion, did not want to impinge on someone else's job.

"I don't keep one onboard, since *Florida Station*." There was bile in Artisius' voice.

Alfred nodded and moved to the terminal. He began the start up procedure. It would take a few minutes before the terminal was ready.

Artisius turned to Draz. "Can you man a gun turret? Not all my gunners made it back onboard from leave on Earth before we left in rather a hurry. I had to leave some crew behind. Those missiles are coming in thick and fast and if you could shoot any down before they hit us that would be great!" he said, partially and order, partially a request.

Draz, still looking queasy from the lurching of the ship, nodded in agreement, and was shown where one of the defence turret control consoles was on the lower level of the bridge, near the main walkway, by one of the guards. She fired up the system and put on the virtual reality headset as the turret came online. She charged the defence lasers in the turret and scanned the space around for incoming missiles.

"Sir," came the call from the Scanning Officer, who was in charge of radar and scanning for incoming objects and other ships. "We've detected part of the Collective Zone fleet starting to reorganise in the orbit of the Moon and prepare to move to an intercept course."

"Damn it, I was hoping to get further before they realised," Artisius muttered. "Keep tracking them, we'll have to outrun them," he called out to the officer. "This ship can go faster than anything in their fleet, they're warships, we're a mercenary frigate, and we're built for speed."

There was a large explosion and the ship lurched forward. "Where's that missile defence!?" Artisius yelled.

Draz nodded from within her virtual reality headset. "Almost online," she yelled back.

263

"Hurry up," Artisius said. He had absolute faith in his crew and ship, but he knew that even the *Green Dragon* could only withstand a certain number of missile and auto-turret hits.

***

Draz swore. She knew how to operate such a defence system, in theory. However, she had never really done it in practice. The virtual reality headset put her in the position of the defence gun on the underside of the *Green Dragon* and with the controllers she could move it around and fire it. The headset imposed a computer generated heads up display over her vision, which informed her of the incoming missiles and their trajectories so that she could shoot them down. It was all fine in theory, but on a lurching and bucking ship, it was harder to aim the defence gun than she had appreciated.

She knew she had to do something, so she locked the turret onto the nearest incoming missile and started to fire. The auto tracking system of the gun aided her targeting somewhat and the headset generated a fake firing noise and sensory feedback to aid the user.

After a few short shots, the missile exploded, and Draz let out a cry of success. "One down!" she yelled triumphantly as the ship took another harsh turn.

Draz, buoyed by her success, kept firing the defence gun and destroyed any missile that came within her line of fire and range. She was getting the hang of this, she thought.

***

"Excellent, keep it up!" yelled back Artisius. "We'll need more than one missile destroyed to get out of this," he whispered to himself. Again, he had confidence in his ship and crew, but he had underestimated the response of the Collective Zone to his escape. Not only did he have to

264

evade this section of the Earth Ring, he had to evade a section of the Great Fleet; the best war fleet in the system.

"How's that zet coming?" Artisius yelled over to Alfred.

Artisius watched as Alfred pressed lots of buttons and adjusted settings on the log in computer.

"Almost ready," Alfred responded quietly. He was plainly concentrating on what he was doing.

Artisius knew, although he now disliked zetters, that one false reading on the unused terminal and Alfred could end up with his brain fried on start-up.

***

"Okay, ready. Permission to..." Alfred paused, that had been his line when he had operated the zet terminal under Hestra back on *Florida Station*. He looked at Artisius. Artisius simply nodded.

Alfred jammed the zetting needle deep into the implant on the side of his head. Once more he felt the rush as the world bled away and was replaced by the circuitry of the unfamiliar *Green Dragon's* computer system.

Alfred raced through the system, soaring, diving and climbing through the endless wires of the ships computer systems. He had never experienced a system like this. He was used to the old and outdated network of *Florida Station*, which was also similar to the network that he zetted back on the Earth Moon, as that network too was very old and cobbled together. This network in the *Green Dragon* was totally different; it was new, modern, and high tech. He could move faster and there was more functionality. He felt an even greater rush than normal, too.

Stopping himself for a second, Alfred paused in his enjoyment of the system he had plugged into. He had to focus, he reminded himself. They were all in danger of being killed. He could not simply enjoy this experience.

Soaring through the system, Alfred checked for anomalies and breaks in the computer network, as he had done countless times before on *Florida Station*. He detected some problems and re-routed the signals and impulses with his mind so that the computer was guiding the ship with utmost precision and speed.

While flying through the engine systems of the ship Alfred paused for a while. Something was wrong with his feedback circuits. There was a slight fuzziness on the borders of his vision. Something like a cracking and blurring of his observation of the network. He tried to refresh his vision systems and reboot his optic sensors in an attempt to clear the problem, but nothing seemed to fix it.

Alfred felt a cold dread creep into his being. Was this another stage of zetting sickness? He did not know. But he had never experienced it before. Perhaps it was the modern system having an impact on his older hardware. He had not updated his firmware in a while and he reasoned that might be the cause of the problem, but he was not sure. He had a terrible feeling that the problem would get worse and now, without medication, he was terribly vulnerable.

Alfred rebooted his visual circuits one more time. This time the problem seemed to lessen, but not disappear. He continued with his job of optimising the network of the *Green Dragon*. He had a crucial job to do, and he would not let those dependent on him down.

***

Draz lurched in her virtual reality headset as she targeted another incoming missile and blew it to pieces with her defence gun. She let out a cry of satisfaction as the missile exploded before making contact with the hull. She was getting the hang of this, she thought. The heads up display and movement of the gun with the hand controls were coming naturally to her now.

Suddenly there were no more missiles. Draz paused a second, rotating her view around to see if anything more was incoming to the *Green Dragon*. Then the heads up display shut down and hands grabbed her virtual reality goggles and lifted them off her eyes. She blinked, trying to adjust her eyes to the surroundings again.

"What's happened?" she asked the attendant. He pointed to Artisius.

"We're out of range of their missiles, Draz," said Artisius from behind her. "Good job! You kept at least two dozen off our ship!"

Draz stood up uneasily and moved with a stagger. "I wish this ship's gravity well generators were better," she said, reaching out to steady herself on the hull.

"They're fine." Artisius laughed, his hips and torso rolling with the action of the ship. "Anyway, now we're out of range of the missiles all we have to do is avoid the auto-turret tracking systems for another few hundred kilometres, then we can activate inter-planetary drives and power away! The Collective Zone fleet won't be able to catch us then; this is the fastest ship in this sector of the system, only some Solar Solutions warships are faster."

Draz nodded, but said nothing; she just wanted the rough ride to stop. "What do you want me to do now?" she asked.

Artisius thought for a moment and his face was illuminated by the light of an auto-turret laser as it streaked past the observation dome. "Nothing much, ha, just enjoy the ride. We'll be out of range of their guns soon and then we can get your friend out of the zet terminal."

Draz gave a sidelong glance at Artisius, not quite knowing what he was after, but she accepted the fact that his words would come true and that they would soon be plotting a less hectic path through space.

Artisius indicated with an outstretched arm for Draz to move back to the command dais of the ship from her defence gun station near the bottom of the bridge. She moved past him, and they walked together back to the command level of the bridge.

Draz looked over to where Alfred was sitting. He was bolt upright and his lips were drawn back in what she knew as the zetter's grin. She had heard of it but had never really seen it. She had known what zetters could do, from her time on Earth, and what they were useful for, but she had never seen one in action before. Draz watched with horror as Alfred's body was contorted into what looked like painful muscle contractions with his back arched and face taught and eyes glassy but wide open.

"Horrid isn't it?" said Artisius behind her. He had noticed what she was looking at. His voice had a note of disgust in it.

Draz nodded. "But he helped me escape the Moon with his...talent. So, I owe him my life." She paused, thinking whether to say the next sentence to Artisius or not. Artisius was saving their lives too and had thrown away his allegiance with the Collective Zone, but Alfred and Draz had only known him a few dozen minutes and she was unclear as to whether she could trust him.

"I think he's dying," said Draz with sadness in her voice. She watched Alfred while she spoke to Artisius, so he could not see her face. She decided to voice her feelings. She either had to trust Artisius entirely or distrust him entirely, there would be no in between as they were destined to stay together until they reached Solar Solutions' territory. "That happens to zetters doesn't it?" She turned to face Artisius, hoping for him to say something reassuring.

"I'm sorry, but yes. I was part of the interrogation back on *Florida Station* before it exploded, and he was ill then," Artisius stated.

It was not what Draz wanted to hear. She grimaced.

"You care for him?" Artisius asked.

The combat outside the ship was forgotten, all that mattered was the conversation between the two of them. The ship rolled again just before an auto-turret laser streaked past the observation dome.

Draz thought for a moment before replying, she looked at Alfred again, who was totally oblivious to their conversation about him. "I owe him my life, and he owes his life to me. Whether it's any more I don't know, but I value his abilities," Draz said.

Artisius nodded.

***

"Sir!" called out the Helmsman of the *Green Dragon*. The past few dozen minutes had brought out the best in his piloting skills and he was drenched with sweat as he had avoided most of the deadly fire that came from the Earth Ring. "I think the fire has stopped."

Artisius turned from Draz and moved to the side of the Scanning Officer. "We are out of range, Captain!" said the officer with unbridled glee. "We made it!"

With a curt nod, Artisius moved back to the command dais and addressed his crew. "Men and women of the *Green Dragon*," his voice boomed over the loud speakers through the craft, "congratulations, thanks to the expert piloting of Lieutenant Orthox," he nodded to the Helmsman who was trying to calm down after half an hour of the most intense flying of his life, "and the expert actions of all of you, we have avoided the worst the Earth has to throw at us. We can now engage inter-planetary drives and power away. Set course for Europa! Yes, the

Collective Zone fleet is pursuing us, but we are faster than them and will outdistance them easily. They are gathered around the Moon, and as such are not in a good position to head us off. Artisius out!"

Artisius looked around the bridge of the craft and saw many of the crew had stood to attention in respect of his words. He indicated with his hands that they get back to work and silently they all sat down and continued with their tasks. He knew that his crew relied on him absolutely and now that he had pulled this off, they would follow him to the core of the Sun if he ordered them to.

"Easy, easy now." Artisius turned to hear the words uttered by Draz as she helped Alfred out of the zetting terminal. He noticed that there was some blood around the implant on the side of Alfred's head. He moved over to help Draz and Alfred. Draz gave him a careful look. Alfred's eyes were glassy, and he moved uneasily. They lay him down on the bridge floor.

"Is he all right?" asked Artisius.

"I don't know. He doesn't look it. I don't know about this stuff." Draz indicated the implant in Alfred's skull.

Alfred blinked. His eyes returned to normal, and he attempted to focus on the pair leaning over him. "I'm...all right..." he stuttered.

Draz smiled, looking somewhat relieved.

Alfred sat up and looked around. "What a rush!" he said with a gasp. He turned to Artisius. "Your system is state of the art and amazing to navigate!"

Artisius laughed. "Glad you enjoyed it, sonny," he said and Draz and Artisius helped Alfred to his feet. "You're welcome to zet there when you are needed," Artisius continued. Alfred licked his lips and tried to steady his shaking hands.

"Are you sure that's wise?" asked Draz.

"I'm not twelve you know, I can decide for myself what I want to do," said Alfred to Draz, she looked hurt. "Thank you," he said, turning to Artisius. "Sorry, but I love doing it!" he replied to Draz's hurt expression. She smiled, at least the rolling of the ship had stopped, and she stopped looking queasy.

"Now what?" Draz asked Artisius.

"Well, we need to get as far away from Collective space as possible, as fast as possible. I suggest we head to Europa, the boarder of Solar Solutions space to refuel and resupply and the head on to Neptune, the Solar Solutions' headquarters and deliver the red drive to them," Artisius replied.

"But the red drive must be destroyed!" blurted Draz. "I mean, cloaking technology is too much for anyone!"

"But think, the Collective Zone might already have the tech, we don't definitively know if they managed to copy it or not, you only think that they haven't. I cannot simply take the risk of destroying the drive if the Collective Zone might have the tech on it. And they have the more military able fleet than Solar Solutions. Sure, it will take them years to implement it and their current fleet will be without cloaking tech; but think of the long term! If we don't aid Solar Solutions then the Collective Zone could take over all space anyway. We have to take a side!" said Artisius.

"It's admirable that you want to help Solar Solutions, sir," said Alfred, "but I spent all my life under them, and they're no better than the Collective Zone. We cannot give them the technology."

Draz nodded her agreement.

"My ship, my rules," snapped Artisius. "I will help you, but first I need to help myself, and I believe that by helping Solar Solutions I do that best. Meeting over."

"But..." began Draz. Alfred caught her arm in an effort to stop her saying anything stupid to their host. Artisius' expression ended any argument.

"Sir!" interrupted one of the flight crew who had approached unnoticed. Artisius turned his attention to the woman. "We may have a problem about going to Europa. One of the missiles punctured the secondary fuel tanks and we're leaking fusion fuel."

"How far can we get?" asked Artisius.

"We might make Mars...With our fuel supplies we can keep the reactors going until then..." said the woman, nervously.

Alfred and Draz looked at each other. They had heard about Mars, everyone had.

"Mars..." Artisius paced the dais. "Mars?" He looked at the officer, Draz and Alfred. "Mars! Fine then, we head for Mars where we will repair and refuel. We should be able to get lost in all the detritus and criminals there. But we must be careful, we cannot attract too much attention, or the Earth Great Fleet will find us before we can pass into Solar Solutions space."

"Mars!?" whispered Draz to Alfred. "It's like the Earth Moon but without the security and not a prison...it's a criminal hideout."

Alfred nodded.

"Yes...so...we must stop at Mars. Not my first choice of port, but if it must be, it must be," said Artisius to Alfred and Draz, there was a little worry in his voice. "It shouldn't be too hard to lose the Collective Zone followers in the mess around that planet."

"How long will it take us to get there?" asked Draz. Artisius smiled as it was clear she was still unsure of planetary distances in her inexperience of space travel.

"About nine months," Artisius said grimly. "We should be able to outrun the Great Fleet all the way and then lose them there. I recommend cryo-sleep for most of the journey. It can be deadly boring otherwise, and it can help with..." he looked at Alfred, "...certain problems."

Alfred nodded his response, without saying a word.

Draz indicated her acceptance of the situation also, with look of anxiety.

Artisius wondered if she had ever used a cryo-pod before.

"Good. We will sleep all the way to Mars." Artisius clicked his fingers in satisfaction. "One good thing about cryo-sleep, it seems to prolong life, it's as if the body doesn't age in it so even though we will travel for nine months, we won't have aged more than a few days. Your hair does grow a bit though, slower than normal but it does grow."

Alfred ran his hand over the stubble on his scalp, still shaved from his prison experience. He wanted his hair back, but it would not grow much in cryo-sleep. Draz seemed at home without her hair, not noticing Alfred's discomfort.

"Now if you'll excuse me," Artisius turned to the pair, "I have to compose a message to be broadcast through a satellite here and bounced off towards Solar Solutions Headquarters around Neptune. They need to know what's been happening from a trusted source rather than any rumours they may hear." He nodded and moved back to the Communications Officer.

Artisius returned after a short time. "Now that the immediate danger is over," he continued, "how about some new clothes. You can't be comfortable in those blood soaked Collective Zone uniforms. And perhaps a wash?"

273

Draz responded enthusiastically to the suggestion of clean clothes, as did Alfred.

"As you're my guests, I'll show you to your quarters. This ship is well decked out and quite comfortable for the star traveller. We'll be in each other's company for a while, we might as well get to be friends," said Artisius, leading them out of the bridge and down the corridors to their independent rooms.

Chapter 28

"Sir! They're extending beyond the range of our missiles and auto-turrets!" cried out gunner Ractar of Epsilon Detachment of Earth Ring Defences. They were all stationed in front of their holo-terminals that each controlled one of the turrets on this station of the Earth Ring. He had more than a little trepidation in his voice. What he said meant that the *Green Dragon* had evaded their turrets and was now unhindered in open space. He ran his sweaty palms over his black uniform to dry them, but it was impossible.

"Damn it!" said his Detachment Commander Lumnor as he walked the row of computer terminals, all controlled by gunners of the Epsilon Detachment. "I'll have to report this to Fleet Command. They won't be happy, and they won't take all YOUR failures lightly." He spun on his heel and addressed his soldiers. They snapped to attention. "That ship destroyed part of Atraxa Prime, part of a station of the Earth Ring, and it evaded us. What do you have to say for yourselves?"

"Sir...we did hit it," came a tremulous voice from the ranks of soldiers.

"Oh, did we? Well, that's great, but it didn't go boom now did it? No, so we all failed," snapped Lumnor.

"Sir!..."

"This had better be good Ractar," snapped Lumnor turning precisely on his heel to face the gunner.

"It's leaking fuel! Sir, I mean, I think I hit it in its fuel tanks, yes, yes it's leaking fuel! I can detect it on the scanner," shouted Ractar somewhat joyously, and somewhat nervously, unsure of how his commander would react.

Suddenly Lumnor was beside him, tweaking the dials of the scanner to get a better image on the holo-screen. "I think you're right...I really do. That means..." he trailed off in thought. "I'll have to report this all to the Fleet Command, as it's up to them now to find and destroy those traitors. Nevertheless, well done soldiers, well done Ractar!"

Lumnor knew that a light frigate type of ship like the *Green Dragon* did not have that much in the way of fuel reserves. It would have needed all its main and secondary tanks to evade Collective Zone territory and head past the asteroids to somewhere around Jupiter or Saturn. They probably wanted to go to Europa first, one of Jupiter's moons. However, the fact that they were leaking fuel meant that they probably had to stop at Mars, he thought as he marched down the corridors of the Earth Ring to the transmission room ready to make his report.

He would inform the Fleet to make for Mars: an unpleasant colony always on the brink of rebellion and full of criminals. It was between the two empires and, as such, was rather lawless.

Lumnor made his report to the Fleet Command. They were both scathing of his failure to stop the frigate but also grateful of the news that the ship was leaking fuel for its reactors. They too realised that the ship would need to go to Mars.

"...and if they get there they can lose us, but they will have to be very careful not to fall on the wrong side of the gangs that rule that part of space..." continued Lumnor.

"Yes, yes, I know," said Fleet Commander Boltha. "I've flown past Mars before." She was the consummate military person. She was tall and wiry; no one really knew her age.

She had had undergone the arduous longevity surgery procedure at least twice, or so the rumours went. Behind her angular face and sharp, piercing eyes was a brain that knew how to conduct fleet tactics with absolute dedication and precision. She had closely shaved hair. She had no time for hairstyles. Hers was a desire only to make war and now, she had the chance. "We will make for Mars. It's unlikely that we will cut them off, but we should be able to blockade the planet and make sure they do not leave. Is there anything more, Detachment Commander?"

She said the words with a little too much disdain for Lumnor's liking. "No, ma'am," Lumnor snapped to attention in front of the computer screen. The messages taking a little while to reach from the Earth Ring to the Great Fleet in orbit around the Moon, meaning a slight delay.

"Good, Boltha out," the video feed went dead.

Lumnor visibly relaxed. He was not sure what would happen now. His part of the fight was over, and they had acted admirably, but they had let the ship escape.

Lumnor looked out the nearest window to the Moon which floated like a great warning to all on Earth and above it to be careful or you would be sent there as a prisoner.

He shuddered and hoped they would catch those traitors and make them pay for what they did.

Chapter 29

"This is Fleet Commander Boltha broadcasting to all the Collective Zone fleet currently in orbit around the Moon. Cease all pacification activity immediately and reboard your troops for preparation to embark upon a mission to Mars. We must stop the *Green Dragon* frigate from breaking into Solar Solutions space. They are leaking fuel, so they have to stop at Mars. Our orders are to blockade the planet until they give themselves up. We are to use all means necessary to achieve our goals." A smile entered her voice. "This is what we've been waiting for. Further orders will come when we have achieved this objective. Boltha out." Boltha grinned, they had been busy making sure the Moon prison got back to order but now, they had a real mission. It had been too long since she had sailed her fleet to war. It was what she lived for. She made her way out of the bridge and down towards the docking bay.

Boltha disliked speeches, so she kept her words to the fleet to simple orders and instructions. She did not believe that her words alone would inspire her soldiers. They were trained to do what they do, and that was that.

Boltha was the supreme commander of the Collective Zone fleet. Maxtria was Master of the Fleet, from Earth. Boltha was Fleet Commander of the fleet, from her command ship. She had final say on battle tactics and manoeuvres. Boltha always wondered at the point of Maxtria, but she respected her Earth bound rival.

The broadcast boomed through all the ships arrayed around the Moon. Immediately the ships' transports picked up the soldiers from the prison and Moon's surface and ferried them back to their waiting warships.

The fleet consisted of thirty odd craft of various sizes, ranging from near *Green Dragon* frigate size to full battleship and battle cruiser sized craft that stretched for nearly a kilometre. They hung in what seemed like suspended animation above the surface of the Earth Moon, waiting for the order to embark on their mission. They glittered in the starlight, light from the distant Sun reflecting off their white, silver and blue hulls.

The pride of the fleet was the *Iron Bastion*, Fleet Commander Boltha's flagship. It was massive. It was a kilometre long and was bristling with weapons. It had enough firepower to reduce a large portion of a planet to glass by itself. It had a squadron of fighters docked on board, along with a whole regiment of soldiers, and was primarily and only a warship of the highest order.

There were only two such craft in the entire Collective Zone's arsenal: the *Iron Bastion* and the *Old Monarch*. One always stayed near the Earth to protect it. The other was able to make journeys into the solar system. This time it was the *Iron Bastion's* turn to lead the Great Fleet.

On the prow of both the *Iron Bastion* and the *Old Monarch* was the symbol of the Collective Zone: the stylised yellow Earth surrounded by the silver Earth Ring.

The docking bay of the *Iron Bastion* was a hive of activity. Dozens of craft were coming in to dock through the magnetic shields on the entrance to the docking bay from the Moon's surface as the troops the ship had deployed returned and readied themselves for inter-planetary travel.

The docking bay was at the front of the *Iron Bastion,* and it looked like an open maw ready to disgorge all manner of fighter and boarding craft towards any perceived threat.

Fleet Commander Boltha oversaw the preparations from the observation deck behind a thick glass wall at the top and rear of the docking bay. She felt proud of her soldiers. They would do justice to their training, their ship, and their Collective. She would bring the traitors to heel and one of her ships in the fleet would bring them back to Collective territory for trial and execution or, if they resisted, she would have their ship blown to smithereens by the many auto-turret and missile batteries on her dozens of craft.

What hope did one puny frigate have against the might of the Great Fleet? Then they would progress with the rest of the fleet into Solar Solutions space and crush that pathetic excuse for a corporation.

"All craft onboard, ma'am," said one of the flight officers. "All ships report embarkation complete."

Boltha smiled a wicked grin. She was going to enjoy this. She left the docking bay observation deck with a sharp spin on her heel and marched the long march back to the bridge.

When Boltha reached the bridge, situated near the rear of the ship to afford a wide view over its hull, it was already buzzing with activity, just as she would have expected. When she entered the black and grey steel room, all the crew and staff snapped to attention.

"Admiral on the bridge!" shouted the First Officer.

Fleet Commander Boltha nodded to him and took her position at the front of the bridge near the panoramic observation windows. From this position she could see the surface of the Moon off to her left, a whole sweep of the fleet off to the centre and right, and the stars glinting off in the very far distance to the right.

Dead ahead was the Earth in the middle distance, a poisoned orb of yellow and brown, but the birthplace of humanity and Boltha's home, she would never forget that, no matter how far and long she travelled with a fleet, it was always the sight of the Earth that got to her. She paused, observing its imperfections, and then addressed the crews of her ships through the intercom.

"We are ready, for our ancient home, we move!" Boltha spoke the few words with reverence and made a signal with her hands. The bridge crew jumped into action and in a moment Boltha could feel the rumble of the ship's engines engage and the fleet began to form up and prepare for the journey to Mars. "They won't know what hit them..." she whispered to herself in a form of promise as the Earth slipped beyond the range of vision of the bridge windows as the ships turned and proceeded to move through the void.

"Ma'am, your cryo-pod is ready," said a technician who had approached unnoticed to Boltha's side.

She did not notice him for a minute and then with a short click of her fingers Boltha spoke. "Good, good. I will be there shortly," she said still staring out the window into space. She could tell the fleet had accelerated to cruising speed by the rumble of the deck under her feet. The technician bowed and moved back into the shadows.

Fleet Commander Boltha always liked the view of space through a starship's windows in a sort of melancholy way. The stars were out there, so tantalising, yet so far away. One day, one day humans will make it to other stars, was the thought that always went through her mind. One day, and she would not be there to see it. It always galled her that her time had been spent just in the Solar System and that she could not go and explore the galaxy.

"One day..." she mouthed silently, turning from the broad windows of the bridge. She began to walk away to head to her private quarters, but she stopped for an instant and looked back out the large windows, all other things to do with fleet action and war forgotten. "One day..." she whispered.

Suddenly her reverie was forgotten, and she came to her senses. She had a job to do for her Collective and she would not fail. She marched out of the bridge and prepared for the nine month cryo-sleep to Mars.

Chapter 30

After a wash and a fresh set of clothing, both Alfred and Draz felt much better. Neither of them could remember when they had seen such luxury. They emerged from their individual assigned quarters, which were next to each other. They were amazed at the luxury and elegance of the quarters of for what was for all intents and purposes a cargo ship. Artisius was there in the corridor to greet them.

"So, you smell less!" he said with a laugh. They both looked rather embarrassed. He led them down the passageway to his own quarters.

"How does a cargo ship, no offence, have such...?" Draz waved her hands around, not knowing the right word.

"Luxury?" aided Artisius. "Well, some things I transport pay well, and have a high demand, so I make a tidy profit playing Solar Solutions and Collective Zone off against each other..." he paused for thought. "But no more. I seem to have thrown in my lot with you and Solar Solutions..."

"Voluntarily, of course...you cannot blame us," said Alfred quietly.

"Yes, yes I know it was my decision, but your arrival rather forced my hand. Anyway, enough of that. The point is I used to traffic some interesting things, and they paid well." Artisius waved the subject away with his hands. He opened the door to his quarters, and they all stepped inside. "Brandy?" he asked.

"What...sort of things?" asked Draz, she seemed intrigued.

"Oh, I suppose it doesn't matter now..." Artisius tried to bury the topic.

Draz had caught a scent and was not going to let go. "What did you traffic?" she demanded.

Artisius sighed. "Slaves, to be turned into tech-slaves. Drugs, all sorts. Lots of different contraband that both sides paid handsomely for."

Alfred was silent. He did not really care. He scratched his implant. He accepted the brandy that Artisius offered. It burned his throat.

"Drugs!?" mouthed Draz, evidently enlivened by the word. "What sort of drugs? Do you have any onboard?"

Artisius looked uneasily at her. "Is that an academic question or is there a more sinister reason behind it?"

"Look, I used, back on Earth, and it's been a while since I last did, but I really would like to again, that rush is unparalleled." Draz looked down at the floor as she let her feelings go.

Alfred looked at her, he had only known her a short time, but he was shocked. This was a weakness to her that he had not expected and had not seen. "You can't be serious?"

"You have your zetting!" Draz snapped, more viciously than she wanted to as indicated by the look of contrition that crossed her face moments later.

To Alfred she looked suddenly fidgety.

"True, but it's a job..." said Alfred. "I work for it; I don't just sniff some chemical."

"But you understand the feeling, the rush and you need it more and more!" Draz sat on the edge of the bed in Artisius' room her head in her hands. "Okay it's my weakness, but we all have them. I had to limit myself in prison, mostly, but now with the mention of it...argh I've always had cravings." She hit herself on the temple with the palm of her hand a number of times.

284

Artisius had moved over to a bedside table and opened a draw. Within was a small silver package. He unwrapped it and within there was a small mound of off white powder. "Perhaps, this can help?" he said coolly.

Alfred looked disturbed.

Draz's head snapped up and stared at the powder. "What is it?" she asked, her eyes flashing. "What strength?"

"Ferkis powder. Alpha grade," Artisius said. "Do you want some? I don't use it, but I keep some of my supply around for...emergencies." He cocked his head to the side while looking at Draz.

Draz nodded dumbly. Artisius scraped off a bit onto a silver plate that was on the sideboard in his room where the drinks were kept. He put away the rest in his bedside table. He formed the pile of powder into a line and gave the plate to Draz.

Draz gave Artisius the most pathetic expression of thanks on her face. Alfred said nothing. Draz snorted the line into her right nostril and her pupils contracted to pinpoints, and she collapsed backwards slowly onto Artisius' bed.

"Well, that's her out of it for a while," Artisius said.

"Why did you do that?" said Alfred.

"Do what? She took it." Artisius raised his hands in mock surrender.

"You offered it. You mentioned it," said Alfred. He watched Draz as she lay on the bed, semi catatonic. He could not help think of his zetting though, and how he loved it.

"Oh, don't get all moralistic with me. I'm a freelance trader. I traffic in unpleasant things sometimes. It's MY job," Artisius sighed, and deflated somewhat. "How's the brandy?"

"Good," said Alfred, "from Neptune?"

Artisius nodded. "Look we'd better get her to her own bed." He pointed at Draz, who was breathing very shallowly and slowly. Alfred nodded.

Alfred and Artisius carried Draz awkwardly back to her own quarters and deposited her onto her own bed; the soft white sheets embraced her in her drugged stupor.

"How long does it last?" asked Alfred.

"About half an hour," replied Artisius not looking at him, instead watching Draz. "She'll have to be sober to go into cryo-sleep though, so we can't do that for a bit. Ah well, want a tour of the ship?" said Artisius in an upbeat way.

"I suppose," said Alfred. "You won't tell me where that red hard drive is...?"

Artisius laughed and tapped his nose. "I need my little insurance policies," he replied, shaking his head a little.

They left Draz on her bed and wandered the ship.

***

Alfred was given a tour of the ship, but he paid little attention. He was more worried about Draz's sudden relapse into drug use. She had seemed so strong willed to him, so sure of herself, and then this happened. Even though he had only been in prison with her a short time, he had not noticed the drug use she mentioned. When he had watched her taking the drug, it was as if she were a different person, a slave. The change was so sudden that he could not believe that she was the same person.

Artisius gave the tour in a distracted way. It was obvious that Alfred was not really paying attention. He paused at the door to the crew quarters.

"You're bothered about her aren't you?" Artisius looked concerned.

"Yes. What happened back there," Alfred waved his hands indicating back at the private quarters, "was unusual

286

and I've never seen her behave that way before. I mean, I've only known her a short time, but she was so headstrong and determined...then...that!"

"Ah...we mustn't judge too harshly," Artisius replied. "We all do...undesirable things. Sometimes it's all about surviving, and what we can do to survive..." He paused in thought and looked at his chronometer. "That's about half an hour. We should be getting back. She'll be waking up again. Then we can put you both into cryo-sleep."

Alfred, looking cynical, said as a passing comment, "What guarantee do we have that we won't end up as tech-slaves or in some other prison or just vented into space?" Alfred gave a sidelong glance at Artisius. "We've only known you a few hours, and although you seem to have thrown in your lot with us and Solar Solutions and abandoned the Collective Zone...you understand my concerns. I've been accused of terrible things in the past and imprisoned, as you know. You took me there."

Artisius, did not look offended, and replied not looking at Alfred but staring off down the corridor. "I understand your concern, and I would have the same in your position. But believe me; the Collective Zone will want my head on a pike by now, so I won't be going back there. And as for the other things, I maybe a freelance trader, a smuggler, a slave trader, and a drug runner but I have principles!" He laughed.

Alfred smiled too, not quite sure why he did so.

"No really," Artisius continued, "I won't abandon you again, I have realised that I have had to choose a side and I need to clean up my life. Too long have I relied on deception and shadowy trading. I believe the ancient saying was 'turn over a new leaf'...And, if I pull off the sale of the drive to Solar Solutions..." he said with a grimace.

"Sale?" Alfred asked, his eyebrows raised.

"Hah, never mind." Artisius furrowed his brow. "Old habits...Shall we go back?"

Alfred nodded and they moved back through the shiny corridors of the *Green Dragon* with little words spoken. Alfred sensed that Artisius was a little ashamed at taking Alfred and the other prisoners from *Florida Station* to the Moon, but he did not raise the issue and Artisius seemed grateful that he did not.

On the way Artisius paused for a moment in a lift and turned to Alfred. "How's the head, the implant?"

"Fizzing," Alfred said, guarded at first, but then after a moment he opened up a little more. "It's deteriorating. Truth is, I'll be glad to go into cryo-sleep, it seems to calm it down and give me a little more life. But the deterioration is noticeable. For example, in the zet on this ship I noticed artefacts in the visual representation of the network."

Artisius nodded as the lift door slid open to the command deck floor, where their rooms were. "How's the memory? I've heard that can go too," he asked.

"Yeah, at the moment it's all right. I haven't noticed much memory deterioration. It's mainly irritation at the moment..." Alfred sighed; he knew what he had to look forward to.

They reached Draz's quarters after a while and walked in to see her sitting up on the end of the bed rubbing her head and looking rather sketchy.

"Well, how was it?" asked Artisius.

"Amazing!" Draz said. "That's the purest I've ever had. Where'd you get it?" She looked up at the pair. Her pupils had returned to normal, but she still moved a little jerkily and her voice was a little cracked.

"The distilleries I get that from are secret and I know how to keep a secret," said Artisius. "I can't tell you everything, only that there's plenty more where that came from."

Alfred shot a glance at Artisius, somewhat angrily. He looked back at Draz and helped her uneasily to her feet. He said nothing about it.

"Now, where's that red hard drive?" Draz said with a smile.

Artisius shook his finger at her. "As I told your friend here, I need some insurance so I will not be disclosing that..."

Draz looked icily at him.

"So, what was that about getting ready for cryo-sleep?" Alfred said.

"Yes, well," Artisius sounded grateful for the change in topic, "if you'll follow me?" He left the room and the pair followed him.

Draz shook off Alfred's aid to walking. "I can manage," she said, a little too harshly.

Alfred let go of her arm.

The trio moved through the *Green Dragon's* corridors to the special room that held all the crew's cryo-pods.

"So, the ship just goes on auto-pilot does it?" asked Draz.

"Sort of, there's a skeleton crew that make sure everything's okay, and that gets rotated throughout the journey," replied Artisius.

"And we just sleep? Do we dream?" asked Draz, there was a tremor of nerves in her voice. "I've never done this before."

"Sometimes you dream," said Alfred. "I did this once on the way to the Moon. It was on this ship. But you just get frozen and then wake up months later at your location."

"But what wakes you up?" asked Draz.

"Other crew, or the computer if it's programmed," said Artisius.

"Right, well I want my computer set to a little early if that's okay!" it was not a request from Draz, she was clearly nervous.

They approached a large door and it opened in front of them. Within the room were rows upon rows of cryo-pods for use by the crew and passengers. The rows stretched off into the darkness. Some were already in use and Alfred wondered the difference between these pods and the pods he and the fellow prisoners had been interned in on the way to the Moon. These were probably more reliable and more expensive, he reasoned to himself, but said nothing.

The trio approached a set of silver cryo-pods, and the tech-slave crews began the start up procedure on them.

Draz looked anxiously at the rows of cryo-pods.

"Why did you do that?" asked Alfred.

"Do what?" asked Draz.

"The drugs," said Alfred. "I did not pick it in you."

"So? I take drugs?" Draz said. "I have for a while now. Before, during and after the Moon, if you must know. I don't care if you have a problem with that," she huffed. "You have your zetting!"

Alfred raised his hands in defeat. "Okay, okay, look, there's nothing to fear about cryo-sleep." He did not mention the small chance that sometimes the person in the pod did not wake up.

"It's perfectly safe," said Artisius.

Draz looked doubtfully at them both.

Artisius gestured for someone to enter the nearest pod. Alfred was about to enter the pod when Artisius interrupted. "Clothes off," he said.

Alfred looked puzzled. "But last time I was in clothing, on the way to the Moon?" he said, creasing his brow.

"That was because you were a prisoner, and we did not really care about you. You're not supposed to wear full clothing in these things. Underwear's fine though," said Artisius.

Alfred nodded and stripped off his clothes to his underwear and stashed the clothes in the locker next to the pod where Artisius indicated. He then climbed into his pod. A tech-slave began making adjustments to the controls on the side of the pod.

Draz looked nervous and, after taking off her clothes down to her underwear and stashing the clothes as Alfred had, climbed into her pod.

"It's like a prison cell," she whispered.

Alfred heard this but said nothing as the pod closed around him and he was frozen in time. Suddenly, there was complete nothingness.

Chapter 31

CEO Gunter awoke with a start. His emergency intercom was chiming, and he rolled over in his luxurious bed to check the time before he answered the pinging machine next to his bed on the side table. It was early in the morning, too early. *Neptune Prime* had not yet moved onto the daytime cycle, and that would not for a good few hours.

Gunter considered turning off the intercom and rolling back over and going to sleep, but he knew that the intercom would not sound unless there was an emergency, and as the head of the Solar Solutions Corporation he knew that he had to answer any emergency call no matter the hour.

He sat up and gave the verbal command and the lights in the room came on. As head of Solar Solutions, he had the penthouse and most luxurious apartment in *Neptune Prime*. His sheets in his bed were silk. The room he was in was full of wood panelling, exceedingly rare at this point in the Solar System. He had the finest drinks in all the Solar System on his drinks cabinet. He had the finest carpets on the floor. He had anything he could ever want.

Gunter looked over across his bed to the young woman lying, still somehow asleep, face down and naked under the silken sheets. He smiled.

Gunter got up and put on a dressing gown. He picked up the intercom and walked over the rich carpets of his bedroom and out onto the balcony that was shielded against the harshness of space, and he stared down at the vast structure that was *Neptune Prime*.

His artificial right leg whirred and clicked on the cold metallic surface of the balcony. He noticed it again. He had almost forgotten about it, but there it was, always haunting him. It was well fitted and should not have caused him any problems, physically. But mentally he hated the thing. It reminded him that he was not complete.

Gunter had lost his right leg in an airlock accident when he was twenty years old. One of the airlocks on *Neptune Prime* had malfunctioned and slammed shut on his leg. The doctors had tried to operate and save it but there was no hope. He had always resented that.

Neptune Prime stretched away down and out from his penthouse suite. He looked back at the view to take his mind off his troubles. It was the largest space station owned by Solar Solutions. It was constantly being updated and modernised. It held approximately two billion people not counting menial labourers like tech-slaves.

The station was of a bulbous construction, which was not elegant or pretty, but it was efficient and allowed for as much space to be used for required purposes as possible. It stretched from the turbulent atmosphere of Neptune, where it generated some of its power through wind turbines laced throughout the planet's atmosphere to Gunter's penthouse apartment at the top of the highest point of the main spire many hundreds of kilometres into harsh space above the equally harsh atmosphere. It was the heart of the Solar Solutions Empire. From it went instructions to all the far reaches of the Solar System and Gunter was the head of it all.

The CEO smiled again as he surveyed his territory. His view from the balcony stretched from the deep blue of the Neptune surface to the dark blackness of space and the pinpoints of light that dotted the sky. All those stars, all those other planets, all those things he would never see.

Gunter was not old; he was only in his mid forties. He was the youngest CEO Solar Solutions had had in a long time. Nevertheless, he knew that even with longevity surgery he would never see the other stars. He had never really seen the Sun closer than the boundary of Solar Solutions space. He had never been closer than Jupiter.

The intercom was still chiming. He decided to answer it, looking back at the naked woman in his bed.

"Yes? What?" he snapped.

The intercom was silent for a second and then came the clear voice of his deputy, Chief Operating Officer Cranmere, "CEO Sir, we have an emergency message for you!"

"Is it really urgent? Or is it another one of those false alarms you always seem to burden me with?" replied Gunter. He liked playing games with Cranmere's emotions.

"CEO Sir." The COO sounded desperate. "This really is important. I can't tell you over unsecured lines, but please come down to Operations and hear the message."

"You can't tell me anything now?" said the CEO. This was different; usually Cranmere would talk on any line. "On my personal communicator?"

"CEO Sir, just come down here!" snapped the COO, a little too harshly for his position, Gunter thought.

The COO realised his transgression and was about to apologise for his tone when Gunter responded. "Good, you're learning how to motivate people, that's good. I will come down presently." He hung up before the COO could continue.

Gunter paused a few more minutes, soaking in the view that he never got tired of. He then turned and went back into his apartment. He dressed in a business suit. He preferred the old style of dress to the more modern, semi military, uniforms that many of the station commanders had adopted. He liked the much older suit and tie that people in his position had worn all those centuries ago back on Earth. He viewed it as civilised. It was pre Collective.

The woman in his bed moved and sat up as he was dressing. "What time is it?" She rubbed her eyes. She was beautiful, like all the other ones that he had procured over the years. He was not even totally sure of her name. He had only met her last night; it was arranged by his boardroom. Whatever he wanted, he got.

Gunter did not want to alarm her, so he simply said, "Early, I'm needed for urgent business."

"Now?" She groaned. "But aren't I urgent business?" She winked at him playfully.

He moved over and kissed her. He lingered. "You are, but my COO wants me," he said as he left the room.

"Do you love your COO more than me?" she said, as he left the room and left the apartment.

Gunter heard her sink back into the bed and fall asleep quickly after ordering the lights to switch off as the door to the apartment closed behind him.

CEO Gunter made his way through the top layers of *Neptune Prime*. He had his own private lifts, corridors, guards, and passageways through to the Operations Deck where much of the running of the space station was done.

As he approached the Operations Deck, flanked by two guards, he was greeted by the enthusiastic yet overly clingy and fat COO Cranmere who, in his attempts to ingratiate himself with his leader, only seemed to embarrass himself.

The Operations Deck was a very large, dark room filled with computer terminals and communications equipment. It was where all the electronic operations for the station were done. It was highly classified and secret and only those with high clearance were allowed in. It had a number of zetting terminals and always had at least one zetter working at any time.

"What's the problem, Cranmere?" snapped Gunter as he was shepherded towards the long-range communications terminal.

"Sir, we have received a transmission from Earth..." began Cranmere, waving the comm-operators away from the terminal and pressing a few buttons himself.

"And?" said Gunter. He was rather surprised, from Earth. Cranmere's half sentence seemed to intimate that he should understand everything due to just a few words.

Cranmere floundered. "And...well...it's about the Collective Zone fleet..." he paused, as if to suggest that there was more but the CEO should work it out from what the COO had just said.

"Look, Cranmere," sighed Gunter, "I'm sure you understand what you are talking about, but I need more information. I'm surprised there's a message from Earth, yes, but I need more info if I'm going to understand. Also, it's 4am standard Earth time and I'm tired. What is going on?"

Cranmere, embarrassed, indicated that the CEO should sit down in the chair and when he had done so, the message was replayed.

The face of Artisius appeared on the monitor. Gunter smiled; he knew Artisius. He sat and listened as Artisius outlined the situation.

"...and so, we blasted out of Earth space. We will seek repairs at Mars but would love to be welcomed into Solar Solutions space..." Artisius explained a few things and continued, "The Great Fleet is on the move, Gunter. They're going to move into Solar Solutions space, and they want blood. They're not just chasing us; they want war. Get your fleet ready. There will be bloodshed. Understand this, I would not be involving you unless it was urgent, but get your fleet ready; and prepare for war." The last thing was

Artisius' worried face staring at the recording screen. The communication went dead.

Gunter looked at Cranmere. They could see the fear in each other's faces. "Ah," is all Gunter said, all annoyance with Cranmere forgotten.

"CEO Sir, what do we do?" pleaded Cranmere.

"Ready the fleet. And prepare a Council of War. We can take them on. We've done it before; before my time...We have advanced warning, we'll probably meet their fleet around Saturn or Jupiter as most of our fleet is around Saturn anyway, with some around Jupiter. We only have the Home Fleet around Neptune at this point." Gunter was babbling. He, personally, had never been to war before. "I need to think on this, get the Council ready. I will confer with them." He moved stiffly and anxiously out of the Operations Deck and back to his penthouse to sleep.

"CEO Sir!" Cranmere saluted. It was an awkward motion, but in the situation, it was the right thing to do.

***

When CEO Gunter walked into the boardroom, the board members there stood for him out of respect. Only Chief Weapons Officer Michael did not stand, for he was old and required a cane to move around. He was an old and experienced member of the boardroom. He knew Gunter's father. And he knew Gunter. Gunter respected the man more than the others.

"So," said Gunter, sitting down at the head of the metal table; his mechanical leg whirring as it compensated for the change in weight. He scanned the faces in the room looking expectantly towards him. The room was sparsely decorated and made mostly of bare metal. It had large windows at each end; one looking out over the planet Neptune, the other looking towards the centre of the Solar System and focused on the small pinprick of light that was the Sun. It was supposed to be symbolic of the position of the Solar Solutions Corporation: one foot on Neptune, but also rooted firmly in the human Solar System.

Gunter did not care for the symbolism much; the room was built long before his time as CEO. He just wanted to get on with living the life of a senior official in the Corporation. "So," he said again, "we've all seen the message."

The board members all nodded in unison and a faint murmur went around the room.

"And," Gunter continued, raising a hand to quieten the murmur, "although the message was dire, I think we should all move a motion to thank the messenger." He paused while the motion was passed unanimously and with much agreement as to the intelligence of their CEO and leader.

"But," Gunter continued again, "I also think that it would be best not to send him aid, as it was his action in escaping Earth that brought about the initiation of the march to war of the Collective Zone." He paused for the expected nods of agreement and praise, that did not come. Gunter froze, would he have to go to war? Could he not get out of this? "Do I detect...dissent?" he said quietly.

"CEO Sir," said a nondescript female board member who Gunter did not really know the name of, and did not really care, "sir," she continued when he looked at her vaguely, "Captain Artisius has gone to great lengths to give us this warning, and you want simply to ignore it by not sending aid? That, with respect, is ludicrous..." she trailed off.

There was a murmur of agreement around the table and Gunter realised that he was outnumbered in his view, and he had to change it fast in order to maintain control.

"My friends," Gunter began again. He always used that term of his board members when he wanted to placate them, and they knew it too. "My friends, all I merely meant was that we should not be rash in our response to the *Green Dragon's* distress signal. I will of course be mobilising our fleet, which at this present moment is located around this planet and also partially around Saturn. The forward portions are even now forging their way around Jupiter." He finished with a flourish of his hands pointing at the window that faced the Sun.

Internally Gunter was screaming. All he wanted was to stay on Neptune. He knew where all this was leading. He could not go to war.

There was silence for a moment, and then the boardroom erupted, not so spontaneously, into applause.

"Now, Fleet Officer?" Gunter turned to a balding and fat man wheezing at a corner of the table.

The man seemed to wake up. "CEO Sir!" He saluted.

Gunter smiled at the man. "What do you suggest we do?"

The Fleet Officer paused in his admiration for a second and coughed lightly.

"CEO Sir," the Fleet Officer adopted a conciliatory tone. "Sir, perhaps we should consolidate our fleet from around our Empire at Saturn. Then we can form up and go further in-system to Jupiter and make our first line of resistance there. If we need to fall back we will have plenty of space to do so."

"Good, then we will withdraw from Jupiter while sending our Home Fleet to meet up at Saturn. Then the fleets, once they have joined, will proceed back to Jupiter to resist on our first line of defence," Gunter said with a smile. He was not stupid; he needed to listen to his officers, as he was not a military man himself.

The Fleet Officer bowed his head and smiled. "Indeed, CEO Sir, I will get on it right away."

"One thing I wanted to ask," said Gunter. "The destruction of *Florida Station*, that couldn't've been a Collective Zone preliminary attack could it? Some sort of commando raid or something? Infiltrating our stations?"

"Unlikely, sir," said a young woman who took up the post of Security Officer. "From what we can gather it was some sort of emergency coolant failure on the main reactor. It's hard to determine as the station was blown to smithereens, but as far as we can tell it was not a Collective Zone plot; more an internal affair. We have it under control. We detected no communications to or from the Collective Zone from *Florida Station* at that time of the explosion."

"Will you be joining the fleet to lead them with your brilliance, CEO Sir?" asked the Fleet Officer, his double chin wobbling mesmerically, breaking Gunter's attention regarding *Florida Station*.

"Do you think I should, Cranmere?" asked Gunter genuinely of the COO who had remained silent yet attentive through the whole meeting so far.

"Well, CEO Sir, think of what the Collective Zone CEO would do and then, because, you understand, that you are so much greater than he is, you would have to do more," wheezed the COO. The other board members nodded emphatically and voiced their appreciation of Gunter's brilliance.

"And what would Uxus do? It is Uxus isn't it still?" sighed Gunter. He did not want to go to war. He just wanted to enjoy himself and let his deputies run the corporation.

"Yes, sir, it is Uxus," chimed in a board member.

"Fine, prepare my shuttle." Gunter slumped in his chair. "I will rendezvous with my flagship the *Silver Ark* and proceed to lead my forces in a glorious repulsion of the

Collective Zone forces. Due to our engine advantage our ships are faster, but their ships have heavier guns and are more armoured."

Gunter did not quite believe what he was saying but he had to do it, otherwise the board could vote him out and vote another CEO in and he could not have that. He would lose his penthouse. Besides, how hard could it be to defeat the Collective Zone? Solar Solutions ships were far superior and as the Collective fleet got further from Earth its supply lines would stretch and his supply lines would shorten.

Although Gunter knew that many of his subordinates were sycophantic cronies, they did want to do the best for Solar Solutions and Gunter knew that if they suggested that he go, personally, to war then it was the best option. He knew above all else that good morale was crucial for the waging of a war, and even if his immediate board room were sycophantic, the run of the mill line soldier on a ship almost worshiped the CEO and if he could inspire his soldiers to do just that little bit extra by being on the front line, then he had to do it. They all believed in him. It was a blessing and a curse. The blessing was that he could do as he pleased on *Neptune Prime*; the curse was he had to live up to their expectations otherwise he would be replaced.

"...CEO Sir...sir?" one of the board members was asking him something, but Gunter was away with his thoughts.

"Mmm?" Gunter said finally.

"Are you all right, sir?" was the question.

"Me? Yes, quite fine..." He did not want to go to war.

Gunter stood up; his leg whirred into action. The other board members stood up too, except Michael, and bowed. Gunter waved to them to stand upright. He had other things to think about.

301

"I will be in my quarters getting ready. Prepare the fleet..." Gunter left the room with a clicking and whirring of his leg and a mind full of thoughts of mild despair.

Chapter 32

CEO Gunter looked out the window of the shuttle he was in as it transported him and a few other board members to the part of the Solar Solutions fleet that was locked in orbit around Neptune. They were all crammed within the tight confines of the shuttle and were headed towards the flagship of the Solar Solutions fleet, the *Silver Ark*. It boasted the common Solar Solutions military ion engines that were fitted to all Solar Solutions military vessels. These allowed it to travel faster than its Collective Zone counterparts.

"Magnificent, isn't it, sir?" said the COO a little too closely to Gunter for his liking. But Cranmere had a point, Gunter had to admit, the fleet looked awe-inspiring.

As they neared, the rest of the fleet became visible. The *Silver Ark* was a massive construction. It was made of bright silvery metal and overlayed with white panels in places so that it glittered in the half-light of the very distant Sun. It was of a smooth construction with a large number of the missile turrets and auto-targeting laser cannons anchored to what looked like large silver wings that protruded from each side of the craft. Its docking bay was slung underneath its main body, a hole pointing forward at the front of the docking bay that opened up into a cavernous space within that held many dozens of smaller craft; troop transports, fighters, bombers, and other supply craft.

The Solar Solutions symbol was emblazoned on the side of the nose of the *Silver Ark*: the symbol of a trident; the symbol of Neptune.

The rest of the fleet looked paltry in comparison to the *Silver Ark*; but the people in the pod knew that the main parts of their fleet would meet up on the journey towards Jupiter.

The other dozen ships surrounding the *Silver Ark* were much smaller than it but of a similar silvery metallic and white panel construction that made them glitter like small stars in the light. The ships had all taken up a guarding formation around the *Silver Ark* to honour the arrival of their CEO to the flagship.

"Nothing can stand against that, sir," said Cranmere in a whisper again in Gunter's ear as they neared the *Silver Ark* and were swallowed up by its cavernous docking bay.

"It is certainly very impressive, Cranmere," said Gunter, rather overcome by the spectacle of the whole thing.

Gunter knew he would have to make a speech to the top brass when he boarded the ship and as he had never been to war he was rather apprehensive about the whole situation.

He did not want to take the pride of the Solar Solutions fleet into a battle where it could be damaged or worse, he could be killed. He knew he was inexperienced in these matters and his inferiors' reliance on his instructions could cost lives, many lives. However, he did not say any of this to anyone; he simply kept the worry inside himself and hoped for the best.

They all had such faith in him. It was uncanny. He had inherited the Solar Solutions Corporation from his father, who had been a good CEO and general; but Gunter was always hankering for the richer things in life: food, wine, women. He liked to party. He did not want to fight; he had no idea how to fight. All those lessons from his father of fleet tactics and things had gone in one ear and out the other. He knew his shortcomings and for some reason none of his inferiors seemed to care, they all trusted him, absolutely.

After a short trip into the docking bay, the shuttle came to rest on the docking bay floor, and they could disembark. The COO, Cranmere, went first from the mouth of the shuttle and then the other dignitaries and board members; last came CEO Gunter. He swallowed hard.

As Gunter stepped out of the shuttle, he saw the soldiers of the flagship's personal guard arrayed in their finest uniforms and the commanding officers of the ship at their head. They cheered. Gunter paused; he was not quite sure what to do. He smiled and raised an arm in acknowledgement of them, and they did the worst thing possible: they cheered more. Gunter had intended to quieten them with his movement, but they kept cheering. Then someone, he did not know who, broke out into applause, and the contagion spread throughout the troops amassed in the docking bay. They cheered and clapped.

Gunter felt a fool. He knew that they could not have that much faith in a womanising partier, could they? He raised both arms and descended the ramp to the docking bay floor. At last, the cheering and applause stopped.

Then Gunter stepped to the awkward podium erected on the docking bay floor. The microphone whined for a second, then stopped. He coughed. He knew that this message he was about to say was not just going to the personal guard arrayed before him. He had spotted the cameras set up at the edges of the group; it was going to the whole fleet around Neptune, and would be shown to the other fleets around Saturn and Jupiter when the broadcast got there.

He coughed again, and began awkwardly. "Men and women of the Solar Solutions military arm, this day we have been tasked with a great undertaking. We must bring peace back to our Solar System. The Collective Zone fleet is headed to the gateway to our great corporate space." Gunter paused and was terrified by the silent adoration that was emanating from soldiers in front of him. He continued, he seemed to be getting the hang of this. He knew he could speak. He felt more confident, "They intend to breach our peaceful space with their military might. I will be joining you on this great endeavour to push them out of our space and back towards Earth."

There was cheering from the group arrayed in front of him again.

Gunter looked into the nearest camera. "Men and women of the advanced war fleets on the border of our space, I know the fight will be hard and you will do your duty. I will be there as soon as I can with reinforcements. Your CEO trusts and believes in you. I believe in you. War is a brutal thing, but we must prevail, for the cost of failure is too terrible to grasp. This is your CEO, Gunter, signing off." He fell silent.

The crowd erupted in applause and cheering. Gunter always knew he had the ability to speak, it is how he convinced people to party and how he got any woman he wanted. He had felt anxious, but the words had just come to him; words of encouragement for his soldiers. This time it did not feel sleazy; it did not feel dirty; it did not feel manipulative; it felt like he was doing the right thing for once.

As he scanned the applauding crowd he felt different somehow; he knew that war was a terrible thing, but if he could be there with his soldiers as they fought, perhaps him boosting their morale would carry the day. He stepped down from the podium.

Cranmere rushed up to him, fawning. "CEO Sir, marvellous speech, truly masterful, the soldiers are inspired by your brilliance."

"No...Are the microphones off?" Gunter scanned the crowd.

"No, CEO Sir? Uh, yes the microphones are switched off" Cranmere looked confused.

"I could have told them they would all die, but I didn't," Gunter told the man honestly. "I said I'd be there with them, and that was all that they needed to hear. War, Cranmere, war makes people do terrible things. I saw it do such things to my father. Perhaps I've just done my first terrible thing. I gave them hope." Gunter watched confusion crawl over Cranmere's features.

"But, sir! We will win! You do believe that, don't you?" Cranmere gasped.

"Oh, I believe it, Cranmere. I believe it. But I don't know it." Gunter waved to the crowd again, they cheered harder. "My father told me about war, and how nothing ever goes quite as you intend. You can plan all you like, but when the bullets start flying, you don't know who is going to die." Gunter focused back on Cranmere, and smiled. "I'd much rather be in bed with a woman and have some good wine. You know that. You know me. I know that. I know me. But here I am going to lead a fleet to war, which we may very well lose. I'm no great general. But, I will do my duty. I will do my best; and, most of all, I will maintain hope!"

Cranmere looked a little lost and crestfallen for a moment, and then regained his composure. "CEO Sir, with you at our head we will have all the hope in the world!"

Gunter smiled and made a motion to leave the docking bay and get settled in to the ship for a long voyage. The clique of officers that had arrived with him on the pod formed up around him and they moved through the docking bay to the lifts that would take them to their private quarters.

The dignitaries and officers peeled off to their own private quarters and finally Gunter was alone in his. It was richly decorated like his private rooms on *Neptune Prime*: wood panelling and rich carpets and leather seats.

Gunter sat down in one of the seats and poured himself a brandy. He tasted it. It tasted of the best brandy.

He looked out the window of his quarters towards the very distant Sun. It shone dimly in the great distance, many billions of kilometres away. He sat, silently, watching, and waiting for the time he was called to the bridge to put the fleet into motion. Then he would go into a cryo-pod for the long journey in-system. He knew that the Solar Solutions propulsion systems were better than the Collective Zone's and as such, they would cover the vast distances in-system faster than the Collective Zone fleet could manage, but would their speed be enough?

***

"CEO, the fleet is ready to depart. All we need is your word." The words chimed over the intercom in Gunter's room.

Gunter put down his third glass of brandy, which he had not yet finished. He sighed. He felt the slight intoxication as the alcohol coursed through his system. He was not drunk. He was used to drinking large quantities of spirits at parties. He was nervous.

He looked out the window of his quarters towards the distant Sun again. "Oh, why has this war happened now?" he mused to himself. He hoped for a good outcome. He hoped.

"I'm coming," he replied to the intercom and rose from his seat. He walked past his bed. There was no woman in it this time. He could not afford to be distracted on war manoeuvres. He wished there was a woman there.

Gunter was still wearing his business suit; his leg was clicking and whirring as he walked. He made his way from his quarters towards the bridge.

Gunter had enjoyed running through the corridors as a child, not knowing what the machine he was laughing in was really for. Now he knew. He knew the only purpose of the *Silver Ark* was to kill. He was not a killer. But that damn fool Uxus was forcing his hand.

As Gunter moved through the passageways, crew and soldiers snapped to attention as he passed. They were counting on him. No matter what he did, they always trusted him and supported him. They believed in him. He needed to believe in them too. He needed to believe in himself.

Gunter steeled himself as he approached the bridge. All the corridors in the *Silver Ark* were of a white construction with metal floors, similar to the outside of the craft, they shone with the lights in the ceiling of the corridors.

He reached the bridge. He paused before entering. The guards on the outside of the doors had snapped to attention. They watched him.

He breathed deeply. Believe in yourself, they do, he thought to himself. He entered the bridge.

"CEO on the bridge!" came the cry from the First Officer. The whole bridge stood to attention and saluted.

Gunter waved them to continue, and they returned to their work as one. They were well trained and well disciplined.

Gunter stood and looked around the bridge. It was of a similar circular construction as some of the colonies of Solar Solutions. It had central walkways that jutted out and cut across an open space with tiers around the outside of

309

the space where crew and soldiers went about their tasks. There were stairways between the tiers. All the walkways had railings to prevent people from falling off as the ship rocked when fighting. The observation dome covered the bridge and allowed for good visibility and was used as the observation point for steering the ship.

Gunter walked out into the open space in the middle of the bridge where the command dais was. It was right in the middle of all the most important functions of the bridge. It had a very good view of the space in the front of the ship through the observation dome in front of the bridge. He felt his mechanical leg whir under him.

An orderly ran up to him and spoke in his ear, "Microphones are open, CEO Sir, ready for your address to the crews of the fleet."

Gunter smiled at the man and nodded kindly. The man bowed and ran back to his position on the edge of the bridge.

"Men and women of the fleet," he said, while staring out the front observation window of the bridge towards the distant Sun, "I addressed you not long ago about how we must undertake this great endeavour to rid the Solar System of war. Well, sometimes to do something noble we must do something terrible. Therefore, we must wage a war on the Collective Zone and defend our space. They will fight hard, but we will fight harder. We will fight them wherever they present themselves. I have been asked," Gunter lied, but it made a good story, "what makes me so sure that we will win? I answer that question with the simple fact, that the outcome will be too terrible if we lose. Therefore, we must win. We must triumph over all adversity, and I will be with you all the way when we engage the enemy fleet. I do not command you to do your best. I ask you," he paused for effect, "I beseech you to do

310

your best, for if we fail, the consequences are dire. I am proud of you, and I know that you will all do your duty. As my father used to tell me: march on!"

Gunter paused for a moment. He looked around the bridge. Many of the crew had paused in their work to watch him speak and they were still pausing when he finished. It was apparent that they adored him. The looks on their faces as he looked back at them were those of semi worship. He felt proud of them. He really did. They were prepared to do anything for him, and he must be prepared to follow through with his promises. He did not want war. He did not want to go to war. But the looks on their faces as he looked around made him feel ashamed of himself. If only they knew the real him. However, Gunter knew, that if they knew the real him, they would lose the war. It was best to maintain the charade of the heroic commander with them until the last. No army ever won a war when the commander in chief was a womanising alcoholic. There was one thing for certain, he could act the part.

Gunter raised his arms and finished his speech. "I command the Neptune Fleet of Solar Solutions, led by the *Silver Ark*, to be set in motion and forge forward towards Jupiter!" He ended his speech and waited for the microphones to be switched off.

The First Officer ran up to his CEO on the command dais. "CEO Sir, that was inspirational! We are so pleased to have you on the ship!"

"Well, I am the commander of this ship and of Solar Solutions, it is my duty," Gunter said, smiling.

"Your example honours us, CEO Sir." The First Officer bowed.

"First Officer, set a course for Jupiter. We will gather more ships on the way. Prepare the crew and soldiers for cryo-sleep and I will be in my quarters. Wake me from cryo-sleep when we reach our destination." Gunter concluded and marched out of the bridge, head held high, as an example to his crew.

Gunter retired to his quarters and undressed to his underwear in preparation for cryo-sleep. The tech-slave in his quarters had prepared his personal pod.

"Remember to wake me before the action hits," he said to the tech-slave, which fizzed at him with understanding and compliance. Gunter shivered; he hated tech-slaves.

Gunter climbed into the pod, and it shut on him. He breathed hard. He hated cryo-sleep, but it was necessary due to the distances involved. He just hoped he woke up. Then there was nothing.

Chapter 33

Europa's Solar Solutions colony, on the moon that orbited Jupiter, sat on the surface of what had been named, many centuries ago, the Great Ice Glacier. It served as a research station and also as another entry point and refuelling station for outgoing ships into the Solar Solutions Corporation that stretched from Jupiter outwards into the Solar System. It was the nearest colony to what had been *Florida Station*.

The complex itself was large, very large. It stretched over most of the surface of Europa, and it drilled down into the icy crust of the moon and even further down into the frigid oceans beneath the ice sheets. It was newer, in parts, than *Florida Station*. The original sections of the colony were similar in age to *Florida Station* but, as it was on a moon's surface, it was easier to add to and the colony had grown much larger than *Florida Station* and was being improved and added to constantly in an effort to keep it as modern as possible.

The population of the colony was large. It was approximately a billion people, but the population could never be strictly measured as it fluctuated all the time with science teams coming and going and ships docking at the upper extremities of the colony while they refuelled their reactors and brought supplies to and fro within the system and the Solar Solutions Corporate Empire.

***

Colony Commander Anya stood on the observation deck of her private quarters in the colony. She stared out into the space around Jupiter with a melancholy expression on her face. Her thoughts were of over a year ago when she had been standing right where she was now and had seen a flash of brilliant light when *Florida Station's* reactor overloaded.

Anya ran a hand through her brown hair. She was tall and wiry and had undergone longevity surgery at least once. She wore the standard black and green Solar Solutions uniform of her position as Colony Commander.

She remembered the calls coming in from numerous ships about what had happened eighteen months ago. They had said that *Florida Station* had simply vanished in a massive explosion, a reactor overload. The first message to come in had been from the *Green Dragon*: a welcome name bringing unwelcome news.

The colony had sent salvage and rescue craft as soon as it had been able. She remembered the reports of the station torn to pieces in a cataclysmic explosion. She had been unable to travel on the craft; she was too needed on Europa to go gallivanting around trying to save people who were already dead.

That was the terrible thing; there was only one survivor from *Florida Station*, one. The salvage crews had managed to detect the faint pulse of a cryo-pod amidst the wreckage when they got there a few weeks later. It took time to prepare a salvage operation, Anya cursed. They had brought the pod onto their ship and brought it back to Europa for attention.

The pod had been placed into deep sleep mode by either its occupant or someone who put the occupant in the pod. This meant that it would take a long time for the person to wake up and thaw out, but the benefit was that the pod's occupant could survive in space or other freezing environments for an almost infinite time without the need to repower the cryo-pod's batteries, as it was cut off from a power supply.

They had set the pod on thaw almost as soon as it cleared quarantine a year and a half ago, but the occupant was only supposed to thaw out around now. Anya looked at her chronometer. Yes, around this date.

She waited for the call and the opportunity to interrogate this survivor about what had happened. She needed to know. Hestra had been her friend, and it was not Hestra in the pod. Somehow, someone who was not the commander of the station was able to survive. Anya's blood boiled at the thought, but she tried to calm herself, if she wanted the anti-aging surgery to last then she had to remain calm.

"Commander, he's almost thawed," came the message over her communicator. It needed no further explanation.

Commander Anya left the observation deck, Jupiter, and the stars behind, and made her way to the science, recovery and quarantine laboratories.

***

Commander Anya arrived at the laboratory where the survival pod was being held. She addressed the employees curtly and moved to the side of the pod. She looked in through the window in the front and saw the face of an older man. She did not recognise him. She had looked in on him many times but now she would be able to talk to him.

The laboratory was a sterile white room with medical equipment around the edges, for any eventuality. Thawing someone from deep sleep mode was tricky and dangerous at the best of times.

"Commander, on your orders, we will open the pod," said the attendant GammaEpsilon89 from behind a mask

315

and medical robes. He was a fattish man with a pronounced limp and a rather asthmatic wheeze to his voice.

Anya nodded her approval. "We need to question this person about what happened," she said calmly, but her heart was pounding. At last, there would be answers.

GammaEpsilon89 and his subordinates moved to the edges of the pod and began the final thawing procedure. It took a few moments to enter the commands but the lights on the side of the pod began to flash and count down.

After a minute, the lights stopped, and the lid of the pod began to move and hiss open.

Anya held her breath.

The attendants waited for a response from the occupant who, now they could see him fully, was an older man in a white robe.

There was a cough and a splutter from the occupant. He opened his eyes. He tried to speak but after so long in deep sleep mode his voice was cracked and unintelligible.

"Easy now, sir," said GammaEpsilon89. "We've woken you up from a long sleep. You set the pod to deep sleep mode, as you wanted to survive space. You'll be better shortly."

The man nodded his understanding and climbed out of the pod with the assistance of some of the attendants. His white robe billowed around his slender frame.

"Th-thank you," he said in a raspy voice, while he smoothed down the ruffled greyish hair that seemed to have a life of its own. He looked around as if he could use some assistance with movement, but none was forthcoming.

Commander Anya, with folded arms across her chest, asked him the questions they all wanted the answer to, "Who are you? And what happened to *Florida Station*?"

The man paused for a second, as if gaining strength to utter the words. "I was the chief priest on *Florida Station*. My name...is Virtus. I will tell you what happened shortly." He grinned. "I am alive...to continue my work."

***

This story is continued in the next novel *Martian Flight: Broken Cosmos Volume Two* by Ian Kennedy:

Alfred, Draz and Artisius escape from Earth in the *Green Dragon* and make their way to Mars as they attempt to outrun the Collective Zone Great Fleet. On Mars, they try to get lost in the criminal gangs that operate with impunity on the planet.

Alfred struggles with his sanity, as his zetting gets more and more enslaving.

Draz fights her own demons as addiction closes in on her.

Artisius' past catches up with him as he tries to protect Alfred and Draz.

Alfred, Draz, and Artisius try to escape the danger of the situation they are in. The Great Fleet of the Collective Zone chases them, as it attempts to recover the plans on the hard drive that Draz stole from the Collective Zone archives.

Virtus' influence continues to ripple across space.

Freedom is many things to many people.

***

Author details and sites:
Website: www.ikennedyauthor.com (mailing list link on website / contact email at bottom of website)
Amazon: www.amazon.com/author/ikennedy
Twitter: twitter.com/ikennedyauthor
Facebook: www.facebook.com/ikennedyauthor

***

Please leave a review of this book (*Florida Station*) on Amazon, I would really appreciate it. Please see the Amazon link above for the link to the book.